Shadow
Trade

Other Books by Alan Furst

Your Day in the Barrel
The Paris Drop
The Caribbean Account

Shadow Trade

Alan Furst

F991sh

dp DELACORTE PRESS/NEW YORK

Published by
Delacorte Press
1 Dag Hammarskjold Plaza
New York, N.Y. 10017

Manufactured in the United States of America
First printing

Designed by Rhea Braunstein

LIBRARY OF CONGRESS CATALOGING IN PUBLICATION DATA

Furst, Alan.
  Shadow trade.

  I. Title.
PS3556.U76S5   1983   813'.54   82–17219
ISBN 0–440–07698–6

The following is a work of fiction. Although
reference is made to covert actions—in Laos,
Angola, and Kurdistan—that are matters of public
record, all the characters are fictitious, and any
resemblance to persons living or dead is
purely coincidental.

Arconada

THAT OCTOBER IT rained steadily and New York was gray and sad; autumn was lost—there weren't going to be any bright, cool, optimistic days—and what lay ahead was winter. Guyer took a cab home through the drizzle. He lived in an old brick apartment house just north of Greenwich Village, in a small studio on the fourteenth floor: a narrow kitchenette, a bathroom, and a room with a sofa that converted to a bed, though it was never folded back into a sofa because nobody but Guyer ever came there. It was an anonymous place, which suited Guyer because he had been an intelligence officer all of his working life.

He got home from the office a little after 8:30—he was often later than that—and after he'd thrown his jacket on a chair and loosened his tie, he thought about dinner. He planned to eat a frozen pizza—he jabbed the *Bake* button on the oven on his way to the refrigerator—but when he looked in the freezer compartment, it wasn't there. He'd eaten it sometime earlier. He didn't remember eating it, but apparently he had. It crossed his mind to go out and buy another one at the supermarket on Greenwich Avenue, but that was too much trouble for a frozen pizza. He stood before the open refrigerator for a few minutes, balked and immobile. Then he gave up on dinner, slammed the door, and rubbed his fists into his eyes, which felt dry and hot. It didn't help. He'd spent hours that day looking at faces on a computer screen and what he needed, he thought, was a rest. He wandered into the bedroom, sat down on the edge of the bed, and fell back until he hit a pillow. He groped on the floor beside him until he found a remote-control set and turned on the television at the foot of the bed. It was a twenty-five-inch color model, de-tuned to black and white, with contrast and brightness adjusted to bring up the shadings. On top of the cabinet was a ruled notebook with a ballpoint pen clipped to its cover. He watched for a minute, flipping channels, then closed his eyes. His mind moved slowly, reaching for a connection that had eluded him earlier that day. Something went with something else, but he couldn't recapture the circumstance. *Christ, I'm tired,* he thought. He didn't want to open his eyes, the darkness felt good. The low mumble from the television was hypnotic, like surf, and he decided that he wouldn't let himself go all the way but would instead drift to the edge, where dreams lay just below the horizon, and float for a few minutes.

When he woke up, he looked at his watch and it was 9:40. His mouth tasted terrible. He willed himself off the bed and walked slowly to the bathroom, splashed warm water on his face, and rinsed his mouth. He shivered, his clothes felt damp and stiff. There had been a time when he was able to sleep for an hour, then come instantly awake and alert. No more. Again, he tried the refrigerator. Standing in front of the open door, he pulled the laces on his shoes and stepped out of them by holding the backs down with his opposite foot. He took out three eggs and a half cube of butter with paper crumpled over one end. He got a spatula from the drawer, scraped at toast crumbs on the end of the butter, cut off a small piece and dropped it in a frying pan. When the butter melted, he broke the eggs into the pan and made scrambled eggs by slashing at them with the edge of the spatula until the whites were no longer obvious. When the eggs set, he tried to flip the thing over but only half came on the first try, and that had brown streaks on the bottom. He shrugged, declared it done, and shoveled it onto a Melmac plate with a picture of a sheaf of wheat on it. He ate standing, using the spatula instead of a fork, listening to a beer commercial from the muttering television in the other room. When he was done, he washed up by turning on the hot tap full blast and letting the water do the work. Then he looked at his watch again. 9:51. The operation was due to go off at 10:00; he could get most of the way toward a shower.

He undressed, hanging his pants up in a clip hanger, hoping that some of the crease would come back, and threw everything else on a chair. He went into the bathroom, wrapped a towel around his waist, got the shower adjusted, then walked back into the bedroom and sat on the edge of the bed closest to the telephones. There were three of them, black Touch-Tone models, taking up most of the space on the night table. The sound of the roaring shower was seductive, and he grunted with irritation and again looked at his watch. 10:03. *Let's go,* he thought. He watched seconds go by on the dial. The phone on the left, 4704, rang once.

"Yes," he answered.

"This is Nagle."

"Go ahead."

"It just went down."

"They're inside?"

"Yeah."

"Can you see in?"

"No. He's got curtains."

"Okay. Anything else?"

"That motorbike is a sitting duck. She didn't chain it to anything, just put the key in her pocket and walked away. Later tonight, pretty good chance somebody's gonna come along and burn it. You care?"

"No. Let it go."

"Okay. If that's what you want."

"That's what I want."

"Exit time the same?"

"2:00 A.M."

"I thought you guys said 0200."

"Anything else?"

"What if he comes out early?"

"Roust him. Drive him around a little, ask him questions. Keep him busy until 2:00. Where's Wynn?"

"In the car. Don't worry, we don't coop on your time."

"Any problem, call."

"Yeah. Talk to you later."

Guyer hung up. Walked to the bathroom, looped the towel over the inside knob of the door, and stepped into the steaming shower. He visualized Nagle and Wynn in their car. They were big German–Irish kids from Yonkers who had joined the police a few years before and worked their way quickly into plainclothes. They went off duty at 4:00 P.M. and after that, sometimes before that, they worked for him. What people in the neighborhood saw were two plainclothes cops sitting in an NYPD unmarked Plymouth. Nothing unusual about that. The very last thing he needed, he thought, was some bearded Hungarian in a trench coat pretending to

[6]

read a newspaper on the corner of 111th Street. Cops had perfect camouflage for the sort of baby-sitting he required, and they were steady and solid. Trouble came, they'd stop it quietly. Private free-lance was cheaper, he knew, but they had a tendency toward weapons and everything went bad when guns came out. He soaped his hair, let the water rinse the suds down his back. He wanted no action, just a clean, cool process of people doing their jobs on time. It should be silent and smooth. When it was finished, he would hand over an envelope and receive an envelope in return. Good business, period.

In the basement apartment, Victor Cruz was dancing. The song on the radio was "The Girl from Ipanema," and they probably should have been dancing a Brazilian samba, but he wanted to hold her closer than that and she didn't seem to mind. She'd made it clear, earlier, that they weren't going to bed. She wanted to drink a couple of beers and dance a little and talk about nothing in particular, but she wasn't going to sleep with him. Not *tonight* she wasn't going to sleep with him. She wasn't uptight about it, he liked her for that. When he'd put his hands on her shoulders and looked at her a certain way, she gave him a nice smile, and a single shake of her head. "Easy does it," she said. "Just not my day for that. Okay?" It was okay, just barely maybe, but it was. There was a hell of a lot of pleasure simply being in her presence and there weren't many women he could say that about. At first, when she came to his apartment to use the telephone, he thought he was going to get really *lucky*. Then later, after they'd been together for a couple of hours, he realized that it wasn't going to happen. There'd been a quick flash of anger, then a mental shrug and a decision

[7]

to enjoy what she offered freely and not to press it beyond that. Not *tonight,* anyhow. What made the decision easy to take was the girl herself. *Azúcar,* he thought. Sugar—sweet, smooth, and pale. She had skin like satin, and thick copper-colored hair spilled down her back. When they danced he could smell the perfume in it. She had freckles clustered across the bridge of her nose and, he saw in the V of her lavender shirt, across the tops of her breasts. She was maybe twenty-one, he thought, and possibly Irish. Sweet to look at. Even on the streets of New York, stunning. *Azúcar that way,* he thought. But also her nature was sweet, the way she was. She listened to him when he talked, met his eyes, and her laugh was loud and uninhibited. She danced with her eyes closed, hummed under her breath, put in a word or two when she knew them. She drank her beer from the bottle, took a good healthy swig and wiped her lips with the back of her hand. And he had the conviction that if—that *when*—they made love, there was yet unrevealed sweetness awaiting him.

The sax solo ended and the singer, Astrud Gilberto, picked up the lyric at the bridge. The song was one of his favorites. He liked the sexy beat, the breathy voice, the feeling of a summer day by the ocean when time stops. His mind far away on a Brazilian beach, the girl in his arms beautiful, her body lightly held against his, moving easily with him—it all added up to a lovely little vacation from the world and if he didn't get laid in the bargain, he could live with that. He felt a drop of sweat start at his hairline, reached up and wiped it away. It was always warm in the basement and that felt good too.

Out in the night, on West 111th Street, a late October wind was blowing hard off the Hudson. It sang through the fire escapes and hummed against the windows. The sky had been low and lead-colored all day and people walking against the wind had knotted faces and raised forearms. That made it feel better indoors: hidden away from the weather and the city. He was having a good time, he realized, as good as any he could remember. Just dancing with a girl and drinking a beer and talking about nothing in particular.

He was forty-four, bald, and beer had made him fat. He worked as a janitor for a service that cleaned midtown offices at night. Weekends in the summer he went to Shea and watched the Mets. There was the occasional woman, one of the ADC mothers in the neighborhood, in apartments with damp walls and sour smells. Life wasn't bad, it went along. Earlier in the evening he had made two sandwiches of bologna and cheese and put them in a paper bag with a package of raisin cookies for his lunch at three in the morning. The crew usually ate at the conference table in the offices of a slick fashion magazine. The janitors joked obscenely about the huge black and white photomurals on the walls: leggy models in scarves and woolly hats throwing snowballs at each other. Lunch made, he had dressed in washed-out blue workpants and shirt with DEPENDABLE OFFICE MAINTENANCE lettered in red across the back and VICTOR stitched in script above the pocket. He'd worked for Dependable for three years and Lefkowitz, the boss, insisted on the uniform. Every once in a while a late office worker would be discovered at a desk and the uniform was meant to be reassuring. By 9:50 he had bundled himself in an old checkered coat, sandwiched a folded *Daily News* against his side, and, head down, walked out into the wind. He turned east toward Broadway and the one-block walk to the subway, and there she was.

Seeing her, he swore an appreciative oath under his breath. She wore a soft jacket of black leather, copper hair whipping its shoulders. She stood with hands on hips, glaring at a small motorcycle that leaned on its kickstand. His eyes ran up the curve of her jeans, swept back down the long legs. Unconsciously, his free hand creased his moustache east and west. What is *she* doing here, he wondered. West 111th Street wasn't a slum or a ghetto, it was a mixed neighborhood: a residence hotel down the block had junkies and welfare people, brownstones like his held Columbia students and a widely assorted lot of younger people, and the tall buildings were family places, inhabited by people who had lived in the neighborhood, and worked downtown, for years. But nothing like her, not at that time of night. He strolled by, savoring the view. Then her head swiveled so fast and her words were so unexpected that he actually jumped. Something in him wanted to run away.

She was angry, mouth in a line. "This stupid thing won't run," she said. Right at him, an appeal for justice. Her New York accent was hard and thick, and that made her approachable. She only looked like a goddess.

"Wass wrong?"

"God only knows."

"Maybe if I push, it starts."

"Nah. It's dead."

He clucked his tongue. "S'brand new."

"Three weeks I had it."

For a moment they stood silent in the wind, mourning bad luck and things that wouldn't work. She drew air audibly into her nose, then sighed it out. "You got a telephone?"

"In my apartment," he said. It occurred to him an instant later that the phone couldn't very well be in his pocket. But he had been imagining her in his apartment and it just came out that way. He sensed what was coming, but he refused to believe it. Not her and him. No way. Life never got that good.

[10]

Life got, as it happened, almost that good. She was a treasure. His apartment—small, hot, cluttered, an army blanket thrown over a cot—bothered her not at all. He knew that, alert as he was for some snobbery or fear in her. She laughed at his jokes. She drank beer with him. They danced to the radio. The combination astonished him: the way she looked, she could have been throwing snowballs with the other models in the photomural; the way she *was,* well she was just like him. There was only one minor irritation in an otherwise perfect evening: His phone wouldn't work. So she couldn't make her call. There was a dial tone, but no amount of dialing altered it. His mind nagged at him to call Lefkowitz and report sick, but that would have required a walk along Broadway in search of a working payphone and that, he knew, would have shattered the spell. He tried, halfheartedly, around midnight, asking her if she wanted to go out and have something to eat. That way he could have managed the phone call. "Unh-uh," she said, after considering it. "But you go ahead, if you're really hungry. Maybe I should get home." So much for Lefkowitz. *For one night,* he thought, *the hell with Dependable.* So they ate bologna sandwiches and raisin cookies and by the time he walked her to a cab, a little after 2:00, he was completely in love.

He would, very early the next day, receive a phone call explaining her presence in his apartment. He'd been tricked. Somebody had wanted silent entry into one of the offices he customarily cleaned, so they'd sent her around to keep him occupied. Nothing ever came of it, Lefkowitz never even found out, it was just one of those nighttime things that went on in New York. And the final surprise was this: It didn't change his feelings for her at all—the glow stayed. In the months that followed, he'd watch for her, anywhere he happened to go

[11]

—all he wanted was a smile and a wave—but New York was a big city and it could happen that somebody you saw once you would never see again, and that's how it turned out for him.

Guyer sat half off the bed, feet on the floor, back propped on a pillow, towel wrapped around his waist. His eyes flickered over the images on the television screen, not engaging them. Somebody in the apartment down the hall was practicing the piano, working the same phrase over and over again. Now and then he walked to the window and stared out at Seventh Avenue. Traffic was thin. It was Monday night, the city felt exhausted, a long week stretching out ahead. People who couldn't get to sleep on Sunday night, a common ailment, went off early on Monday night. Guyer knew there was percentage there and he took it, running operations on Monday night when that was possible. Outside, the streets were slick and wet, another tilt in his favor: rain fouled security systems run on telephone lines, humidity set off false alarms, and security personnel tended to ignore the lights and buzzes after two or three bad signals. He'd waited for a little less than four hours. Everything in the intelligence business happened too slow or too fast, principally the former, so he'd spent years learning to wait, though he'd never learned how not to hate it. When 4161 finally rang for him, he had the receiver off the hook before the ring ended.

"Yes?"

"Fillipelli here."

His mind raced. He found it just as the voice returned. "Doorman at 9 East."

"Oh, yeah."

"I was supposed to call this number when the man in

the baseball hat went into 14 East, across the street."

"And?"

"He just went in. About a minute ago."

"Okay. You'll get another envelope, tomorrow."

"I don't come on until four."

"After four, then."

"What time you think you might get here? See, sometimes I go down the basement to warm up."

"We'll find you."

"If I knew the exac' time, see, I'd be right there waiting and save you the parking or whatever."

"It'll be okay. Just after four sometime."

"Hey, uh, anything else you need, feel free."

"We'll keep it in mind."

"Fillipelli."

"Yeah."

Guyer hung up. He glanced at his watch, 1:48, climbed slowly to his feet, and stretched. Arconada, the man in the baseball cap, would need only a few minutes once he was inside the office. That got him out at 2:00 at the latest. In a cab at around 2:05. He should be at the Belmore, an all-night cafeteria, at around 2:20. So, he realized, he had only one call left: Nagle, confirming that the girl was safely out of the basement apartment. He was looking forward to the Belmore. He could have a roast beef sandwich and french fries and read the early papers. He dropped the towel on the floor and went to get his pants out of the closet. The crease hadn't come back at all, now he'd have to take them to the dry cleaners, then remember to pick them up. Working as hard as he did, it was the sort of errand that became impossibly difficult. He dressed slowly, except for the tie, the same clothes he'd worn that day. He turned off the television, patted his pocket to make sure he had what he needed, and sat on the edge of the bed, staring at the telephone. The urge to be up and moving, to be doing *something* after a long night of

[13]

waiting, was overpowering. It was 2:06 before the phone rang.

"Yes?"

"You have Prince Albert in the can?"

"Everything okay?"

"Yup. She came out about five minutes ago. He was with her. They stopped at the scooter, we were afraid she was gonna forget and *start* the fucking thing and ride away."

"But she didn't."

"He walked her to the corner, she got in a cab."

"He use a payphone?"

"No. Just turned around and went home, we waited until he was inside."

"Thanks. I'll be in touch."

"Okay if we pay ourselves tomorrow?"

"After 11:00."

"That'll do. The girl you got, she has a name? A phone number?"

"Both, I'd guess."

"She's a real good-looking girl, is what I mean."

"Yes."

Nagle sighed. "Okay, be that way. We're gonna head uptown."

They hung up simultaneously. Guyer set the locks on his door, went out into the carpeted hall and pressed the elevator button. The worst part of dealing with the cops was that it was hard to pay them. They didn't like coming around to offices, you couldn't go handing cash to detectives in public restaurants, so they'd set up a joint account at a bank. Guyer deposited cash, Nagle took it out. He'd need a paymaster tomorrow, he realized. The bank deposit had to be made, envelopes distributed to Fillipelli and Maggie. The telephone man, who'd cooked Victor Cruz's line, would restore service at 5:30. He liked to be paid at the end of the month, not as a convenience to Guyer, a problem of money in his hands passing magically into bookies' pockets. Guyer listened for the elevator, heard it climbing slowly to his floor. Nagle was right, he thought, the girl was beautiful. He'd never actually met her, she'd been recruited by his associate, who had arranged for Guyer to be present at a bar while they had a drink. Every man there had looked at her, some openly, some surreptitiously. There were other good-looking women in the place, but she was special. Something about her, he thought, what was it? A certain quality: raw, tough, street-smart. It had to do, also, with how she felt about how she looked. She didn't flirt. She did not seem to have—he'd watched her carefully—a repertoire of hair flips and princess moves. She knew what she looked like, that was apparent, but she wasn't going to take any points for it, that was apparent too. Underneath, he felt, there was something else, which would fight hard for what it wanted, even if it knew it was going to lose. He laughed at himself silently for building cloud castles. After all, what had he seen? A woman across a room having a drink. He gave up looking for words, maybe the best things about people didn't have names. The elevator whined upward, bumped to a stop, and the door opened. Guyer took one beat to check the corners, then stepped inside.

Daniel Arconada pushed the baseball cap back on his head and ran one finger along the *R*'s in the filing cabinet drawer. It had been a long, humiliating night and by now he was so enraged that he was having trouble concentrating. All he wanted to do was find the *chingada* file so he could get away from this *chingada* office, leave behind the doubly *chingada* mop and bucket, go see that *chingadon* Guyer and get his *chingada* money. One thousand dollars. A lot of money? *Not enough.*

First of all, he hated to be taken for Puerto Rican. Guyer couldn't have known, but it was the worst thing about New York—you were Hispanic, people thought you were Puerto Rican. Sometimes cabs didn't stop. Sometimes people were nice, too nice, in a frightened sort of way. He was from Uruguay, a professional thief who made covert entries as a sideline. His hair was curly and black, and he was five feet five inches tall, but his nose was longish and delicate, his skin was pale, and he had very little *Indio* in him to speak of. As far as this *chingada* city was concerned, however, he was Puerto Rican.

Still, *chingada* though it might be, the city had advantages for him. In Montevideo the police were ferocious, adamant, they'd clip a field telephone to your balls and crank the handle. For a thief, life could be nasty. Here it was much, much easier. The pickings were fatter, and home burglary was a virtually uninvestigated crime. Better yet, local people practiced at the art of being victims. A few months earlier he'd broken into an apartment in the East Thirties and the occupant, a middle-aged man, had come home in the middle of the day and caught him red-handed. He hadn't bothered to jam the lock from inside. The man, hearing him at work, panting while he wrestled with a big television, backed out of the door and waited in the hall. As Arconada, heart walloping, ran out of the apartment he saw the man, standing stiff and scared, his back turned so that he would not see the robber's face.

The bad night had begun for Arconada when he arrived at the tiny midtown office at 10:30. There was a line of janitors entering ahead of him, almost all of them were Puerto Rican. At the door, Lefkowitz was waiting. He was one of those men who must shave twice a day while their hairline recedes. Every night he stood by the door and, by way of employee relations, greeted each of his workers in a reedy Long Island accent: *Buenas noches, José. Buenas noches, Luis.* On entering, Arconada saw his opportunity to normalize relations quickly and gave out a cheery *Buenas noches* of his own. Lefkowitz was visibly startled, Arconada could read the thought as it crossed his face: *Oh my God here's one of my PR's and I forgot his name.* Arconada jumped right in, in his best East Harlem imitation: "I yam Lopez."

"*Quien . . . ?*" Lefkowitz had said the word for "who" but the rest of the Spanish eluded him.

"Cruz cousin. He got the flu. Tell me to come in."

"Oh. Uh, *Victor* Cruz?"

Arconada almost broke out laughing. Lefkowitz made the name sound like it belonged to a Spanish aristocrat, such perfect Castilian delivered through pursed lips. He let his face go all happy and excited: "*Sí, sí,* Victor Cruz! My cousin."

Lefkowitz had now regained his poise. "*Su hijo esta enfermo,*" he said firmly. Arconada heard the men behind him stirring angrily in the cold wind. Lefkowitz honored their heritage, they mopped floors. And they had had enough Spanish lesson for one evening. Lefkowitz had said: "Your son is sick."

"*Es verdad,*" Arconada said, moving into the office.

A few minutes later, his janitors gathered, Lefkowitz wrote the night's assignments on a small blackboard, explaining carefully as he went. Arconada privately sighed with relief. He was assigned to clean his "cousin's" usual offices. If the boss had crossed him up, he would have had to return another night and break in. Because it was a dental office and would normally stock narcotics, it was probably all wired up and difficult. He relaxed and waited for the truck to take him out.

But from 11:00 to 1:45 he did not relax. Life was

pure hell. For months New York had been corrosive to his pride, now here he was, on a cold, dark night, swabbing floors and driving a stiff brush around the insides of toilet bowls. He had soft hands and the cleaning fluids burned him. Working legitimately, with the lights on, made him nervous. He was used to moving like a cat, on the balls of his feet, but the masquerade demanded that he clump around like a janitor. His back hurt. *Never again,* he swore to himself. But he knew it was a lie. A good thing he had with Guyer. He needed the thousand. He could steal like crazy in New York but was taking a terrible beating on the resale because he wasn't locally connected. He dealt with fences who bought from junkies, thus were spoiled by the weakness of their clientele and would pay only ten to fifteen percent of value.

Find the goddamn file, he told himself, *and get out of this.* Once that was done, all he had to do was meet Guyer and get his money. Then he had to call Cruz when they put his phone back on in the morning, explain that he had taken his place but had stolen nothing. Cruz would have no choice but to go along quietly, and agree to confirm to Lefkowitz that his cousin had subbed for him. Otherwise there would be police, suspicion, a lost job. Cruz, he imagined, would tell the boss that his cousin had become frustrated by the work and left early. He would, Arconada thought, find the most appeasing lie.

His index finger traced the tops of the folders: Reber, Resterman, Rewell, Reznick, Ricard.

Ricard.

He stopped still, concentrating, sorting the background into constituent parts, checking each for normalcy. Outside, on the side street, a light patter of rain. East one block, on Madison, a bus pulling away from the curb. In the building itself, only the sound of a refrigerator running in a storage area. Everything normal, as it should be.

He did it. Withdrew the folder from the drawer and laid it atop the filing cabinet. Opened it. There was a billing copy, and four X-ray photos with rounded corners. He reached around his back and withdrew an envelope from the place where his pants were belted snugly against his spine. From the envelope he took four X-ray photos and laid them on the left side of the folder, then took the others and put them in the envelope and wedged it back beneath his belt. He resettled his shirttail, closed the manila folder and dropped it back into place, then slid the drawer closed.

Altogether it took less than a minute. A small act. Silent, fast, inconsequential. Arconada knew there had been preparation and several other people involved that night. Quite a lot of motion, actually, when you considered that the result was four black plastic sheets out of a folder and four others in. It was, he guessed, somebody covering his tracks. Dental X rays were often used for identification when fingerprints were unavailable.

He glanced at his watch. 2:10. A momentary temptation to relieve the dentist of his Percodan. It could be sold very profitably. Temptation resisted. As a point of curiosity, he peeled back a thick drape to check the system protecting the tall window. Two wires, red and blue. He laughed to himself. *Dentist,* he thought, *you have no class*. He took a deep breath, listened again, then walked out of the office, through the front door, and down three stone steps onto the street. Casually, without stealth, in case somebody was watching. When he'd entered the building, equipment dangling from both arms, his peripheral vision had picked up a doorman who seemed to be studying him from beneath a canopy across the street. Arconada went to Fifth

[19]

Avenue, turned south for two blocks, then raised his arm for a cab. The fourth one stopped, Arconada got in. He made the driver for a college kid.

"Third and 30th," he said. The rule was: Never go from where you have been to where you are going. Sometimes the drivers actually wrote down accurate street addresses on their trip sheets. He wanted a cigarette but was afraid the kid might hassle him about it. He did not want to be remembered. He'd wait, he decided, until he got to the Belmore. But he really wanted one. He felt let down and very flat. Usually, when he stole, there was a rush, a triumphant high, something in him danced and twirled. But that night's operation was without honor, without meaning. This "Ricard," or his friends, had missed a detail, so they'd thrown him a thousand-dollar bone and told him to fix it up. It made him small and insignificant. He felt like a clerk.

The Belmore Cafeteria, on Park Avenue South at 28th Street, was packed with cabdrivers, all of them eating and talking at the same time. They were mostly older men, who had begun driving in the fifties, planning always to be doing something else by next year. They were mainly Italian, Jewish, and Irish. At one time they'd lived in the middle-class parts of Brooklyn and Queens, most of them now lived on Long Island. They were eating big plates of scrambled eggs, corned beef sandwiches, french fries, buttered bagels, seven-layer cake; and drinking coffee with cream, or iced tea, or diet soda. Guyer, who looked tough and sour and a little overweight, did not seem out of place. He wolfed down a big roast beef sandwich on rye bread, then took his time with the french fries, picking them up between thumb and forefinger, one at a time, and dunking them in a small pond of ketchup he'd made on the edge of the plate. While he ate, he glanced through an early morning paper and listened to the drivers at the next table. They were telling cab stories, cursing and laughing and shouting at each other, their fares that night the dumbest, meanest, cheapest bastards that ever rode taxis.

Something made him look up from the newspaper. Arconada had materialized in a chair on the other side of the table. He was sitting back, arms folded across his chest, baseball cap tilted forward so that it shadowed his eyes, and he wore a nasty little grin. When Guyer looked up, he started to whistle "La Cucaracha." He dropped one hand behind him, then brought it back with a small manila envelope held between index and middle fingers. He circled it in the air for a moment, then, as he whistled the last seven notes of the melody, his hand moved forward and dropped it in front of Guyer. After it hit the table, he leaned toward Guyer and said, *"Olé."*

Guyer slid the envelope toward him, with one hand spread the end apart slightly until he could see the negatives, then closed it.

"Where's the waiter?" Arconada asked, lighting a cigarette.

"You have to get it yourself."

"Hunh," he said, but made no move to get up.

"Went off okay?"

"Easy."

"When you go, take the newspaper with you."

Arconada moved it a few inches toward himself, his hand gesture a parody of Guyer's. "What denomination?"

"Hundreds."

Arconada nodded, poked at the newspaper with his finger. "I found it," he said, like a little boy.

"Not enough?"

Arconada shrugged, the answer beneath his dignity.

[21]

He reached out, took a french fry off Guyer's plate, swept it back and forth through the ketchup, then ate it. He made a face. "You got something else coming up?"

"I think so," Guyer said. "Couple weeks, maybe." It was a lie. He'd let Arconada find that out for himself. "You call Cruz at six."

"Yeah. I know."

"Call me on 4161 after you've talked to him."

"Yessir."

They sat for a minute, silent. Guyer picked up the envelope and slid it into the side pocket of his jacket, then he stood. "Talk to you later," he said.

Arconada made a two-finger salute, flipping it up off his forehead. *"Buenas noches,"* he said, his voice like a teacher on a language record.

Guyer went out the revolving door behind a cabdriver. Once on the sidewalk, he said, "Going west?"

"Why not," the driver said.

Guyer watched the empty avenues go by as the cab pounded across the cracks and potholes of the side street. He felt drained and tired. He'd have to set an alarm for 5:45, he realized. The cab roared through the last second of an amber light on Fifth Avenue. Somewhere a siren started up, the canyon effect of the tall buildings making it impossible to locate the fire engine. Guyer leaned back against the seat and closed his eyes. The man paying for the operation was named Langer, though Guyer felt he was working at someone else's direction. He had always done that, had never been out on his own as far as Guyer knew. He also knew that Langer had killed a lot of people. He was a mercenary, of the officer class, who had fought in secret wars all over Africa and Asia. Being in New York, hiring someone to run a penetration, that was new. Evidently he'd found a different sort of sponsor. Guyer wondered, idly, who it was. He realized that he would probably never know that. He wondered whose X rays he had in his pocket. That, too, he was never going to know. The envelope had to go back to Langer before the second half of the fee could be paid. That had to be done right away, they were out a thousand each for Arconada and Maggie, two-fifty for the phone man, the cops split another thousand, and fifty bucks for the doorman. Guyer would have paid him more but didn't want to stimulate his imagination. *Funny,* he thought, *how you make your own price.* He opened his eyes as the driver ran a red light and swung south into Seventh Avenue, in time to make the downtown light.

In June of 1977 the Central Intelligence Agency had discharged eight hundred and twenty Clandestine Services officers in a single day, declaring them redundant because of new technological capability. Guyer had been one of them. His own dismissal, he felt, was not entirely based on simple reduction in force. He had made a bad enemy, a small dainty man who had come to believe Guyer a coward, a man with influence on the personnel board that did the dirty work. Of course, he could never know for certain because Francis Mains, the small dainty man, was the very model of obliquity. What he had taken for cowardice in Guyer was, in fact, shame and fury over the pointless death of an unimportant man, a thing that was allowed to happen as a courtesy to other intelligence services. Guyer had made no secret of his contempt. In return, he believed, the man had destroyed his career.

A few months after he was terminated, he started his own company, to do for the private sector what he had done for the public. He had spent his working life in the intelligence trade, it was what he knew, and it was what he did best.

Delatte

7:45. THE OFFICE. An old narrow brownstone at 74th and Madison. Outside, the hiss of tires on the wet pavement, the roar of accelerating buses, New York going to work. Inside, blinds drawn, lights out, Guyer drinking coffee from a Styrofoam cup, his mind clearing slowly. He could not, after Arconada's call at six, go back to sleep. The office was the next best thing, better than staring at the ceiling and tormenting himself with the day's problems. The office was his true home. When they'd leased half the building, four years earlier, the previous tenant had been an ambitious publisher of horticultural magazines, whose garden had grown only the tall stubborn weeds of Chapter Eleven. The furniture had, as part of the lease agreement, remained, so the office had a dowdy faculty-lounge feeling to it: area rugs, battered oak desks, aging leather chairs, and Robert Furber botanical prints on the wall. Except for the computer console area, where the floor was shiny gray asbestos tile, the walls were covered in sheets of hard white plastic, and the console itself was computer blue. If the decor was a little schizophrenic, he'd always thought, then it was only so much so, and in the same way, as the business itself.

At one end of the office a young man in a white shirt was setting up a film projector. The young man, Kevin Smith, worked for Guyer—answering telephones, processing mail, helping with keypunch—and he was very good at things like setting up film projectors. In his middle twenties, he was tall and thin, kept his dark hair short and slicked down on either side of a perfect white part. His office uniform never changed: dark suits, white shirts, and a blue tie with a sailboat on it. Sometimes he tucked the tie between the second and third button of his shirt. He wore glasses with heavy black frames, addressed Guyer either as Mr. Guyer or sir, and was altogether a very serious young man. He came from a large family in Jackson Heights and still lived there with his mother, who, Guyer supposed, ironed the white shirts, their perfection obviously beyond that obtainable from commercial laundries. He had studied for the priesthood, an unspecified life crisis had turned him aside from that, and he now attended Fordham Law School at night.

Richard List, Guyer's associate in the business, was virtually his opposite, night to his day, and was casually cruel to Kevin's somber image, referring to him in private conversation as Kevin Smith, Boy Undertaker, as though he were the living embodiment of a luck'n'pluck book, as St. Kevin of Robert Hall, or as God's Covert Angel. But that, Guyer knew, was just Richard List being Richard List—a day without epigrams was a day without sunshine—and Guyer didn't take it very seriously.

"Mr. Guyer?"

He came to attention, he'd been deep into an early-morning stupor.

"Ready any time, sir," Kevin continued.

Guyer made sure he had pencil and paper handy, then told Kevin to go ahead and run the film. The Delatte film—it was well known within the intelligence community and bore that title—differed greatly from most covertly achieved documentation. First of all, it was film and not videotape, the medium of choice for surveillance. Second, it was in color. Secret video was done in black and white, which was attainable at normal levels of indoor lighting. Color would in many instances be preferable, but a subject entering a motel room for clandestine purposes might become suspicious on discovering the interior lit by four thousand watts of illumination. Third, the camera was handheld and followed the action. Hidden cameras had to be in fixed positions—the ancient man-behind-the-one-way-mirror-taking-movies trick had, deservedly, comic overtones in the industry. The Delatte film had been taken by a German tourist who was visiting Damascus. He had a 16mm Arriflex loaded with Ektachrome 7255 and a glittering, sunny day. Also in Damascus that week was Hamoud Ghazal, nominally a Libyan commercial attaché, in fact a colonel in the military intelligence service. The German tourist entered Qasim Square from the west, following a Syrian guide and several other tourists.

Guyer watched the leader-strip count backward to one, then the film began with a slow pan up a white mosque to the blue-and-white-tile mosaic on the dome. Then a pan around the square: on three sides a columned arcade, a waterless fountain with a stained rim at the center. An old dented Citroën, color faded to matte by years of desert sun, can be seen briefly, parked on the south side of the square. The softened blue and gray of the dusty car contrasts nicely with the yellow

[29]

wall of the arcade. The film jumps suddenly to two fat women in white mesh sun hats, drinking mineral water at a round metal table, the wall of the cafe to their left briefly visible. The one on the right laughs and waves the photographer away, but the camera moves closer, then rises above their heads—a moment of blue sky— the focus adjusts, three men are entering the square together from the far end. They are strolling casually, the pace suggests a conversation, begun indoors, was thought to be more fruitful if continued outside. One of the men is talking, his head slightly inclined toward his listener. He wears Syrian army uniform, khaki and red, with flashes and insignia indicating considerable rank. The listener is walking with hands clasped behind his back. He is wearing a tropical-weight tan suit, a white shirt open at the neck, and sunglasses. Slightly to their left and behind them is another officer; by position and uniform it is clear that he is junior to both men. A momentary adjustment in focus (the lens initially turned in the wrong direction) as the tourist becomes interested in this grouping. The senior officer now gestures with his left hand, a rolling motion, as though paying out invisible fishing line. Apparently even more interesting to the tourist, who uses the instant zoom conversion on the Arriflex. The civilian has cropped curly hair, a high forehead, and is surprisingly young. The officer is dark, with a pitted complexion and a thick moustache. He takes off his sunglasses in order to gesture with them. Several frames of blue sky follow, the camera jerks, a flash of yellow building facade, what looks like the back of a man wearing white and, again, the three men. They are caught at the moment of collapse, falling sideways in unison, hands thrust palm-out to one side as though to ward off invisible blows. At their feet a small storm of dust dances across the cobblestones. The senior officer's face is in the foreground, his lips drawn back, teeth locked together, eyes pressed shut so hard the upper part of his face is distorted. The camera swings violently left, finds two men in pale shirts and dark pants walking backward. Each holds a short-barreled machine pistol, a long stream of shells ejecting from the chamber. For a foot in front of each barrel a thin current of visible air vibrates in rhythm to the rounds passing through it. They stop firing simultaneously, raising the ends of the guns slightly. The camera moves right. The civilian in the tan suit lies half twisted, his face to the sky, mouth open wide, eyes closed. The senior officer is facedown on the cobbled street, arms at sides, one foot resting on its toe. He has fallen with his face inside his upside-down officer's cap. The junior officer cannot be seen. The camera pans back left, finds the Citroën. The front door opens, a man in a suede jacket climbs out. His motion is efficient but not hurried. He opens the rear door, says something briefly, the two men with machine pistols enter the frame. Both have styled hair, one is quite tall and wears a closely trimmed beard, the shorter of the two is much younger, obviously a teen-ager. They carry their machine pistols loosely, by the gravity point in the middle. From their physical attitudes, what is on the street behind them has ceased to be interesting. When the man in the suede jacket closes the door behind them, he is seen in profile. His face is not remarkable: curly, sandy hair of medium short length, thin lips, delicate features, a European face. He turns, sees the camera and stares directly into the lens. His eyes have fine, webby lines at the corners, as though he has spent much of his life squinting into the sun, or as though he has found life faintly amusing. The face changes subtly, the expression around the eyes hardening, the head tilting slightly to one side. The film ends abruptly.

Guyer sat in the dark, staring at the empty screen. He'd seen the film many times before, it always brought the same question to mind: Why did the leader of the assassination team not take the camera away from the tourist? Probably it would have been bloody, a few more people would have been killed. That wouldn't have bothered the man in the suede jacket, but the slaughter would have been reported by the press in a very different light: an act of terrorism rather than an act of politics, and, Guyer knew, the southern rim of the Mediterranean was sensitive to such distinctions.

Legend that accompanied the film had it that the tour guide wasn't a tour guide at all, but a minor security operative. As soon as the Citroën drove from the square, he'd collected every single camera from the German tour group. From the guide the film went to Syrian intelligence, and from there to associated intelligence services with whom the Syrians shared product. Eventually someone produced a few copies. Spies are human, something really good cries to be shared. As for the man squinting into the afternoon sun, that was Raoul Delatte.

When Guyer was first approached about the Delatte project, the man was not unknown to him. His reputation defined him as a sometime criminal, sometime mercenary of the middle rank: not a bit player but not yet a star, certainly not a celebrity of the Carlos class. He had been born and raised in Corsica. Then served in the French military in an elite paratroop unit. From there he was dishonorably discharged, on pretext of minor theft of supplies. Rumor had it, however, that the discharge was in fact for undertaking, at the behest of the South African government, an assassination in Munich. He then served in the Spanish Legion, fighting Polisaro guerrillas in the Sahara. Eight months later he was forced to resign that commission, accused of excess brutality during the interrogation of civilians. To be accused of excess brutality by the Spanish Legion was in itself an eloquent comment on Delatte. Next, he worked for the French, this time under a private contract, with commando units in Chad. He disappeared from there to resurface, allegedly, at a major bank robbery in Antwerp, said to have been committed by a group of French ex-paratroopers. Two years later, during which time he was doing nobody knew what, he led the team that assassinated Hamoud Ghazal.

Delatte's decision not to expropriate the German tourist's camera had been a grave career error. It was not known who wanted Ghazal assassinated, or why they wanted him assassinated in Syria. The two gunmen were believed to be Iraqi Palestinians but that, in the Middle East, could mean almost anything. What *was* known was that the governments of Libya (Ghazal was a Libyan), Syria (the host country), Belgium (the Antwerp robbery), and France (on general principle) wanted him and wanted him badly. Intelligence agencies from many countries were made aware of the value of producing him. In that way Delatte became a non-person: unable to contact former associates, unable to disappear and resurface under a new identity, in hiding so deep it served as de facto death. He was an extremely valuable man at that point, worth so many dinars, Syrian pounds, francs, and dollars that he could not go out into the street.

Guyer's copy of the film had come from a man named Benauti. He had approached Richard List, Guyer's associate, in a restaurant in the East Fifties and handed him a reel of film. They'd spoken only briefly, then Benauti had left. List described the contact as tentative. He had inquired about Benauti and learned only that he was half French, half Tunisian, perhaps the son of a Tunisian NCO in the French Foreign Legion who had chosen the wrong side at the time when France was being kicked out of its North African colonies. Benauti was reputed to make a marginal living by acting as a go-between on the fringes of the intelligence community. Otherwise very little was known about him.

The film itself was a de facto indication of what Benauti was after. Guyer's company, in four years of operation, had acquired millions of photographs. By the use of a computer they were able to find individuals who, in a photographic context, could serve as doubles. Apparently, Benauti represented Delatte. Apparently, the reel of film was a probe to see if Guyer could come up with a suitable stand-in. They had run the facial image from the film through their computer and found a few faces that were close, and one that was very close. When Benauti called a few days later, Guyer suggested they meet.

Over dinner in a French restaurant Benauti explained that a deal was in progress to rehabilitate Delatte's reputation. A man of his talents, it was reasoned, should not remain forever invisible. He had now acquired the beneficial interest of "a significant client." This entity had the assets to meet Delatte's due bills from the various countries in which he'd operated. Negotiations would be undertaken, it was a certainty that directly concerned parties could be mollified by receiving something (more likely, someone) in lieu of Delatte. As for the French, well, all one needed there was money. Benauti (pronounced, he informed Guyer, in the Arabic fashion, accent on the final syllable) then proceeded to sketch out the delicate arrangements for Delatte's return to grace. For twenty minutes he spoke in the sort of soft generalities favored by State Department bureaucrats—where "sober discussions" meant fang marks on the throat. Reference was made to "certain accommodations," "proper climates," and "special conditions." Guyer listened hard but heard nothing.

[34]

Benauti was thin, his hairline receded to the middle of his head, he was dark-skinned, dark-eyed, and had a smooth, oily complexion. He spoke French-accented English, in a whisper, with such conspiratorial urgency he made Guyer uncomfortable.

For his part, Guyer took Benauti back over the ground as best he could, making very clear that the safety of a substitute individual was not to be compromised. Benauti dismissed that with a flick of the hand. It was a matter of photography only, no more. Delatte would appear at a certain time and a certain place to signal his assent to the arrangements offered. Why, Guyer wondered aloud, could he not appear himself? Benauti laughed, implying that men of the world do not ask such questions. Guyer persisted. Benauti diagrammed his answer by moving a fork through the *petits pois* on the expensive china: if, and it was unlikely, a hostile element should observe the substitute, the latter would be no more than followed, and he simply had to go home for it to be understood that he was a null. It was, Benauti insisted, the photograph that mattered. "Chames Bund will not shoot him with a fountain pen," he said with a condescending smile. Guyer probed once again. Benauti dug his heels in. They would likely be paying, he pointed out, a considerable fee, therefore they should not be pressured to reveal too much information. They were trusting Guyer, he would have to trust them.

The dinner was $189.40, Guyer paid the check. After they parted, he walked a long time before going home. He knew there was something wrong with the project, knew it for a certainty. He also knew there was a forty-thousand-dollar fee involved. The business had to have the money to stay alive, whether he had misgivings or not, so they would do it, but he knew in his heart it was going to end badly.

[35]

                              *   *   *

10:00 A.M. The coffee shop. Six blocks north on
Madison. List and Guyer met there most mornings,
usually on their way to work. It was a way to talk about
the day's problems away from the telephones. List ate
breakfast, Guyer drank coffee. By arrangement with the
cashier Guyer had copies of the *Times, The Wall Street
Journal,* and *The Christian Science Monitor* waiting for
him when he came in. If you took all three versions of
international events, Guyer believed, and accepted two
thirds of it, you would have a remote idea of what the
reality might be. It wasn't so much the facts—those
meant little in isolation—but the mood, the drift of the
wind, he was after. The problem with facts was that
every nation in the world had an intelligence apparatus
that understood perfectly that an effective press release
was worth ten thousand bullets. What Guyer most
needed to know, in fact, was what other people who
used the same resources *thought* was happening.
    Guyer drank black coffee and read the papers. Being
in the restaurant relaxed him. The tables were covered
with green-and-white-checked oilcloth. The salt and
pepper shakers were little ceramic windmills. There
were always paper place mats with games on them to
entertain the solitary diner: *Can You Name the Capitals of All Fifty States? Column A Lists the Capitals . . .*
He glanced up and watched List enter the restaurant.
At this time of the morning the coffee shop was a
popular spot for women shopping in the neighborhood.
Since the neighborhood was Madison Avenue in the
Seventies, they wore quiet clothing and quiet perfume,
and they spoke and laughed quietly. Guyer liked the
undercurrent they created, though that wasn't quiet at
all. When List entered, heads turned. With grace and
gentility and apparent lack of interest, but they moved

to where they could get a look. Guyer watched one woman in particular, in a knit suit the color of a clamshell, who stared, moved her eyes away, then went back for another look, without pausing in the story she was telling her friend.

List stopped for a beat, then moved forward. It was an actor's entrance. He had longish, dirty blond hair swept across his forehead like an English schoolboy. His skin was blue-white, a condition acquired during his heroin days. He tended to dress carefully, in British-cut tweed suits and thick cotton shirts with monochromatic wool ties. Often, though not today, a belted trench coat worn cape-style over the shoulders. What really set off his presence, however, was the cane. And the limp. The last a degree more extreme than polite or intriguing. In the Laotian town of Khong Mat, on the Cambodian border where the Mekong River branched to the west, he had been standing in front of a tiny cafe, staring at an old man eating a steamed bun, when a twelve-year-old boy came up silently behind him and hamstrung him with a sugarcane knife. List had collapsed, the tendon behind his left thigh severed. He must have moved involuntarily, because the boy had meant to do the job completely but the knife passed through the right pants leg, barely breaking the skin. Sitting in the dust, he had stared in shock into the boy's face. He had no idea what had been done to him, but there was blood on the knife and he knew it was his. He thought he was dead. He'd seen people mortally wounded who for a few minutes after the hit were normally and perfectly alive. "Why do you not run away?" he said to the boy in Lao. The boy returned the knife to a sheath on his belt, turned, and ran. List killed him on the second step.

"Good morning," Guyer said as List settled himself in the chair. He hung his cane on the edge of the table.

"Morning, Captain."

"Chilly out."

"Getting winter. The man on the television says that caterpillars are growing long fur this year."

A waitress appeared. She topped off Guyer's cup from a steaming Silex and said to List, "Ready to order, dear?"

"A number six," he said, "with a toasted English muffin instead of toast, butter and raspberry jam on the side." That was his usual. A poached egg and one strip of bacon. The muffin was his daily indulgence. "What news of the world?" He gestured with his eyes toward the mound of newsprint in front of Guyer.

"General Moreno, leader of the Bolivian junta, has not been heard from since contact was lost with his plane somewhere over the Andes. Prime Minister Korvas, in Malta, has managed to form a new government by making concessions to the Social Democrats."

"Do we care, this morning?"

"We are concerned, but not involved."

"So far as we know, that is."

"Amen."

List sipped at his coffee. His eyes narrowed. "Captain, where did you get that suit?"

"This? A store near my apartment."

"You must let me take you shopping. For the good of the business."

"Pretty bad?"

"You look like Bob Hope in *Road to Rio*."

Guyer shrugged. He felt that List had sufficient style for both of them, and it was enough to have one person in the office who looked like a spy.

"Maybe," Guyer said, "next week." It was a polite way to say no. List was his associate, in the strictest paper terms of the business, but had long ago become his spiritual partner in the actual running of the company.

List read his mind. Raised two fingers tight together.

"Scout's honor I won't try to make you look like one of us." He was grinning.

"I'm not worried about that," Guyer said levelly.

"Did the work go well last night?"

"Everybody was where they were supposed to be, we got what we went after. . . ." He shrugged. They both knew an operation stayed warm for several months after the action terminated. It could still, with fangs and claws, come roaring back to life.

"What's the disposal procedure?"

"Who knows. Langer said he'd be in touch, we'll just hang on to it until then."

"Dental X rays," List mused. "Somebody covering their tracks."

"I would think."

They were silent for a minute, Guyer's eyes fell back on his newspaper. Disarmament talks. Japanese trade incursions.

"Where are we with Delatte?" List asked.

"Pretty much ready to go. Benauti is due to call. Maybe today."

"*Meester* Benauti. The Peter Lorre spy. Life imitates art—"

"Yeah, well—"

"—and gets it wrong again."

Guyer's laugh was halfhearted. He'd seen what could happen when superficially silly people weren't taken seriously. And List's wisecracks put him in mind of Arconada—he knew that contempt was an indulgence, a luxury they couldn't afford.

"By the way," Guyer said, "we're not going to use Arconada anymore."

"Oh dear. What happened?"

"Nothing substantive, but . . ." Guyer circled his finger in the air. The gesture meant intuitions of danger, negative vibrations. He knew that if he started up a lecture on employee attitudes, List would make jokes.

List's breakfast arrived. Guyer watched him work butter onto a cooling muffin half and felt a pang of simultaneous hunger and nausea. He took a sip of coffee.

"Can we afford this fussy taste in thieves?"

"I think we better," Guyer said.

"I mean, your traditional ex-agency spook, you know, he'll do you a nice penetration. But the rates are very uptown. I'm all in favor of going upscale, nothing I like better, but you start talking to these characters and it's a guy in a car, a guy in the building across the street, walkie-talkies, dry runs, damage control, bow-wow woof-woof . . ."

"You can't tell me our friend is the only semitrustworthy burglar in New York." Guyer's voice had a slight edge. Darkside recruitment was List's responsibility.

"No, no. It's around. How'd Maggie do?"

"Great. No problems. But the other thing, maybe you'll work it into your schedule to stop by Monte Carlo."

"If I must, I must." He shook his head. "The Waltz of the Slavs."

The Monte Carlo was a restaurant in the East Fifties. It looked from the outside like a thousand other places in Manhattan, a sort of continental bistro with a maroon awning. People who'd lived in the city all their lives routinely passed by such places and wondered, *What is this one all about?* It had low lighting, red carpet, white tablecloths, old waiters, and a Franco-Italian menu with cheesecake the recommended dessert. What it was, in reality, was a demilitarized zone for New York's covert community. A spot where people could find each other without prior contact. The clientele ran to the requisite "chauffeurs" from the Eastern Bloc diplomatic community, third world bureaucrats attached to United Nations agencies, private-for-profit intelligence people, CIA junior staff, and a small army of free-floating spooks of every possible affiliation. By unspoken but rigid agreement no operations ran inside the Monte Carlo. No electronics, trick photos, potions in drinks, or body snatchings were allowed. One game run would have been enough to ruin everybody's office away from the office. There was graffiti in the men's toilet, center stall, that said, "You are in the safest place in New York City." Below it were two words in cyrillic alphabet with an exclamation point, the Eastern European equivalent of "right on."

List finished his muffin. "Arconada's replacement. You have something for him?"

"No. We'd be better off never doing that garbage, but"—he spread his hands—"semper paratus and all that."

The waitress appeared with the Silex and refilled both their cups. List put three spoonfuls of sugar into his coffee, then caught Guyer watching him. "Extra energy," he explained. "It's going to be a long day." Guyer looked at him for an instant longer than necessary. They both knew that drug addicts craved sugar.

"You can relax, Skipper," List said, one eyebrow rising slightly, "that's all in my sordid past." Guyer took one sip of the new coffee, then stood. List said, "You going now?"

"Yeah, might as well. You want any of this?"

"Leave the section of the *Times* with the crossword."

" 'Kay. See you at the office."

"I'll be along."

Guyer paid and walked down Madison toward his office.

The ground floor of Guyer's building was occupied by an art gallery called Galani, its name spelled out across the window in gold block letters. Guyer's entrance was around the corner on East 74th Street. There was a small vestibule, and a stairway up to the second floor, where Kevin worked in the small reception area. Most of the second floor was storage space for the gallery. Guyer occupied the top floor. The companies located at 40 East 74th Street received an enormous volume of mail. They were phantom companies, set up by Guyer to do exactly that. At first they'd used a post-office box, but quickly learned two things: (1) the general public distrusted post-office boxes, response to a street address was considerably better, (2) the sheer bulk of the mail made the PO box a nightmare. So they'd gone to a street address and let the postman do the work. Bottles of Johnnie Walker Black Label for Christmas and July Fourth assured excellent service. Considering the nature of the firms, the volume of mail wasn't that surprising. There was the American Institute of College Yearbooks; Photofile, a stock house; Portrait Studio Contest of America, Inc.; Consolidated Clipping Service, which specialized in Chamber of Commerce magazines and newsletters, community newspapers, and the Business and Life-style sections of daily and Sunday newspapers. And Intercast, an economic forecast group that subscribed to endless trade and industrial journals. It usually took Kevin three trips to bring the mail upstairs, though certain times of year were heavier than others. In late June and early July, for instance, every college yearbook in the United States was mailed to the American Institute of College Yearbooks. Not only did AICY subscribe, and prepay postage, they awarded a thousand-dollar prize for "Excellence in Annual College or University Yearbooks." List, in a parody of manic indecision, always made the choice on the last working day in August. The previous August the University of Tulsa *Pawnee* had taken first prize, with Texas Tech's *Blue and Gold* walking away with a five-hundred-dollar second place. In December, envelopes pleading "Photographs—Please Do Not Bend" would arrive for the Portrait Studio Contest of America. Again they spread prize money around, making sure that geographical distribution was maintained. A few hundred dollars spent in St. Louis one year brought floods of entries in the year following, from cities and towns throughout Missouri and Kansas. Again, word of mouth. They kept a job printer in Brooklyn very busy in certain seasons, with certificates of merit, excellence awards, first, second, and third prizes, and honorable mentions. The more they gave out, the greater the number of participants. The commercial world had, apparently, a great appetite for hanging framed documents on its walls. Three years earlier they'd brought into existence a company called Seaboard Demographic Research, Inc. With that, they were able to buy driver-license duplications from those states that used photographs on their licenses, most of which, for revenue purposes, permitted sale to private corporations. SDR had also been able to obtain, from a medium-size credit corporation, photo-ID tapes taken by store cameras at point of sale. One night when Guyer and List were working in the office at midnight, List had looked up wearily from a staggering pile of correspondence and said, "At last, Captain, the craft of intelligence." That was fact. Ninety percent of contemporary intelligence work was compilation of one sort or another, drawn from trade journals, newspapers, satellite-site photos, or microwave-sound interception. The number of facts held had become exponential, banked in the computers of intelligence and security agencies everywhere.

Kevin was busy at the reception desk, logging in manila envelopes with a date and number stamp: inventory control had become a necessity early on. He looked up and said, "Mr. Guyer."

"Kevin." He picked up a short stack of phone messages and began to browse. "What's the mail like?"

"Normal day, sir."

Guyer's eye wandered to the telephone. One line was lit, another was blinking on hold. Only Mrs. Foley was up in the office, who did she have on hold? "Anything in the mail for us?" He meant the business itself, which ran under the name Metro Data Research, Inc. They'd found they could do very nearly anything in that name, in terms of purchased services and equipment, and nobody found it odd or unusual. Kevin answered the phone with the last four digits of the number.

"Yessir," Kevin said, thumbing quickly through a small stack next to the bulk of packages and large envelopes. "Brokerage house acknowledgments."

"I'll take those," Guyer said. The company was paid in that format. Cash in large amounts drew too much attention from the wrong people. There was a quiet buzz and one of the lines lit up.

"9930," Kevin answered. Then, "One moment, sir, I'll see if he's available." He popped the line on to *hold* and said to Guyer, "A Mr. David Sears."

"Hunh. Sure, Kevin, ask him to wait, I'll take it in the office."

He heard Kevin relay the message as he trotted up the stairs to his office on the top floor. He moved quickly to his desk, picked up the telephone and said, "Guyer."

"This is David Sears." The quality of the connection told Guyer the call was long-distance.

"Hello, David, how've you been?"

"Just great. How are you?"

"I'm fine. Nice to hear your voice, what's it been, six years?"

[44]

"Seven. Seven this spring. In D.C., I think."

"You're right. Are you still there?" A very slight accent on the last word.

"No. I left there about two years ago." Sears stressed the word *there,* as Guyer had.

"Oh?"

"Yes. I resigned."

"Sorry to hear that. You seemed pretty squared away."

"I guess I was. But it changed. Or I changed. I don't know. I got divorced, among other things." He paused. "It wasn't a redundancy, my resignation, they didn't want me to leave. I burned out a little on the office politics. Maybe that."

"Happens." Guyer's voice was sympathetic.

"The work itself, well, I liked the work. Maybe *like* isn't the word. I was very involved with it."

"Unh-huh."

"And I was sorry to leave that part of it." *Who got you?* Guyer wondered. *Did I know him?*

"Where are you now?"

"That's a funny one. I'm at Memphis State University."

"Teaching?"

"Well, some of the time. Actually, I'm a graduate assistant here, in the department of education. I'm working on a Ph.D." Guyer computed an approximate age, came up at forty-five. "So," Sears continued, "some quarters I teach a beginning class, and I do some research."

"That's terrific. A completely different sort of thing."

"Oh, you'd be surprised, a lot of it's analogous."

"I guess it would be." Guyer glanced at his watch. 10:17. Very close to bank time. Where the hell was List? Was he going to hang out at the coffee shop the whole morning?

"Actually, the reason I'm calling, I ran into a mutual acquaintance and I heard you'd set up your own business."

"Yes, that's right."

"Well, it's not that I'm unhappy here, but it's getting to be something of a financial burden. I guess I got used to a more, uh, to a different sort of life-style and"— Guyer heard a faintly perceptible hitch in his voice as he prepared to take the plunge—"well I was wondering if you might have something available for somebody with my particular background. Nothing spectacular, of course. I feel I can be a constructive addition. For the right sort of people, of course."

"I appreciate your thinking of me," Guyer said. He didn't want to let Sears work into the full pitch, wanted to keep him as unhumiliated as possible. "I don't think I can give you much of an answer right now. With what we have right now we're running staff at the limit. So if things get a little better, I'd say there's a reasonable chance we might take on somebody. I had no idea you were available, David. Is there a number where I can reach you?"

"Yes. I'm at 901-555-3136. Best time is in the evening."

"Okay. All I can hold out is that there's a fair possibility we will get some kind of upswing here. At that point . . ."

"A probationary period, you know, wouldn't bother me at all. I realize I'm going to have to sacrifice a little to get back into things. So please don't think of it as a major salary investment. Once we both know where we're going, well we can talk about that."

"I appreciate the flexibility, it certainly would help us to go one step at a time. Meanwhile, look, if you get to New York, it'd be nice to sit down and talk. Do you get up here at all?"

[46]

"No. Not really. Maybe I could call again, say in sixty, ninety, days, just to check in."

"Sure. That'd be fine. I'm glad you called. Always good to hear from old friends."

"And good to talk to you. Sounds like you're doing very nicely."

"Not too bad."

"Then I'll be in touch."

"Yeah. Let me know where you are if you move or—"

"I will. Good-bye. And thanks."

"No problem. Talk to you soon."

"Take care now."

"I will. And good luck." Guyer placed the phone gently on the cradle and felt a brief shudder go off inside him.

He checked his watch again. 10:18. In ten minutes he'd have to go himself. He wrote David Sears's number and name on a piece of paper, walked it over to Edna Foley's area. She was seated in front of the console that spoke to the computer downstairs, running a series of black and white photos under a scanner hood and punching in codes. Mrs. Foley was in her early fifties, a large woman who carried her weight well. The widow of a merchant seaman, she lived quietly somewhere in northern New Jersey and took a Trailways bus into Manhattan every morning. Guyer did not speak when he placed the note in her in-tray. She had made it clear to everyone in the office that she was not to be disturbed when working at the console. Guyer acknowledged that he was a little afraid of her. While she was not at all temperamental, she implied somehow a temperamental streak and was able to bully Guyer and List into giving her considerable latitude.

Sears's entry would be encoded as it went into the computer. You could, Guyer thought, have the deepest cover and the finest security in the world, still, only a fool would keep a Rolodex in this business.

List came through the door as Guyer returned to his desk.

"Don't sit down," Guyer said.

List raised his eyebrows.

"Would you walk a thousand up to the bank and deposit it in the Nagle account?"

"Okay."

"I told Nagle he could withdraw at eleven."

"That's fine. How's it set up?"

"Joint partnership account. Hurwitz and Russo doing business as Plymouth Dry Cleaning. We're Hurwitz. The checkbook is in the drawer with the petty cash. Oh yeah, count the deposit slips. I think I remember it being low."

"Any special account to write it out of?"

"It'll have to come from Metro Data. The charge-back code is RIC. Make sure, Richard, that that gets on the check. It has to wind up on the Ricard/Expense side in the books."

"Anything else while I'm out?"

"Uhhh, no. We take care of the phone man at the end of the month. Maggie and that doorman get envelopes today, but I'll probably run them around myself. Right now, let's just keep Nagle happy. Will they clear that check into the account?"

"They always have. That branch is a whorehouse."

"Make sure. I don't want to run Nagle into any of that uncollected funds bullshit."

"The true peril we face, Captain, right at this moment, is that you'll keep me here so long, while you play warthog in the bushes, that I'll wind up standing behind Nagle in the bank line. Okay?"

"Sorry. Talk to you later."

List limped to the spare desk, opened a drawer, and began rummaging through various checkbooks, bankbooks, brokerage house statements, and other financial accounting paper that tended to accumulate there. They would, one of these days, Guyer thought, have to clean up that drawer. He felt that a well-ordered office was a good adjunct to morale. But unless Mrs. Foley became annoyed by the mess, it was generally a lost cause.

Guyer shuffled the phone messages into a working priority, then took a to-do list from a stack of filing trays and placed them side by side. If the fates were kind, some of the items on the list could be crossed off by calling back some of the people on the pile. He ran an index finger down the list, and peeled messages off one by one. The fates were not kind. Back to the first item on the list, Thomas Novotny. Telephone number with a 305 area code. That meant Miami. What the hell was he doing there? He'd had the feeling, all along, that he was dealing with an Eastern European exile group, probably based in Chicago. He dialed.

"Good morn-ing. The Beach-wood." The operator was so wired on customer relations she was practically singing like a bird.

"818, please."

"Thank you. One mo-ment."

"Hello?"

"Mr. Novotny?"

"Who is this?"

"Your friend in New York—who arranged a guest appearance."

"Hey, hello."

"How are you doing?"

"Great. It's just fabulous down here. Warm and sunny. Beautiful. I'll tell you a crazy coincidence."

"What's that?"

"I was just getting ready to call you."

"I'm glad we connected. What were you going to call about?"

"Next Thursday, absolutely, I'm going to take care

[49]

of that brokerage house situation. You use Hulin and Associates, right? I want to check that account number with you, I think I have it . . ."

"I assume you're referring to the entire obligation."

"I'm gonna try. I know I can get most of it."

"Fifteen thousand dollars."

"I'm at eight five as it stands today. Tomorrow I have lunch with a man here. I think all our problems will be solved."

"Mr. Novotny, it's been two months and a few days. I appreciate your difficulties but we can't wait longer than Thursday. Our business won't run without cash, it's that simple. We did our job to your satisfaction, now we have to be paid the second installment. Okay?"

"Okay. What about this, Monday I'll put through the eight five, then two weeks later you'll have the rest, that'd be six thousand five hundred."

"No."

"I don't want to hold your money. Why not make it like a loan? We'll figure it at two percent a month, that way everybody benefits. So you'll have the eight five, and the rest with interest. Now that's fair."

"I want it Thursday. All of it. No interest, just the entire fifteen thousand. Please."

There was a long silence. Guyer willed himself not to break it. Novotny held out for twenty seconds.

"Well . . ." he said.

"We have an agreement now, is that right, Mr. Novotny?"

"Okay. How late are they open on Thursday?"

"Until five."

"All right, there's a way. . . ."

"Good."

"I'm really sorry about this. We've had some un-anticipated problems."

Guyer hung up.

He walked over to the small table where a half-full

Silex rested on a coil heater, wedged a conical paper cup into an orange plastic holder, and poured a cup of coffee. His eyes rested for a moment on an open jar of nondairy creamer with a spoon rising from its rim, but he foresaw disappointment and returned to his desk. For a time, in the beginning, they'd had mugs: nice thick white ones that recalled diners and roadside cafés, but nobody really washed them, and the rinse-when-needed program at last offended everybody. He'd better, he thought, have a look at the brokerage house acknowledgments. He scanned the desk, no envelope. Began lifting the corners of various papers and peering underneath. Goddamn it, Kevin had handed him the envelope, where was it? He slid open a drawer, then slammed it. He was about to become very angry when he noticed a slight weight dragging at one pocket of his jacket. He made a sound of relief, withdrew the envelope, and opened it.

The tidal motion of vast sums of money was one of the great studies in the intelligence business. Given: A must pay B. At arm's length. Ideally, without meeting. With the faintest possible track left after the transaction was completed. Numbered accounts in Swiss banks were essentially remnants of another age. There was, after all, so rarely a Swiss bank on the corner when you needed one. The torch had passed to the financial institutions of the Cayman Islands: a nation with twice as many bank accounts as citizens. Somebody had to notice, and of course somebody did. Investigative reporters were followed by investigative investigators. In the hide-the-money game, fashion was unusually fickle. The problem was compounded by certain banks in certain countries who let it be known that your money was hidden when stored in their vaults. Unfortunately, it rather often turned out that your money was hidden from you as well. And it was worse than pointless to shoot the teller. Guyer and List had worked out a format that served them adequately. It wasn't perfect, but it satisfied the clients because it protected their anonymity. The client simply walked in to any one of a number of brokerage houses and purchased bearer bonds in thousand-dollar denominations. These bonds tended to be for gold (essentially warehouse receipts of a negotiable sort) or U.S. Treasury paper. The broker selling them the bonds would ask for a name, they would give him a name, he would write it down. The bonds were then taken to a small brokerage house that Guyer had found. There, the depositor requested that the bonds be placed in a numbered account. For the client, that was that. The bonds were then registered under what was known in the business as a "street name," in fact the name of the brokerage house, and cashed. The broker then mailed a check to a false company at an accommodation address. Now *he* was off the hook. The checks were then remailed to Guyer's bank, the brokerage acknowledgments remailed to Metro Data Research. The omniscient third party to all such transactions, the IRS, was neutralized by the clever ruse of paying income taxes on time, quarterly, and forswearing the kinds of deductions that historically drew return fire. The IRS, they found, cared not what you did as long as they got their piece of the action. As for the system protecting Guyer and the company, it didn't. Any sensible FBI bloodhound could easily enough sniff out the path their money took, but they felt that by the time anybody cared enough to do that, the game would already be up. What they did, their business, rested in a very gray area of the legal spectrum, except when they were forced by a client to do the sort of damp work Arconada had managed the previous night. But all things considered, their payment procedure worked: it spared them retrieval of envelopes taped beneath park benches, and shifty-eyed hoods carrying wads of cash into the office.

[52]

Guyer looked at the brokerage house acknowledgments. There were four. He had a fantasy, for a moment, about the day when there would be hundreds and he would have to hire an accounts receivable clerk to manage this side of things. It would amount to hiring somebody to count your money. *It will come,* he thought, *just be patient.* He placed the statements on a pile headed for Mrs. Foley, then checked the second item on his list, meanwhile wondering where Kevin was with the rest of the mail. Most of the mail that came in would be meaningless, the real action took place on the phone or in person. Still, if you had an address, you had mail and, since some attention had to be paid to the maintenance of cover, it had to be answered. But that was for later. The second item facing him was in a sort of personal code. He had to have an employer-employee talk with List. There was no major dereliction of duty, but that only made it harder. Rather, it was an accumulation of small sins, as though List's attention were elsewhere, and his work seemed generally half-hearted. Guyer hated this kind of discussion. List would resent it. He himself would wind up being apologetic, it probably *was* his fault, after all. . . . The intercom buzzed.

"Yes?"

"Mr. Guyer, you just had a request for a call-back."

"Okay."

"A Mr. Johnson is at 555-8232. Please contact him. He requests that you use a neutral phone."

"Thank you, Kevin." *Mr. Johnson,* he thought, *Mr. Jackson and Mr. James, Mr. White and Mr. Green.* He dialed the number. *Neutral phone,* he thought, *how about a black phone?* He counted six rings. Out there somewhere, he knew, a paranoid was biting his nails and waiting for the call. Well, he had it. Now it remained for the man to rev up his courage, swallow his fear, and answer the goddamn thing.

[53]

"Shamrock," a voice growled. A bar and grill, Guyer thought.

"Mr. Johnson there?"

"Hold on a minute." There was a plastic thud as the receiver was dropped on the bar. He could hear a juke-box playing Tony Bennett in the background, and a low murmur of voices. "Hey, we got a Johnson here?"

Guyer heard a laugh. Then the bartender came back on. "Here he comes," he said, and dropped the phone again.

"Here is Mr. Chonson." Benauti, he thought. De-latte's representative. He hissed his esses like a stage Frenchman.

"This is your friend you just asked to call back."

"Mr. G.?"

"Yeah." He imagined Benauti in his four-hundred-dollar overcoat with the satin collar, brooding over a ginger ale in a high wooden booth, his great beak of a nose trying not to breathe the beer and bourbon fume of the place.

"My client would like to know if we may proceed. If you have what we will require."

"Yes."

"You can prove this?"

"With a document, yes. How should we handle transmission?"

"Pardon?" He said it in French.

"What do you want us to do with it?" He spaced each word carefully.

"We must meet."

"Okay."

"Op-servation deck. Empire State Building. Three P.M."

Guyer groaned silently. It would leave him down-town in the rush hour with small chance of a cab back to his office. He decided to at least try. "There's a bar in the Sixties, on Lexington Avenue—"

[54]

"Pleece." The voice was intense. "The rendezvous as I have said."

"Okay. Three."

"Thank you," Benauti said, and hung up. Guyer sighed. There went the afternoon. He put the phone back on the cradle and the intercom buzzed.

"Yes?"

"A Mr. Francis Mains holding on 34."

"Thank you, Kevin." His stomach twisted inside him. He jabbed the 9934 button before he could think about it. "Guyer," he said.

"Mr. Guyer? Mr. Francis Mains calling, one moment please." It was a woman's voice, low and cool against the ocean background of a long-distance line.

Okay, Guyer thought, *now I know you have a secretary.* But it was a defensive thrust. His heart was thudding. He closed his eyes for a second.

"Good morning." Mains's voice was as he remembered it. Strong and aristocratic at the center, faintly insinuating at the edges. With, overall, a strange quality: as though it were attempting to fade, disappear, be soft enough so that you had to lean toward it. When you listened to Mains, he thought, you heard a battle between power and discretion.

"Hello," Guyer said, consciously pitching his tone to mean absolutely nothing.

"What's the weather up there?"

It's raining blood. Guyer closed his eyes again, tried to settle himself mentally. Went up a level, criticized himself for the depth of his reaction. It helped. He waited a beat, then said, "It's cold. Gray skies." *What the hell do you want?* he thought. First Sears, now Mains. From nowhere, his past was flooding back at him.

"I love New York in late fall," Mains said, "here it's overcast and humid. I really believe the ills of American government are due to the weather in D.C." There was a brief silence, to give him time, evidently, to meditate on Mains's epiphany. "That aside," he continued, "how is everything with you?"

"I'm doing fine."

"So I hear, so I hear. And the dreadful Mr. List?" The voice was playful.

"He's fine too."

"You know, of course, about Mains, Gulbenyan and Associates."

"Yes."

"Somewhat strange, being in business for oneself, after all those years. I imagine you find it so as well."

"A little."

"I'd much rather have located in New York, but of course a great deal of what we do is centered here. People must be seen constantly. Steal a bureaucrat's free lunch, you know, and you have stolen his soul. So I am here for the duration, as they say. Still, the ideal thing would be to have some obligations up there. Enough to justify a weekly trip. All the culture here is imported, it has that feeling. I miss the theatre, the nightclubs, the galleries on Madison Avenue."

The galleries on Madison Avenue. Guyer knew he wasn't hypersensitive. With Mains, accidental inference did not exist.

"It's all so alive," Mains continued, "vital." He let the word hang in the air.

"Yeah," Guyer said.

"I really think," Mains went on, as though Guyer hadn't spoken, "the optimum situation would be to have affiliation in both places. One could be down here, where the funds flow in, and up there, where they tend to flow out. Thus nature strives for perfect balance. You understand what I'm saying."

Did he? His mind locked on the word *affiliation.* It yielded nothing. It was a rubbery word, would fit endless possibilities if you tugged at its meaning.

[56]

"I'd think it would be easy for you to find something here."

"Any old thing, yes. The right thing, that's another matter. Mains, Gulbenyan has been a success, you see, and it turns out that success spawns a lot of damn obligations. Corporations are finicky eaters. I must add that all of this, ah, these sorts of arabesques, come to me late in life. Government service turns out to have been simpler, comparatively speaking. Do you find it so?"

"Yes."

"The private sector makes demands. No room for those who won't act with decisiveness. What is it the Rotarians say? Has he ever met a payroll? Very maturing thing. I'm sure you find yourself facing realities with a much colder eye these days."

"Not really."

"Well you will, you will. Tell me, do you get out into New York, New York very much? I hope you do. A pity if you don't. Isn't there a wonderful aquarium up there?"

"I think there is. I've never been there."

"Then you must go. It will do you good. All the clichés, sense of peace, what have you, come true. Go at five, if you can. Five o'clock at the aquarium, sounds like a Stevens poem, doesn't it. Well, it is like that, full of passing images, with a lesson if you can perceive it." He stopped abruptly. The silence grew.

"I'll make it a point to get there, sometime."

"You really should. Make sure to go at five, that's when it's best."

"Okay."

"Well, I'm being called into a meeting. That much hasn't changed. If you see a company you think might be interesting, give me a call, will you?"

"Okay."

"Good-bye, Guyer."

They hung up.

Guyer took his hand off the phone. At some point Kevin had come in and left a stack of mail on the catchall desk. *5:00 P.M. at the aquarium*, he thought, *has nothing to do with meeting anybody.* He could confirm it with a phone call, but he didn't need to do that. 5:00 P.M. would turn out to be feeding time. When big fish ate little fish.

The last time he'd seen Mains was near a small city called Agadir, on the Atlantic coast of Morocco. They were a mile out of town on an empty beach of brown pebbles. The sea was calm, the waves coming on shore only a few inches high. A hundred feet away an old Fiat was idling. The sun had just risen. Guyer could smell exhaust from the car, it irritated him, but he didn't ask Mains to turn it off. They were waiting for a Navy helicopter that would take Guyer back to Algeciras, where he'd catch a plane to Barcelona. For a time they didn't talk, then Mains said, "I'd think, at this late date in your career, it should hardly be necessary to remind you that we do not make policy, we only implement it. Policy is made at the State Department, period." Guyer said, without heat, "Policy didn't do it. You did it. It wasn't necessary, it wouldn't have hurt anything to let the man find his way home." Mains peered at him intently for a moment. "Are you sure you have the stomach for this business?" he said. Guyer lost one edge of his control. "We didn't gain anything," he said. "It was just cold-bloodedness for its own sake." Mains shook his head slowly and laughed quietly, moved by the irony of everything. Guyer spit on him.

* * *

2:45. Waiting for a cab. His appointment with Benauti in fifteen minutes. It started to snow, big wet flakes that melted when they hit the pavement. Empty cabs disappeared, so Guyer waited under the awning of a European pastry shop until it became clear that the snow wouldn't stop. Then, head down, he walked over to Fifth to try and catch a bus to 34th, the Empire State Building. *Of all the goddamn places,* he thought.

As he stood at the bus stop, Guyer's sense of time pecked at him. The snow fell faster, traffic jammed and clogged. His shoes were getting wet, and he was afraid he would be late and that Benauti, nervous at the best of times, would take flight. Then the whole exercise would have to be repeated. He peered fiercely up Fifth Avenue, but there wasn't a bus to be seen. A few minutes before three he gave up on the bus and started walking south, from bus stop to bus stop, pausing at each to look over his shoulder in case one appeared. The first bus passed him on 61st. He ran after it. It pulled away. The second one went by while he was between the stops on 55th and 53rd. He swore at it and accelerated to a sprint just as a cab pulled up next to him and deposited an old lady with a fox stole around her shoulders.

By the time he walked from the elevator on the 102nd floor of the Empire State Building, it was 3:20. He saw Benauti immediately, pacing nervously back and forth. He looked pathetic, thin shoulders hunched together inside his expensive coat, dark eyes flashing with anxiety. With the snow falling, the Manhattan skyline was nearly invisible, but a Japanese tour group was clicking cameras energetically. How many photographs, Guyer wondered, were taken in the world today?

"Yes, yes," said Benauti, instead of hello, scolding Guyer for being late.

"The weather," Guyer explained.

[59]

Benauti blew on his hands. "I have been living in a warmer place."

Looking over Benauti's shoulder, Guyer saw a small head with glossy black hair pop around a corner, scowl dramatically for an instant, then disappear. Guyer suppressed a laugh. It was a Japanese kid, about eight years old, who'd had no trouble at all making Benauti for a spy.

"I think we better take a little walk around the corner," Guyer said. Benauti cringed. "Easy," he soothed. "Just for form's sake." After they turned the corner, he handed an envelope to Benauti. Inside was a photo. Behind Benauti, the Japanese kid was edging along the wall like a western gunfighter, his back pressed against the glass of the interior viewing-platform. Guyer reminded himself to tell List about it. Watching Benauti's tense face, and the kid imitating him at the same moment, almost proved too much. He looked down at his feet.

"If my client approves," Benauti said, "how shall we proceed?"

"Deposit in our account at the brokerage signals your agreement. First half of the fee."

"Very well."

"But there's a time thing here. Maybe we better assume everything's going to go, because if you have foreign travel in mind, that'll take some time to set up. Passports, various things. What you don't do is come on the phone telling me the deposit is made and asking for action that night. Can't be done. Yes?"

"All right."

"It helps us with the lead time to have an idea of what we're into."

"Next Friday," Benauti said, after a pause.

"Christ," Guyer answered. Benauti didn't want to tell him where Delatte was, he realized. But if he had a

[60]

notion of *mailing* the photo someplace, especially out of the country, and waiting for a reply, the whole deal was screwed. Guyer didn't want this one to die. Too many times they were approached, negotiations commenced, developmental money was spent, and nothing happened. In the intelligence world for every action undertaken a thousand plans were laid, but in the vast majority of cases the product of conspiracy was air. Benauti raised his hands helplessly. Procedure was procedure, what could he do? "What I'm saying," Guyer sounded very patient, "is that it would not be premature to give us some idea of what we're facing." If Benauti committed information, he reasoned, he'd work hard to have the project accepted. The "lead time" ogre was simply a pressure point that was universally respected—they could move like a streak once the money was paid.

Benauti looked at his watch. "It is 3:31," he said.

"Yes."

"By 6:30, then, you'll have an answer." Which meant, to Guyer, (1) Benauti himself was making the decision, or (2) he had access to a secure teleprinter, which implied embassy, which in turn implied that the "significant client" sponsoring the rehabilitation was in fact running the play, or (3) Delatte was in New York.

Guyer thought, *What the hell,* and fired his final shot. "Good. That'll allow us time to do the job right. You can give us detailed instructions over the telephone." He watched the last word move across Benauti's face.

"We can meet," Benauti said, but it was tentative.

"No."

A puff of wind lifted an oiled strand of Benauti's hair up straight, then dropped it. "Very well," he said with resignation. "Your individual must to take a flight from Rio de Janeiro, on Varig, next Saturday, 3:30 P.M."

"Not this Saturday."

"No. One week. It is the 29th of October."

"Okay. Let's both remember that we agreed that the fee to our person is additional to the main payment."

Benauti acknowledged that with a nod of the head. "When can we expect it?" Guyer said.

"Ten thousand dollars."

"Correct."

"Why do we not divide it as the main fee is divided?"

"Okay. Anything else we have to know?"

"The man must come back into the United States under a certain cover."

Guyer knew what that meant. It made him furious. First Langer paid them to penetrate an office, now this little weasel was about to stick him with procuring a passport. It was like being in public relations or some goddamn thing like that—initially clients wanted press releases, but after they paid you, they wanted tickets to football games. *It wasn't what they did.*

"Something is wrong?" Benauti said.

"He'll need a passport," Guyer answered.

Benauti shrugged. Apparently it wasn't a problem. "I can give you that now, if you like."

Guyer's anger turned to exultation. They had the job. He almost smiled. "Just hand it to me openly," he said. Nothing provoked unwanted attention so much as public stealth.

With a great show of casualness Benauti reached into an inside pocket and handed Guyer a passport. From the cover Guyer recognized it as Canadian. "Thank you," he said. He put it in his pocket. Realized with a start he was still carrying the dental X rays.

"There are, uh, directions," Benauti said. "Can you remember them?" There was a mean little sulk in his voice as he said it, and Guyer realized he had gone much too far, telling him how to hand over a document in a public place. Guyer was briefly annoyed with himself for the lapse. He knew he could take care of business—do good work at a fair price on time—but felt he graded C minus in the probably more important art of ego massage. And if *he* was bad, List—prickly, sensitive to slight, and constitutionally arrogant—was worse. He felt that if their business ultimately failed, an inability to flatter would be at the root of it.

"Just say it slowly," Guyer said, a rather limp attempt at being self-effacing. He'd wanted to make some verbal gesture indicating that they all had their difficulties in the base-level techniques of the trade, but once he got the answer out, he realized that he'd landed well wide of the mark. For one thing, there was very damn little he couldn't remember. He'd been through the mnemonics courses at the Company Farm near McLean and still knew the names of the Cleveland Symphony Orchestra, the Detroit Lions, and the weekday Pan Am schedule from Houston of that year.

"Number one," Benauti said, holding up his index finger, "we must have a, how is it said, path?"

"Track?"

"Yes, a track that begins in Rio. So when he arrives, that should be Friday the 28th in order to return early on Saturday the 29th, he must register at a hotel under the passport name, which is Gerard. He will, of course, fly to Brazil using his own name."

"Of course," Guyer answered mechanically. But it bothered him. It meant that Benauti, or his associates, would have permanent access to the substitute. They could go right around him and approach the man directly. Cutting his fee, for starts, and God knew what else after that. After all, his resources were his business, so he would fight to protect their secrecy. And there was a way, there always was. He could send the substitute off under a cover identity. But a "good" passport (one that would slide easily through Brazilian customs control) wouldn't be cheap. In fact it would blow the budget all to hell. The two- and three-thousand-dollar payments out of a solid five-figure fee ate their profit margin: what List called "death by nibbles."

"He will," Benauti said, bringing him back, "be paged at Kennedy or met by somebody."

"And then?"

"Over one or two days, some appointments, some going around, enough exposure to be seen and photographed. It is very easy."

"Considering your client's problems, maybe we should anticipate the potential for difficulties at the airport."

"Not in Rio," Benauti said.

"What about Kennedy?"

Benauti laughed. "America is a free country," he said.

A response Guyer found troubling. It implied that U.S. security people were lax, that the borders were easily penetrable. That was true, in a general way, but why would Benauti focus so immediately on U.S. security people? In Benauti's place he would worry about the intelligence services of the countries that wanted Delatte. If the track begun in Rio had to run under the designated cover, that could only be because the cover was recognized, a signal to somebody somewhere. Airlines clerks were venal, and underpaid, thus passenger manifests were easily come by.

Guyer shrugged, fought off his intuitions. "Do you have a preference for where he stays in Rio?"

"No. On the beach, perhaps, among the tourists. The Royal Guanabara is nice, quite nice. It hardly matters, all registration cards go to the same place." Benauti smiled at the thought, apparently amused by the fact that hotel registrations went to the office of state security. "No need to stay in the room. He is a man who just made ten thousand dollars for taking two plane rides. So, a pair of prostitutes, a little chemin de fer, champagne for dinner." He rubbed his hands and leered.

"Anything else?" Guyer asked. He was suddenly conscious that he was getting wet and chilled. Behind Benauti the north end of Manhattan was spread out in square blocs of lights, blurred and softened by the falling snow.

"No, that is all there is to it."

" 'Kay," Guyer nodded slowly, apparently fixing the arrangements in his mind, in fact working up to what he had to say next. "Please keep this in mind: Our assets are not jeopardized."

"We know this," Benauti answered.

"I want to be sure that you understand it completely."

"Oh, yes, yes, absolutely."

It crossed Guyer's mind to close Benauti right then and there. The 6:30 phone call was clearly a tactical fiction, on one hand a cover for retreat if necessary, on the other a mechanism to maintain the illusion of powerful forces gathering for consultation and study of the photograph. But he knew the photo was very convincing. And Benauti had given him everything, the deal was essentially made. But, he thought, better to leave it alone. Benauti wanted it. He realized then that he wanted it rather badly, had given way every time. Funny, he'd arrived at the meeting with the idea that the project might not go through, but was now aware that that had not been the case at all. "Okay then, I'll expect to hear from you around 6:30. If it's go, then you'll be making the brokerage deposit on Monday."

"Bearer bonds," Benauti said.

"Yes. Whatever's available." They really did have it, Guyer thought. Once you discuss method of payment . . . "You want to leave first?" he asked. An espionage courtesy. By tradition the more important of the principals always left clandestine meetings first. This meeting, he supposed, was clandestine. It was certainly cold and wet enough to qualify.

Benauti extended his hand and they shook briefly. "Until then," he said with a slight bow of the head, very formal and continental. Guyer watched him leave, his walk casual, almost a stroll, nearly a parody of studied innocence. The Japanese kid followed him all the way to the elevator, his posture and stride matching Benauti's perfectly. *Jesus,* Guyer thought, *a bad spy. Obvious, emotional, overcautious, inept. Who the hell is using him? Somebody poor? Somebody naïve? Somebody stupid? Somebody very, very smart?*

Roser

COLONEL OTTAVIO ROSER, labeled by writers of Marxist pamphlets as *Cuchillo Blanco*, the white knife, brought his wife to New York City in late October in order for her to go shopping at Saks Fifth Avenue. The annual trip to *Norteamérica* was customary among the military and governing classes of his country. From the rank of lieutenant colonel and ministerial deputy down, they went to Miami Beach. Once they rose beyond that, however, social circumstance and ritual demanded that the pilgrimage extend to New York. Only the bankers and the members of the junta went to Paris. In that country, dedication to authority ran deep and hierarchies were observed.

Colonel Roser had married into power; courting, then winning, Rosalia María Llaves y Vilet, the daughter of Dr. Ramon Vilet, owner of a molybdenum mine and Ambassador to Chile. The pamphlet writers at their mimeograph machines in basements near the university called him *Cuchillo Blanco*, for two reasons. *Blanco* because of his customary white suit, white shirt, and white tie. *Cuchillo* because that was how detainees were tortured in that country—also, as it happened, in basements, in this instance beneath police stations. The nickname made reference, in addition, to his reputed association with the White Hand, a terror squad that operated throughout Central America.

Fourteen months before Colonel Roser came to New York, the publisher of a newspaper in the capital had angered the government by running a series of editorials demanding the free elections promised for a year earlier by the generals in the junta. It had been explained to the publisher by a high government official that the elections just recently held *were* free, the country's voters having been freely permitted to choose the correct people. What, exactly, was his problem? The publisher, in the raptures of some political foolishness much abroad that year, responded to correction by printing an editorial cartoon of one of the country's Simón Bolívar statues with tears running down its marble cheeks. Many powerful people were annoyed by this cartoon. The publisher suddenly experienced wildcat strikes at his plant, and a series of misfortunes befell his delivery trucks. The publisher, for one week, stood grave and defiant. Then his daughter returned home from elementary school one day to report that two men had taken her from her classroom and, in the corridor, had requested that she "ask her papa to be a better papa." The next morning he was in Mexico City, where his fortune had preceded him the week before the first editorial ran.

He got out by crossing the border at night through a little-used customs post, his exit lubricated by extensive *mordida* for the lucky soldiers on duty, and only later did it occur to him that he could have saved his money, "out" was where they wanted him. His wife and two daughters were to leave the following day from the airport, in the normal way. The publisher had some knowledge of border guards and did not want to risk his family coming to their attention in case things went badly for him. He believed that the government would not prevent a woman of his wife's class from boarding a plane. But he was wrong. At the airport a courteous official explained that technical difficulties with their passports required that new forms had to be filled out. Sadly, such forms were not now available, but the government printing office had promised them for next week. He was terribly sorry, but the señora would have to return home, he hoped that she would forgive the inconvenience.

In Mexico City, the publisher opened negotiations at the country's consular office. Patiently, he worked his way upward through the bureaucratic layers until he reached an official who knew something. The official knew that the publisher should continue his researches by telephone to the various ministries in the capital. It occurred to him one day, as the line went dead while he was holding for the deputy assistant to the Minister of the Interior, that they were punishing him with great dexterity and vigor. The publisher had studied his philosophy at the university, and knew that the presence of a watch on the beach implied, somewhere, a watchmaker. This particular watchmaker began to show a style that he thought he recognized. Three days later his suspicions were confirmed. Twice. First, when the Vice-President of the Senate suggested that a certain Colonel Roser, in the Bureau of National Security, might be able to aid him in his difficulties. Second, when the telephone line to his house in the capital produced only a recording saying that service would be discontinued while the system received its annual maintenance.

When, after some time, he was able to reach Colonel Roser personally, his situation was made clear to him. He could remain in Mexico City, nothing would be done to him there. His family would stay where they were. As long as he did not choose to make himself into some caricature of a national symbol, most especially in the press of the United States, they would not be harmed. They would in fact continue to receive funds from the operation of the newspaper, where, he might be pleased to learn, certain editorial refinements had been made, a few changes in staff effected. It would probably be best for him, Roser pointed out, not to plan on returning anytime soon. The climate was poor, hot and humid, very unhealthy. The publisher responded that he was concerned with his health and that of his family and would, in future, follow the Colonel's guidance in these matters. The publisher lost his self-control only once in the weeks following: On his forty-eighth birthday, alone in a rented villa, he called Roser and pleaded with him. The Colonel let him go on for a considerable time before hanging up, saying that he was late for a luncheon appointment.

The first stage of exile he bore heroically. He embraced political parallels—Trotsky, Solzhenitsyn—saw himself to be a Figure of History, and retired to the study to write his memoirs. Then, one day while he was out, the manuscript disappeared. So he moved to the garden, read mysteries, and worked crossword puzzles. Days passed, he wasn't entirely sure how they were spent. He visited, unsuccessfully, a prostitute. Gambled listlessly. Got drunk at a very fancy restaurant and wept while a waitress comforted him. The pain of loss, of loneliness, of isolation, was unceasing. After several months of this, however, his pride of manhood, the

[72]

fulminous Latin American *machismo*, finally saved his life. He decided to fight back. Moving with great secrecy, he converted American and Japanese stocks to cash. Then contrived to make a friend or two in Mexico City's bustling, conspiratorial diplomatic community. That city is, after all, the Zurich of the Americas, and international types of all sorts abound there. He began to be invited to parties, endless parties, held as backdrops for the constant diplomacy and spy games that ran all day every day. Soon enough he found what he wanted: a real, live intelligence officer, a Peruvian, as it happened, who served on the staff of an inter-American agricultural agency. This man, in the best KGB/CIA tradition, he *cultivated*. Took him and his wife out for elaborate dinners where they drank up French wines. Took him to the racetrack and made bets for him, absorbing the losses, passing on the winnings. Treated him to sporting nights at one of the city's most exquisite brothels where, the publisher discovered, his initiation of a counteroffensive had apparently restored him to his previous abilities. Of the subject eating at his heart, he said nothing. He was, to the world at large, a man hellbent on amusement, and he found it amusing to indulge his friends. The Peruvian, who had been this way before, relaxed into the rhythm of it and waited to see what would happen. Finally, curiosity began to intrude on his pleasures, and at a fabulous lunch of lobster tails and grilled *espada,* he lit a thin cigar and asked the publisher what he wanted.

The publisher spoke for an hour, coldly, factually, unburdening himself for the first time since the editorials had run, more than a year ago. The Peruvian listened and smoked. Once it became clear who the publisher was and what he wanted, he briefly excused himself to the men's room, where he turned off the tape recorder in his pocket. It seemed, in fact, a legitimately personal matter. Over cognac he told the publisher what to do and how much it would cost. Expensive, certainly, but who could put a price on the love and warmth of a man's family? Alas, Roser was an animal, but no more than a creature of the times. The eternal instability of certain countries allowed such men a free hand in the affairs of their betters, which was a cruel and sad thing indeed. Some day there would be land reform, clinics, model schools, and all their nations would join hands in progress, peace, and prosperity. Until then, however, here is what he must do.

The publisher flew to New York. Visited a dark restaurant in Manhattan's East Fifties, ate the mediocre "continental cuisine," and mentioned a name to the maître d'. The man he sought did not appear that night, or the next, but on the third night he entered the restaurant a little after 9:00 and was pointed out to the publisher. The publisher invited him to have a drink. He was not a very comfortable man to be with: reserved, almost deathly pale, he used a cane and limped badly and was, perhaps, *maricón*. But he had the answer to the publisher's problem. Over the next few days he helped him to obtain, for cash, from the intelligence service of his own country's neighbor and mortal enemy, a series of photographs of Colonel Roser. A strategy was conceived, terms agreed on, deposit made in a local brokerage account. The fee was as the Peruvian had said. The publisher spent his final night at a musical show on Broadway, then went home to Mexico City to wait for October.

Colonel Roser, one afternoon in late October, was sitting comfortably on the edge of his bed at the Waldorf. He was wearing a silk bathrobe, drinking a Budweiser, and watching a quiz show on television. He did not understand very much of the English but enjoyed the women contestants as they jumped up and down gleefully and embraced the emcee. It was 4:30. He knew he had another two hours of peace and quiet before his wife returned from a fitting, at a department store, of a gown she had purchased the previous day. Two hours at *least,* he thought. His wife was a woman who demanded a great deal of service, and because of her shape, some considerable alteration was necessary.

Colonel Roser was a short man with a big stomach. Because he walked with shoulders well thrust back and held himself always at full height, the stomach appeared to precede him, seemingly to announce that an important man was following close behind. He was mostly bald, attempting to soften that impression by a judicious pasting of remaining hairs across his scalp. He cultivated a thin line of moustache above his upper lip. He was, he knew it, a bit of a cartoon. Sometimes people did not take him seriously. That rarely worked to their advantage—Colonel Roser had had two hundred and twenty people put to death that year alone, and it was only October. Many of them, at the very last, perceived that he was to them a man of very great importance indeed. Then they begged and pleaded and cried for mercy. But he never relented, for he was a man of very strong character.

The Colonel hoped that his wife found the alterations satisfactory. She could be difficult when balked, and he went to great pains to maintain her placidity. She was, after all, a Vilet, and her father, a very old-world gentleman, had made clear to Roser that her happiness was paramount. The Colonel managed quite well. After sixteen years of marriage his wife still giggled as he prepared to perform his Saturday-night duty. He had on one occasion attempted a discreet love affair with the daughter of a British automobile salesman, but she had left a love bite on his neck and he had gone about terrified for a week with adhesive tape and gauze hiding the mark. After that he consoled himself during his weekly domestic trysts by acknowledging that power had its costs.

[75]

At 4:35 the telephone rang. It was the desk clerk, two gentlemen wished to visit him in his room, Señores Martinez and Mendez. This did not surprise the Colonel; information, denunciations, the business of state security, sought him out wherever he was. A few minutes later there was a courteous tap at the door. He opened to find two rather ordinary men, conservative in dress, respectful in demeanor. One of them carried a film projector, the other, a portable screen.

"Good afternoon," they said.

"Good afternoon. Please come in," he answered. He noted that the Spanish they spoke was educated. They were not, he sensed, from his country. They were, in fact, employees of a private investigative agency in Mexico City.

"Please forgive the intrusion," said the one on the left, who wore a pale blue tie, "but we have come to show you a film."

"A film?"

"Yes. It is not of great length. We are here at the request of a friend of yours, a publisher of newspapers, who now resides in Mexico City, where he misses his family and hopes that they may be permitted to join him there. He wishes you to know, in addition, that his long-standing interest in politics has declined. He has found philosophy. And now begs sincerely for your compassion and forgiveness. For his previous indiscretions he feels remorse, and hopes you will be understanding, and knows that you join him in the belief that a man's family is the rock on which his life must be built." This was a pretty speech, Colonel Roser thought, obviously memorized, but delivered with just the right blend of conviction and humility. He was, after all, something of a connoisseur of such apologia.

"Very well," he said. "It will be considered." After a pause he added, "And is this film a gift to make such considerations easier?"

[76]

"It is that," said the man.

Now the Colonel was curious. Which of his enemies would be doomed by the film? "Is it a film with sound?" he asked.

"No, it is a silent film," said the man.

"Has it a title, then?"

"No. It was felt that the Colonel may wish to title it himself."

"Please proceed," he said.

They set up the projector on a dresser, then stood the screen against the far wall, setting the tripod legs firmly into the plush carpet. "May we turn out the lights?" one of them asked.

"Naturally," he answered, "the switch is on the wall."

They threaded the film, turned on the projector, let it warm for a moment. Before pressing the starting switch, the man in the blue tie said, "Please forgive the quality of the print, the original is much better, but it was felt that the value of the negative made travel unwise."

The Colonel nodded graciously.

Black numerals ran backward on white frames, the projector whirred quietly, and the first image appeared. The Colonel, sitting upright in a comfortable chair, his robe draped decorously over his bare legs, leaned forward with interest. The two girls, about fourteen, he guessed, wore the blazer of the Academia de la Virgen Enamorada, one of the better private schools in his country, run by Josephite nuns. The emblem on the breast pocket, a Sacred Heart with thorns and fire, was unmistakable. At the same moment the provenance of the film became clear. He was quite used to covertly acquired film, and he recognized the various characteristics of the technique: camera situated high in the room, for a full view; grainy, ill-lighted images; grayish white and faded black coloration. One of the girls, in response to something said offscreen, looked over her shoulder, then she began to undress. The other girl, by facial similarity perhaps a younger sister, followed her lead. They were attractive children, with clear skins and carefully brushed hair. As they undressed they folded their clothing neatly and placed it in two piles on the floor at the end of a bed. Colonel Roser shifted his position in the chair, crossed one leg over the other. These were children of his country's aristocracy, and he saw the type often enough in bathing suits by swimming pools, but their complete nakedness was new to him. They had firm, high small breasts and narrow hips. Again he sensed the presence of a direction given from outside the room. He cleared his throat. The girls obediently positioned themselves on the bed. From the left, a man appeared. The Colonel began to anticipate greedily, the publisher's gift was really too good: clearly there would be deflorations, clinically observed, while at the same moment a man of power would be delivered into his hands. The two sensations met so pleasurably within him that a shiver ran across his shoulders. The man entering the room wore a white bedsheet around his shoulders so his body could not be seen. His face, however, was clearly visible once he walked to the other end of the bed and turned to face the girls, and the camera. Colonel Roser's breath caught in his throat, his mouth opened, and he felt the unbreathed air expand in his chest and stab against the inside of his breastbone. His left hand rose to his heart. The film was less than two minutes long, but the man in the sheet managed to engage in a considerable variety of unnatural acts for such a brief period. Even in the midst of waking nightmare it occurred to the Colonel that jumps in the film indicated editing, so that only the most interesting parts were shown. The man, it was clear, had the tastes of a beast. The man was a voyeur. The man was, to a mild degree, a sadist. The man was a pervert. The man was Colonel Roser.

[78]

Then it was over, the film end flapping sharply until the power was switched off. A thousand gothic possibilities raced through the Colonel's mind: the unknown twin, the schizophrenic episode, secret hypnotism, but these were merely low tickings of the question *how,* which faded almost to silence beneath the mighty roar of the clear evidence *that.* The film *existed.* He became conscious of the thick sound of his own breathing in the silent room. The lights came on, the two men busied themselves with the equipment. The man with the blue tie unhooked the top of the portable screen and lowered it carefully. The Colonel stood, walked across the room, and punched him on the mouth. The man backed up a step. The Colonel drew his arm back, the man raised his hand like a traffic policeman, and the Colonel's fist stayed where it was. The man took a folded white handkerchief out of his jacket pocket and dabbed at his lip. He looked at the handkerchief, but there was no blood on it, so he returned it to his pocket. The other man said, "Is your wife returning soon?"

"Yes," said the Colonel.

"Then we will leave now so as not to disturb her."

The Colonel nodded slowly, sat down in his chair. His hands were shaking, so he put them in the pockets of his bathrobe. He closed his eyes. The image of his father-in-law awaited him. Dr. Ramon Vilet had wavy gray hair, brilliantined then brushed tightly back. His chin was carried high, his lips turned slightly inward as though words of contempt or controlled anger were about to be spoken. His look was unwavering, fierce, judgmental. And cold. His conversation confined itself to seven areas: morality, piety, family, order, authority, respect, and stability. Colonel Roser opened his eyes, the men were moving their equipment toward the door. "Forgive me," he said to the man in the blue tie, "for striking you."

"It did not happen," he said.

"Please say that my fullest cooperation can be expected."

"Very well. Is that all?"

"My apologies."

"Yes?"

"Travel documents will be facilitated."

"When will that be?"

"Immediately. Tonight."

"That is kind of you," said the man.

"Good-bye," said the other man. They went out the door and closed it politely behind them.

That same evening, while Colonel and Señora Roser were just beginning their endive salad at La Grenouille, Ray Whiting was signaling the bartender at The King's Grotto for another Seagram's. Ray had the third chair at Ken's Barbershop and he often stopped by the Grotto after work, and he often stayed late.

"I damn well knew you wouldn't believe it," he said to the man on the next stool, his best friend, a Louisville cabdriver.

"It don't happen in real life," the friend said.

"Hell, I'm not so sure I believe it myself," Whiting said. His friend laughed softly and rattled the ice cubes in his glass. "But every time I don't," he continued, "I just look out in that parking lot and see that Camaro and you know damnsure that didn't just fall outta no thin air."

The office was quiet at 6:30. Kevin and Mrs. Foley had gone home. Guyer's shoes were drying by a heating vent. He was leaning back in his chair with his feet on the desk. One of his socks was blue, the other black. List was sitting on the other side of the desk, drinking coffee from a Styrofoam cup. The small radio on a shelf was playing a classical station. It wasn't quite tuned in, there was a hum and intermittent static, but neither one could be bothered to get up and deal with it.

"I'll be happy," Guyer said, "when we're rid of Benauti."

List made a face. "Dreadful little man."

"Where do you suppose he lives?"

"God only knows," List said, "and He'd rather not. Hotels, I imagine. Yes, I can see him in hotels. In the Bahamas, maybe, or Costa Rica. Hotels with commercial traveler rates, not out on the ocean, in town. That's where I see him. Having his laundry done by a valet service. Killing the morning with a shoeshine. Reading a newspaper in the dining room. Undertipping everybody in sight."

Guyer took the Canadian passport and the envelope holding the X rays out of his pocket and placed them on the desk. With his index finger he moved the envelope toward List. "You take charge of that, okay?"

"What is it?"

"Last night's work. Goes back to Langer. You can go over to Monte Carlo, like we talked about this morning, maybe you'll see Langer there. Kill two birds with one stone."

List put the envelope in the inside pocket of his jacket. Guyer opened the Canadian passport, turning the cover back delicately with one finger. "Mr. Gerard," he said, "is going to Rio de Janeiro."

"I loved *Black Orpheus*," List said.

"You ever been there?"

"No."

Guyer turned the page. "Neither has Mr. Gerard. He went to Rome, last year, for two weeks. Year before that it was London."

"I'm sure he enjoyed it."

"Yeah." Guyer turned the page back and stared at the passport photo.

"That a righteous passport?"

"For all I know about Canadian passports—"

"I mean it isn't spelled C-a-n-o-d-a or anything."

"Unh-uh."

"I don't know that I trust Benauti to get it right."

"I don't know that I trust Benauti to chew gum and walk, come to that," Guyer said. He closed the passport, looked at his watch, and flicked the telephone with his middle finger. "Ring," he said.

"What do you think—" List said. The phone rang. Guyer picked it up immediately.

"Yes?"

"This is your friend," a voice said. It was Benauti.

"Everything okay?"

"Please proceed. All as we have said."

"Okay. We'll have him on that flight. You make a payment tomorrow. When he takes off again, that's when the second part comes due. Agreed?"

"Yes."

"Look, if there's a problem of some sort, how can I reach you?"

"When will you know?"

Guyer looked at an appointment calendar on the wall. "Monday, I should know."

"Then I call you Monday."

"Okay," Guyer said. Benauti hung up. Guyer replaced the receiver, left his hand on it, then drummed his fingers.

List said, "Zo, you haf ze documentsss?"

Guyer kept drumming, in a rhythm like a horse galloping. "You in a big hurry to be anywhere?"

"No. I have to run by Maggie's place, and I have to pay the doorman."

"Give me Maggie's envelope. That's over on Second Avenue, in the Seventies someplace, right?"

"Yes."

"Well, I have to be over there anyhow." List handed

him a long white envelope with ten hundreds inside. "It's just," he continued, "this Delatte business . . ."

"What?"

"It gives me a bad feeling. It's off. I had Kevin run the film for a while, but of course there's nothing new there. Later, I pressed Benauti. Like squeezing a handful of water. Do you know what I mean?"

"What can we do?"

"I don't know. Is there anything else in there?" He nodded toward the computer console on the far wall.

"You already gave them a sample, didn't you?"

Guyer shrugged. "We find a perfect substitute, it doesn't matter." He thought for a few seconds. "As far as I get is that we're working down on the hyena level. I like a client with an office. Or somebody like Langer, who's always going to be around. Somebody who knows that if they pull some kind of tricky shit we'll have somebody coming around and asking why. But with Benauti it's all amorphous. Anytime he wants, he's gone, invisible. There's no string to pull him back with. Then there's Delatte, you look at that film, you see his face, nothing matters to him. He has the balls of a gorilla, just goes ahead and does whatever it is, anything. But for all that he isn't very good. How could he be? If he was, we wouldn't know anything about him. He's a guy who pulls the trigger, that way he's solid, but *then* he gets into trouble. Maybe he looks for it, just enough so that everybody knows what a big-time desperado he is. Now, all of a sudden, he wants a stand-in. And he hires *Benauti* to make his deal with us. With Benauti, it's *we* this, *we* that, *we* the other thing, you get the feeling it's not just him and Delatte, it's him and somebody very big-time. *We.* Me and the Union of Soviet Socialist Republics. Now the logical reason for that is he's trying to get some respect by pretending that he's got major-league affiliations, trying to back us down a little. Like some guy who makes eight hundred a month will say, '*my* attorney,' as though he kept some lawyer on a retainer. It's all huff and puff and bullshit. But that's an assumption. And every time I find myself making an assumption, I kind of wonder if somebody isn't helping me a little. Then I ask myself if Benauti *isn't* bluffing, if there is real weight in the background, what the hell are they doing hiring somebody like him? You see? It doubles back on itself somewhere."

Guyer stopped short. List paused a beat, then said, "So?"

"So," Guyer said after a moment, "we have a building payment on November fourth and a computer payment on November sixth."

"Where's the jeopardy?" List asked.

"I don't know. I suppose if I tried I could make you a dozen or so scenarios."

"And I could make you two dozen. Where does it get us? The way it is, of course, is that everything, everything we do anyhow, evaporates into night and fog. Much better to be in the steel business, when every time you get a case of the galloping ghoulies you can go down to the foundry and pick up a hammer and whang the bejesus out of a piece of steel and hear it go *bong*. Reality time, you know? Much better, maybe, but too late for us. It happens that we're in a shadow trade, after all is said and done, and that's the business of making shadows appear where there isn't any light."

"I know, I know," Guyer said, resigned and gloomy.

"You're not worried that we're going to get screwed out of money, are you?"

"No."

"What about, uh, what the hell's his name, the Czech."

"Novotny?"

"Yeah."

"He's in Miami. I called him this morning. Maybe

he'll come through, maybe he won't, but that's fifteen thousand."

"Not enough."

"No."

They both sat and thought for a minute. They'd done it before, up against a money wall. "Francis Mains called me this morning," Guyer said.

List's face was expressionless. "What's he want?"

"Us, I think. If I read his hieroglyphics."

"A project?"

"No. Us the company."

"There's money."

"We'd start out thinking that, then somehow it would all spin out into deep space. He'd wind up with the business. We'd wind up looking for lawyers willing to spec the case for half. You know who he is, you know who he was, everything the man touches turns to pain."

"What the hell does something the size of Mains, Gulbenyan want with us anyhow?"

"Another small service to offer their clients."

"Who's stopping them? They can pay us to do it and say they did it."

"Corporations don't think like that."

"Okay, then, Delatte."

Guyer put his fists against his eyes, realized he'd had only three hours of sleep the night before. There was still a lot that had to be done. He wanted three or four doughnuts and a big cup of really good coffee. "Let's do this," he said quietly, eyes still shut tight. If he pressed his knuckles in a little, he felt better. "We'll run through a few samples and see what's available. I think maybe my whole problem here is that I talked to the guy in Wisconsin, just to make sure he was possible, and for some reason I liked him, and when I thought about him in the same frame with Benauti and Delatte, an alarm went off."

List pushed himself upright and limped to the console. He never used the cane when they were alone in the office, getting where he had to go by grabbing chair tops and leaning on tables. Guyer followed. The floor was cold when he left the rugs and stood on the tile in front of the console. List adjusted the chair, then started punching buttons on the keyboard. On the left side of the screen a photo of Delatte appeared, a freeze-frame from the German tourist's movie. He was staring into the camera, it seemed, and squinting slightly. "Take the first hundred," Guyer said. He stood behind List—close enough to smell his cologne—and watched the screen over his shoulder. As List typed the computer repeated his instructions and provided information, in large green figures on a black background, on the open side of the display.

```
RUNNING SUBJ 775 270 8465
SOURCE FILM 6/19/80 IN
DELATTE RAOUL 0 MIDDLE NAME
0 ADDRESS 0 CITY 0 COUNTRY
0 OTHER FILE
A/P KEY: 77 INX-SEE 778 & 690 INX
RUN NEAR 100 BY SQNCE
TRANS 1584 10/18 6:42 PM RLIST
```

A photo came up on the right side of the screen. The man wore thick glasses and was not smiling, his eyes centered on the camera in a way that usually meant a passport photo or a driver's license, where the subject is asked to stare at a fixed point. The man did not resemble Delatte at all. They'd learned long ago that no matter the precision of feature measurement, there was an unnameable quality in a face that existed but could not be identified, what computer people call an *exotic*. List called it, ironically, *the soul,* and claimed the existence of an unduplicable category—sharing no similarity of class, vocation, nationality, or age—who had some-

[86]

thing going on inside them that made their faces literally unique.

Photos appeared at three-second intervals, a tiny chime signaling each change. The first man was replaced by a second. Then a third. Both wrong.

"Hit the index," Guyer said. List punched a button, the original instructions returned. "Let's see a different A/P. Try 778."

List typed. A new photo appeared. "Oh look, a bow tie," he said. Guyer was silent. More faces came up.

"I like that," List said.

"Hairline," Guyer said, "let it run."

It ran through another six faces. "Turn that fucking bell off," Guyer said. List hit a series of keys, the chiming stopped. The series ran on.

"There," List said, hitting the *hold* key.

"That's Wisconsin," Guyer said. The face was replaced.

List hit the *hold* button again. They both stared silently for a few seconds. Guyer stepped back a pace and squinted, blurring his vision slightly. The working version, he knew, would not be this defined. "What's the intended product?" List asked.

"Probably photo from a distance."

"Might do. See up there? The eyebrows run a dot or two long at the outer eye, but it's not bad."

"Yeah. Let's see."

List popped a single key, working his hand like a stagy pianist.

RUNNING SUBJ 865 239 8679
SOURCE NEW ORLEANS MORNING
TRIBUNE 7/16/79 PGE 22
8/14/79 IN
0 FILE
CAPTION: SGT RJ BERNIER FOILS
ROBBERY AT SOUTHEND MARKET

"I rather think not," List said.

"False flag, maybe," Guyer said. "Tell him it's CIA."

"Captain, the man is a *cop*. People tell him they're the CIA every twenty minutes."

"Put him on the left, get Wisconsin back and put him up on the right."

"What's the cryptonym?"

"W-i-s, slash, D-e-l."

The faces rearranged.

"All three," Guyer said.

They stared. "Okay," Guyer said, "what's the rest?"

List hit the buttons, then said "Oh Christ, the guy is six feet five."

Guyer sighed. There was something like Mozart playing through the static on the radio. The computer hummed. A police siren wailed a few blocks away. "Run Wisconsin," he said.

A photo appeared on the left, legend on the right:

```
RUNNING SUBJ 795 241 8472
SOURCE WAUKESHA WIS CHAMBER
OF COMMERCE NEWSLETTER 5/3/80
PGE 1
7/2/80 IN
FILE SEE DEL/BEN
CAPTION: SHOE STORE OWNER BILL
ELDEN NAMED MERCHANT OF THE
YEAR!
```

List locked his hands behind his head, then leaned backward to the full tilt of the chair. Guyer stood silent, staring at the screen, then slowly undid his tie, rolled it into a circle, and slid it into his jacket pocket. "What was the phone call like?" List said.

"Told him I was a TV producer. We were packaging a celebrity look-alike game show. We'd seen his picture in a Chamber of Commerce magazine. He asked what celebrity. I told him the singer, Tony Shaw. Said he never heard of him. Asked if he ever got to Vegas. Said he didn't. But, oh yes, he was *extremely* interested."

"The famous Tony Shaw," List said.

"Where are you headed?"

"Off to the bars."

"Would you lock up?"

"Sure. See you tomorrow."

"No. I'm flying to Wisconsin."

"He know you're coming?"

"Unh-uh. I don't want Aunt Hilda there to see the man from L.A."

List leaned forward and started punching keys, words ran across the photo.

ALL AROUND THE COBBLER'S BENCH THE MONKEY CHASED THE WEASEL

The computer, humming quietly on the ground floor in its air-conditioned room, used an internal screen for its facial comparisons. The screen was divided into minute electronic dots, called pixels, which functioned as a more accurate version of the lines on a television screen. At 12 pixels per inch, a photograph will appear blurry. At 500 pixels per inch, the image would be down to pores if the original had high enough resolution. This particular screen had a square of pixels 1024 by 1024. Which meant that the computer would read a total of 1,048,576 (1024×1024) tiny sections. Then, based on a comparison of light and shade, the computer would rate the similarity on a basis of 1 to 8, eight gradations, or "bytes," for each pixel. Thus the computer made what amounted to 8,388,608 decisions, at a rate of 10 million decisions per second, then assigned a million-digit number to each face and stored it in numerical sequence, eliminating the need to search all data each time a request for comparison was received.

Facial-imaging technology in computers was readily available. When Guyer and List first approached the problem, they borrowed elements from a Japanese system called Identicast, which used a computer for criminal identification by re-creating faces on a feature-by-feature basis. Similar programs were available to beauty parlors, where a client could see her own face in a variety of hairstyles. But use of this technology brought Guyer and List face-to-face with the real difficulty: Their system made near-perfect comparisons between photos and photos, but when they contrived to see the people themselves, they discovered that people often do not look like their photographs. And if faces were similar, body shape could vary wildly. They knew, however, that given a skull, forensic pathologists are able to project a physical size based on anthropometric measurements. Thus they wrote a program called A/P Factor, for anthropometry, which calculated distance from feature to feature and arrived at body shape from there. And they decided, in the first sixty days, that they would work only in reproductive format: video, still photograph, film. Since stolen images were a staple of the intelligence industry, this refinement did not hurt the business.

Initially they programmed in ALGOL, a scientific language, but more particularly (this was List's bias) a *European* language, the distinction akin to that between European and American bread. From there they went to assembly language because it was faster. They were trying to work the computer closer to its capacity, which was measured in Megaflops: one Megaflop equalling 10 million floating point transactions per second. To make the electrical ions move that fast, the computer's metallic areas had to be chilled with liquid helium. Such speed created heat: enough BTU's to warm the building in all seasons, even though air conditioners ran constantly in the computer room. The computer itself was a grand old Cray, built by Seymour Cray of Minneapolis. If IBMs and Univacs were Fords and Chevrolets, the Cray was a Cord or a Jensen: you didn't see that many, but adherents were fanatic.

Finally, they wrote their own language—for reasons of speed and encryption, and because what they did in their small corner of the technology, nobody else could do. When they were sure they had something, when it actually, one time out of three, *worked,* they wanted to make it their own in every way possible. The principle was simple: Sooner or later everybody seems to run into somebody who looks exactly like them. The 250 million people in the United States share about 75 million faces, with moustaches, suntans, uniforms of formal or informal sorts, providing sufficient camouflage that each citizen may feel comfortably unique. These faces are living realizations of geopolitics. You may see, if you watch carefully in an art museum, a fourteenth-century peasant staring at a painting of a fourteenth-century peasant. Nikita Khrushchev emerges from a delicatessen in Brooklyn. Louis XIV will check your oil in New Orleans.

The *concept* of a double was as old as MGM, perhaps even older. (It was John Kennedy's *double* killed that day in Dallas. The real Kennedy is held in a dacha in Novosibirsk. Everybody knows that.) But, of course, in person you couldn't fool anybody—each human such an anthill of personal tics and quirks that the notion of a real-life replacement was absurd. But in the sector of covert photography, image-theft, it could be made to work. When the camera caught normal circumstance it found mumblers, hat-wearers, people who looked at their shoes, touched their faces, and milled with obscuring crowds. Thus, playing to a hidden lens, a counterfeit could suffice. The objective wasn't necessarily "By God that's Melnikov!" for in most instances "Could that be Melnikov?" would do just as well. Typically the product fell into one of three categories: subject observed with someone he wasn't supposed to be with; subject observed in a place he didn't belong; subject observed in the act of sexual mischief, the documentation of which was called, by MI5, *son et lumière*. If it didn't absolutely persuade, it created doubt and suspicion. And it put the subject in the absolutely foul position of having to say the words "That's not me. That's a double." In the fun-house mirror that was the intelligence community, doubt and suspicion were often tantamount to guilt. Took a bit of money, but if the gray world had nothing else, it had that and lots of it. When List finally finished writing the new computer language, it needed a name. He suggested UMBRA, which the dictionary defined as "a phantom or shadowy apparition as of someone or something not physically present." But nobody ever called it that, or anything else. When they actually got down to business, they found that problems, hence discussion, centered outside the mechanics of the computer. Their grief was caused by people, not microchips, and they came already equipped with names.

Guyer got out of a cab and walked a block to Maggie's apartment house, an anonymous high-rise in the East Seventies. He felt better—talking it out with List always helped; his tendency to "find eight things wrong with this picture" pruned back by a dose of List's casual irony. Meanwhile, the weather had shifted into neutral: the snow was gone, the wind had died, the temperature stuck at forty-two.

The doorman had something wrong with the left side

of his face. He inventoried Guyer from the shoes up and said, "Yeah?" but he said it with respect. Guyer didn't exactly look like a cop, but there was something about him that made people give him room.

"Maggie home? Fourteen G?"

"You expected?"

"Call," he said. "The name is Guyer."

The doorman pressed buttons on the lobby intercom phone. Guyer pivoted and stared out the glass doors. Somebody looking at him. His eyes flicked across doorways on the other side of Second Avenue. He checked the double-parked cars. Looked up for backlit outlines in windows. Checked the telephone booths. There was nobody hailing a cab or peering into darkened shop windows. There were some dog-walkers, late shoppers, couples going out for the evening, one jogger with earmuffs.

"Mr. Guyer is here," the doorman called into the intercom. Then, to Guyer, "Okay. Elevator on the left."

He took the elevator to fourteen, waited until the door closed, to see if it might go back downstairs, then return. But it stayed put for thirty seconds, then went up. He opened the fire door that led to the back stairway and counted to twenty, then pressed the lock button so that it wouldn't open out, and closed it tight. He pushed the doorbell, heard a double-tone chime sound in the apartment. A moment later the peephole slid open, closed, then the door swung wide. She was wearing a yellow quilted bathrobe with a red towel wrapped around her head.

" 'Mon in," she said. Her hard New York accent came from an angel's face.

He passed through a narrow foyer with shiny tile floor, then entered the living room. There were Danish chairs and modular couches upholstered in synthetic blond leather. The walls were covered with high-gloss wallpaper, red printed on silver. There was white shag carpet on the floor and two black ceramic lamps with low-wattage bulbs. Airport music played softly from hidden speakers.

"Just a sec," she said, "I'll put something on." She disappeared down a hallway. The stereo rested on several levels of a wood-grained cabinet. Guyer casually touched a finger to a place on the back of the receiver. It was cool, she'd apparently turned the music on after the doorman had called upstairs. His eye traced the edge of the ceiling where it met the walls. There was a smoked bronze mirror on one wall. He strolled across the room, settled himself on a squat couch directly below it, then reached up and pushed the mirror frame gently. It moved. He disliked being in places with fixed mirrors.

Maggie returned, shaking her wet hair back. She was wearing jeans with a man's blue dress shirt hanging outside. It was so big, shoulders resting midway down her upper arms, that she seemed lost in it. On her feet were huge fur slippers, imitation bunnies, faces and everything, with tail scuts made of pom-poms resting high on the instep.

"Aren't these a bit?" she said, following his eyes. She did a few dance steps. She was, he noticed, a little clumsy.

"Nice apartment," he said.

"I'm still tryna get it the way I want it," she said. Then, "Want a little Amaretto? Or maybe you're a Scotch and soda type."

"Whatever you're having."

There was a rolltop desk in one corner. She opened it to reveal a bar. She poured Amaretto into two tulip-shaped glasses.

"Here," she said.

He took the glass with one hand, offered the white envelope with the other. "Thank you, sir," she said with a suggestion of a curtsy. Being a little too cute was a nice way to handle it, he thought. She laid the envelope on an end table, then curled into the corner of the couch's ell, tucking her feet beneath her so that the bunnies were lying on top of each other. She lifted her glass like a toast, then raised her eyebrows and drank. He took a sip.

"So what kind of a day did *you* have?" she said.

He thought for a second or two. "Oh," he said, "about a B minus."

"I call that good."

"Oh yeah. Me too. There was a lot of running around in circles and general head-scratching. But I guess something got done." He thought for another second and laughed. "Or did it?" He mocked looking puzzled.

She was silent for a moment, watching him. Then she said, "Tuesday's such a low-energy day. That's my theory."

"Oh?"

"Yeah. I mean Monday's *supposed* to be the worst. So everybody expects it to be bad. Everybody watches out for it and talks about it being Monday. But Tuesday is almost like that. And nobody ever says anything about it being Tuesday."

"You're right," he said. They were both quiet. This apartment, he realized, made him feel secure in some way. He took another sip of the Amaretto and let his head rest against the back of the couch.

"That makes Tuesday worse than Monday," she said.

"Mm," he said, eyes almost closed.

"I was shopping today, downtown." She stopped and shook her head, her eyes lit with sharp points of anger as she remembered what happened. "Ran my day right into a killer salesgirl. I must've been feeling too good, I think. You know how that offends some people?"

"Oh yes."

"Those big stores, on Fifth, you know, I wanted to

write a check. So she sends me upstairs to this *credit* department, and I have to talk to a guy, like he's *Mr. Credit*. All over the universe, Mars, Venus, everywhere, you have to see *him*. You're, uh, one of those little space monsters, buggy eyes on wires, right? And you wanna pay with a check you have to see this guy and show him your cards."

Guyer smiled.

She shook her head again. "Really, my whole life is to beat them for a hundred and twenty-five bucks. That's all I go around doing." She paused again. "He says to me maybe I should clear this with your bank. And he gives me a look. Like I'm gonna fall down on the floor and kick my legs in the air. Oh please, Mr. Man, not my *bank*. Right? So he looks at me and I look at him, and I'm Mrs. Composed. And he says, okay? So I tell him the telephone number and the name of the bank and I say ask for Mr. Diskin there because he's the officer that handles my account. So fine, I think, let's call. So what does he do? He lifts the phone off the hook and he looks at me, like *this,* kinda sideways, like he's saying are you absolutely sure you want me to make this call?"

She stopped. Looked over at the radio and said "This Muzak is driving me crazy. Do you mind if I change the station?"

"Go ahead."

She went to the radio. "What about some MOR rock?"

"Fine." Apparently, he thought, the other station had been for him.

"There," she said, after tuning. "That I can live with." She walked back to the couch and resettled herself carefully. "So anyhow the guy. After he gives me the eye I look back at him like he's some kinda cock-a-roach and he drops the phone back down and says some b.s. about how they have to be careful what with the blah-blah these days and he makes little initials on the corner of the check and gives his pen a click, like now it's okay and everybody in the whole world is gonna be rich and famous and happy forever because those little initials are there. And he goes back to shuffling papers. Meanwhile, I sit. Now we have a waiting contest. Finally, when he can't stand it anymore he picks up the check and hands it to me. I take it like this, with two fingers like a scissors, and I leave. Go down the elevator. Find the salesgirl. I don't say word one. Just show her the initials in the corner. She reaches for it. I move it away. Tear it lengthwise. Give her both halves. Then I make eyebrows at her, See, bitch? Then I walk."

"You let her know," he said.

"Really. I don't believe these people stay in business, handing out aggravation all day long."

"It's their security department," he said. "They'll memo the sales people with profiles of certain shoppers. What they wear, what they buy, time of day, everything. Based on who they think is stealing from them that week. With bad checks, or shoplifting, or whatever it is. If you happen to fit that week's profile, you're due to be hassled. They lose business over it, but they have inventory shrinkage, and they have to do something. Pity of it is, the inventory shrinkage is mainly walking out the door with the employees."

"Yeah well," she said, meaning it wasn't her problem. "You eat?"

"Not yet."

"If I'd known you were going to visit a little I'd of tried to get it together for cheese things or something."

"That's okay. Hey, I'm not, ahh—"

"No, no. Glad to have the company."

"Tell you what. Maybe we could go and get something to eat someplace."

She gave him a look. "Well that I really *would* like."

Something fluttered briefly at the top of his stomach, then stopped. "What do you like? French? Italian? Chinese? We could eat steak. What?"

"French."

"Okay."

"Tell you what," she said, moving over to the bar and returning with the Amaretto bottle. "Lemme top that up for you"—she did it—"and you can watch the TV while I dry my hair and get dressed. Okay?"

"Okay."

She pulled a TV on a rolling stand away from the wall and turned it on, adjusting the position so he could see it. "There's something or other on there," she said, "just switch to anything you like. I don't get Thirteen. Well, I get it, but . . ."

"That's just fine."

She smiled at him and left to get dressed.

The show on television was about two detectives in Los Angeles. The police made a roadblock by parking two cars across a highway with their hoods facing each other. The criminals, two men in their thirties with razor-cut hair and glen plaid suits, drove their car through the roadblock by punching between the parked cars, shoving them out of their path. The detectives chased the criminals in their car. Crossing intersections, they slewed around trucks and cars, tires squealing. Both the criminals and the detectives were driving Pontiac Grand Prix's. They entered a highway with curves. Both cars skidded as they went around the curves. Then the criminals' car failed to make a curve. It broke through a guardrail and rolled down a long hill, winding up on its roof. Then it blew up and caught fire. The flames roared into the air with sharp edges, as though they came from a big bonfire of wood.

* * *

Guyer had worked for the CIA as a debriefing analyst in Vietnam, based on a DER-type destroyer off Phan Thiet in the South China Sea. DER meant Destroyer Escort Radar, a small ship built in the early fifties, with a forest of communication antennae riding high above the superstructure. Guyer was stationed in a tiny, sweltering office belowdecks—the air-conditioning functioned about an hour a day—at a metal desk with a telephone and a tape recorder on it. A landing pad had been mounted near the fantail, and helicopters brought in mercenaries all day long. They'd see a doctor, a paymaster, and a debriefer, catch their breath overnight, then be taken out to wherever it was they were going next: home if they were banged up or burnt out, back to the zone if they were able. Guyer's role was not evaluative, his job was simply to put in time on the other side of the desk as the Company rep, probing for substantive response—*What time of day exactly? How far from the village?* The tapes themselves were transmitted in scramble back to Langley. The mercenaries came to him right off the choppers; some still ratcheting with amphetamines, some with involuntary tears of fatigue running down their cheeks, many without any affect whatsoever. They wore tennis sneakers and blue jeans and Windbreakers, and carried Swedish K machine guns. He interviewed Americans, Australians, South Africans, Koreans and Taiwanese, and the occasional Frenchman, still hard at it seventeen years after Dien Bien Phu. There were, during that period, many operations running in Southeast Asia. Some, like Operation Phoenix, which assassinated Viet Cong political cadres, became famous. Others never came to light. It was said, in the middle and late sixties, that there was hardly a decent mercenary to be found anywhere else in the world, they were all busy padding up and down the trails of Laos and Cambodia and Vietnam in their tennis sneakers.

List stayed on the DER for about a week. His skin was the color of white wax and his eyes blinked incessantly. After being cut, he'd lost so much blood that he'd been transfused at a jungle hospital with coconut milk, a common plasma substitute in field situations. The doctors on the ship prescribed whole blood and a one-week rest on the ship before he went on to a proprietary hospital in Osaka. Guyer ran into him late one night, sitting with his back against a gun emplacement shield and drinking a beer. He had three six-packs of Iron City he'd bought off a sailor, and he invited Guyer to join him.

For a long time they just sat and drank beer. There was no wind that night, and the air hung thick and wet with humidity. They were sitting on the starboard bow, above the crew quarters. Some of the sailors below were playing tapes—they couldn't hear any distinct song, but a throb of low, tinny noise flowed up at them through the deck plates. In front of them was Vietnam: darkness cut by the land-smell of rotten fruit. Then an artillery mission fired, pinprick flashes that lit off the undersides of the low cloud followed by distant flat thuds, like thunder after lightning, and they could see the humped black outline of the landmass.

"Asia," List said.

"Yeah," Guyer said. "At least you're out of it."

"Oh yes."

"Glad?"

"Sort of. The decision was made for me, you see."

Guyer didn't say anything.

"I got what I came for."

"Oh?"

"Yes. Money and morphine. And the God-given right of every man not to be in California."

"Whatever," Guyer said, after a moment.

"I went to school out there. The University of Asia. The way they tether a pig in Laos is to run a thread through its eyelid. If the pig moves too far, off comes the eyelid. It can sense that, of course, and stands still. That the sort of thing you hear all day?"

"No. Not really. It's more like, we were here and then we went there."

List laughed, suddenly, then stopped abruptly. "Too true. We *were* here and then we went *there*. Oh yes." He put an empty back in the pack and peeled the tab off another can. "You ready?" he said.

"Not yet," Guyer said.

They drank in silence for a while. Then List said, "Laos," and shook his head. "Maybe even Burma. We went up through the top of Thailand one time, after a Pathet Lao town in the north, and I do believe we might have been in Burma."

"Really?"

"Well, not for the record." He paused. "Is there a record?"

"Yes."

"Right now?"

Guyer looked at him sharply. "No."

"I talked to someone here. For the record. You?"

"No, not me. There's a few of us."

"Bush spooks."

"Not really."

"The secret war in Laos," List said. There were ironic quotation marks around the words, as though they'd been said on the nightly news. "We liked to do them when they came out in the morning for their shits. They'd stroll out together, chatting, very relaxed, and they'd find a place in the morning sun and squat there. And when they were settled we'd do them from the tree line—pop, pop—the American Cong."

"Americans?"

"No. Just me. The team leader was a New Zealander. I was the sergeant, and the rest were Chinese. From Chiang Kai-shek's army that came down out of China, after they lost the war, and settled in the golden triangle. The second generation, this was, sons of the original soldiers. *They* know."

"What?"

"Everything. All of it. That the soul just leaves, flies away, and there's a body on the ground where it used to be, and if there's sorrow in those who stay behind it's a teaspoon of water in an ocean. You know, man, *Asia.*"

Guyer shrugged.

"Don't you see? I mean we're *Americans,* as far as we're concerned, we're eliminating the Pathet Lao political infrastructure. For them, it's something else. Some sort of music that never stops playing. If we weren't paying them, they'd be fighting the Hmong in somebody's heroin army. They're born to it." He was silent for a moment. "So, who's gonna win the pennant this year?"

Guyer took a long pull at the beer. Put the can on the deck. Locked his fingers on top of his head and leaned back against the metal of the gun emplacement. He fought the desire to scratch at the heat rash under his arms, when he moved the sweat ran down it and it burned, then itched. On shore, the artillery mission was completed. There was a starburst flare, drifting down on its parachute, then blackness.

"What'd you do before this?" List asked.

"This. Someplace else. You?"

"I was a graduate student, I was. At Stanford. Computer logic and systems analysis. The binary life, in Palo Alto under the palm trees."

"Hunh."

"Yup. I was very, *very* good at it."

"Something to look forward to, now."

"I rather think not. No, I don't see it."

"Then what?"

"I used to wonder about that, walking through the

jungle. They have that triple canopy up in Laos, of course you know that, so there's no light. It all rots in there, and it smells the wrong kind of sweet, like bubble gum. I liked it, in my way. Like walking through your imagination, if you're Baudelaire. *Fleurs du Mal*?"

"What?"

"Never mind."

He stopped and seemed to drift off, but Guyer said nothing. He was used to that: sudden stops, pauses while a hidden apparatus whirred and ground someplace, then re-ignition. Interrogating, he waited through these lapses all day.

"Where was I?"

"What you thought about in the jungle."

"Oh yes. Well, I did think. Two choices in there, lots of thinking, keep those cognitive wheels spinning, boys. Or else shut the mama down and run on backbrain only. It's the cervical cortex makes you duck when somebody pulls a trigger a quarter mile away. The front brain won't do that for you: it'll hang on to sanity but it won't save your life. Even so, I kept thinking. Hump along in there pouring sweat with all that ammo hanging on your back, and every once in a while you hear a jungle scream, when God-knows-what kills God-knows-what, and maybe you better keep your mind busy. What I thought was, what the hell am I going to do if I get out of this alive? What's *next*? My life seemed to be one minute I was a graduate student then the next minute I was waiting in the tree line for the sun to come up. And I would keep coming around, again and again, to the same place, not that it made any real sense, but the phrases kept playing: I want to be rich. I want to live on the top floor of a hotel, a good hotel, and I never want to speak to anyone again, ever. So rich, you see, that my needs are understood, met silently. I'm crazy, of course." He laughed at himself.

Not crazy, Guyer thought, shattered perhaps. From

what he'd seen, the American mercenaries came in two categories: those with no imagination, and those with too much. List was of the second category. He was like a sailboat with no tiller, swept by the wind. Maybe the war had made him crazy, but Guyer had seen a lot of them who came to the war in order to be crazy, who hunted down the crazed edge of the war and made a home there.

"I take your silence for agreement," List said.

"Don't," Guyer answered.

"Matters not. Truth is, I came over here to die. I fucked that up too." He wiggled the foot on his damaged leg. "Oh well. God plays pranks."

"You didn't get all the way back here by trying to die, friend."

"You're right. I was so goddamn scared I lived."

"What happened to money and morphine?"

"That's bullshit," List said. He paused. "Just something I told myself at the time. Correction, something I told my *friends*."

"Then why, really?"

List's voice was soft. "I don't know." He shook his head. After a moment he said, "What's in it for you?"

Guyer thought for a bit. "It's something I happen to do well."

"That's all?" The tone was mocking, teasing.

"Oh, I suppose if you really dug down you might find a little love of country in there somewhere."

"Just maybe."

Guyer laughed. "Yeah," he said. "Just maybe."

They were silent for a long time. They had come to an understanding, a delicate thing that further bantering would ruin and they both knew it. List, the crazed adventurer, Guyer, the stolid soldier, opposite lives, fighting in the same war, on the same side, an experience so ancient it long ago passed reason of any sort.

Guyer realized he was beer drunk, on one can of

beer, muzzy and slightly stupid. It was fatigue, he thought. Nobody on the ship slept the night through. The wet heat woke you up, you staggered into the shower and stood under the tepid water in a daze, then tried to sleep again. At dawn, just about the time you went under for real, there was strange yellow light and the rhythmic whisper of the first choppers coming in. He closed his eyes for a moment. Then List touched him on the shoulder. There was a piece of an envelope in his hand.

"This is my sister in Portland," he said. "She always knows where I am. Get in touch sometime."

Guyer took the piece of paper. "Thanks," he said. He was moved by the gesture. The fact that somebody like List—brilliant, flashy, tortured—liked him well enough to do that made him feel appreciated; it flattered him.

List stood, hopping on his good leg, and picked up the remaining beer. "Maybe I can sleep," he said. "I'm supposed to be flown out tomorrow."

"Best of luck," Guyer said.

List smiled crookedly, as if to say that if everything he'd seen in the last few months were possible, maybe that was also. "You too," he said.

He lost the phone number, but he didn't forget the evening. It stayed with him. When he thought about the war, years later, the best image of it, of what it had been, was fixed in that brief conversation with Richard List. Six months after that night he was transferred out of the Southeast Asia theatre. His new assignment was in Barcelona, as part of a working group called SAGSE —Site Analysis Group/Southern Europe. "Site" meant they worked right where they were, in Barcelona, on station. When their product was in turn analyzed, in Langley, it became "intelligence." Eventually, weighted estimates were made available to senior analysis groups, and from there the information ultimately worked its way to the people who made policy and told the President's staff how things were that week. It was work in fine detail, concentrating on the infinite conspiracies of various diplomatic cabals: the temperature of relations between the economic attachés of East Germany and Austria in Spain was, evidently, an indication of political sickness or health elsewhere in the world. Guyer worked at it, but it was during this period that he started to lose interest. The work began to seem circular, self-perpetuating, and finally meaningless. To save himself, he signed on for a special emergency mission in North Africa. It did not save him. What it did do, paradoxically, was ruin him. When he was terminated, two years later, he wound up in New York. He had a vague notion of starting his own business, and to that end was involved with one or two people who'd come out of Clandestine Services at the same time that he did, but it was mostly talk. He went, during the weeks that followed, to a great number of movies. One night—it was a sweltering August—he walked out of an East Side movie theatre and saw a familiar face, in line for the 10:00 P.M. showing. He had to stare for a moment to make certain. The black hollows under the eyes were gone and the face had filled out a little, but it was Richard List.

List recognized him. They shook hands, List suggested he would be just as happy to skip the movie, would Guyer like to get something to drink? They found a bar and talked for a long, long time. Awkwardly at first, because their experience in Southeast Asia had been totally disparate. When Guyer mentioned a business, however, List became very animated. He was unemployed and nearly broke. He wasn't, he admitted, exactly what most conventional employers were looking for. And, as a systems analyst, he was so advanced that he needed something fairly significant. But his job, school, and military history frightened off corporate employers and New York was thoroughly overstocked with independent computer consultants. Did Guyer, he wanted to know, have any intention of using EDP applications in the business? He was willing to work very cheap if he could just get something going for himself. Guyer laid out his idea, first warning List that it was a bizarre notion and might not work at all. List was visibly excited. That was, he said, *precisely* the kind of thing that computers could do successfully. They planned and schemed together for hours. They were both, in the context of the normal business community, homeless orphans. And they recognized in each other the willingness to work and sacrifice that might just make a private venture successful. Their emotional commitment to a business came from a common anger: They'd been declared misfits, outcasts, and both resented it bitterly. That they had been declared so for different reasons was not important to them.

What made it possible, in the beginning, was Guyer's severance check and pension fund payout. They managed to lease an office and a computer, from there it was a month-to-month struggle to create a business and actually earn money at the same time. Working together day and night, they discovered they liked each other, the edges of their particular personalities fit together to make one extremely efficient entity. Guyer was persistent, List was brilliant. Guyer could keep track of endless detail, List could make intuitive connections that worked. Guyer could get up in the morning and talk on the telephone, List filtered easily through New York's night world. It was not, of course, all sweetness and light. Six months in, Guyer began to fret and, to put his mind at ease, had List quietly checked out. That mostly confirmed what he already knew: Richard liked it out on the edge. But as long as he did nothing to damage their common interests, that really didn't matter very much.

On the screen, one of the detectives was now engaged in a shoot-out in an underground garage. The man he was shooting at wore sunglasses. One would pop up, shoot, and hunch down. Then the other would do the same thing. Guyer, a little gone on the long day and the Amaretto, thought such terms of conflict rather decent. The popping up, shooting, and hunching down could continue only so long as ammunition held out, an implicit limit of sixteen sequences, given eight rounds per combatant. A benign duel, something of the eighteenth century in it. Honor satisfied without a wound unless one of the participants lost track of the rhythm and popped when he should have hunched. Or could one of the men have more than eight? He leaned forward and squinted to check the pistols. The detective was well armed with a magnum .357. He could have, if he chose, shot his opponent by firing at the car, since the round would pass through the engine block. The criminal had something long and snouty. Guyer didn't know what it was. It reminded him of some sort of gas-operated target pistol. Maggie burst into the room like someone coming indoors on a very cold day: face flushed, walking fast, a whirl of radiant energy. She came accompanied by a delicious cloud of perfume.

Out in the street, Guyer again felt eyes. But since people were staring anyhow, there was no point in trying to find out who was doing it. Maggie had on a soft black leather jacket, her copper hair streaming down the back, white pants, and supple suede boots with tops folded over. She was wearing a beret made out of gold threads that glittered in the light of the streetlamps. She walked with her head up and shoulders back, in long strides. And she walked very close to him. Everybody looked at them. Guyer became conscious of the tie rolled up in his pocket.

The street life flowed around them: two dignified men with silver hair, one wearing an ascot, who were holding hands; a young dog-walker wearing sunglasses, eight leashes in hand, attached to everything from toy poodle to bull mastiff; a beautiful young woman, blond and green-eyed, wheeling a small maple tree on a mover's dolly.

"Where are you from?" he asked.

"Brooklyn," she said, gesturing south with her head. "Park Slope. What about you?"

"I was born in Cleveland," he said, "then we lived in upstate New York for a time." It wasn't true.

"Like Elmira? Buffalo'n' that?"

"Yeah."

"Brrr."

"How'd you meet Richard?"

"At a weird party."

Guyer wasn't surprised, List constantly came up with acquaintances from his nightly crawl through the city. "Weird?" he said.

"Oh, you know. Costumes and stuff." They stopped to let traffic flow by on Second Avenue, then trotted across together. "It was a break," she said, "running into him like that. I'm takin' these really expensive singing lessons, and I was doing cocktail waitress. Yech. Then all of a sudden I'm Mata Hari. Fantastic!"

"Mata Hari," he snorted. He felt her tense at saying the wrong thing. "I think her name was Gertrud Zelle. Zeller? Something like that. She was Dutch, the mistress of a French colonel, in Paris. What she was, was an exotic dancer, and by all reports a fat one, in her forties. Something, this is during World War One, went on the fritz in French intelligence. So they looked around for a scapegoat and found her. It was pathetic.

She wasn't a spy at all, but some people thought she was German and not Dutch. Anyhow, they executed her." He shook his head. "The French," he said.

"Funny," she said. "I always imagine her in those floor-length shimmery things that look like nightgowns."

"I know. I have a hunch that most people somehow got to thinking that Mata Hari was Pola Negri."

"Who?"

"Silent-film star. A vamp. Maybe because the names are similar."

"Oh yeah," she said. "That's probably it."

They walked in silence for a minute. "Course," she said, "I wouldn't be the mistress of a colonel."

"No?"

"Unh-uh. General, maybe," then she added, a small sigh in her voice, "or more likely a private."

The maître d' at La Coquille was not happy to see them. He gave them a once-over—Guyer rumpled and tieless, Maggie in her shining gold hat—noted the chasm in age and demeanor, then tried to look at his eyebrows.

"Good evening, monsieur," he said. "You have a reservation?"

"No."

"Ahh."

Guyer looked pointedly over the man's shoulder. There was a lawn of white napery and shining silver, about twenty tables, diners at half of them. "Looks like you might be able to help us out."

"Umm," said the man, and went off toward the small bar. Their way was blocked by a velvet rope. Guyer was mad. The sleek little shark was trying to hold him up for money. He figured that what he had here was a sales manager out for the evening with a bimbo, and if they were going to dine with the crème de la crème, there would first be a cash transaction. Then suddenly the man returned, unhooked the rope, and said, "Follow me, monsieur." They were led to a table near the kitchen, but that bothered Guyer not at all. They were given menus, the man said, "Paul will take your order for cocktails," and marched away. What, Guyer wondered, changed his mind? They studied the menu, printed in thin, spidery script, that sang of quenelles, and timbales, and *émincé* of this, and *estouffade* of that. They studied and talked and decided for quite some time. Paul did not appear, though waiters flowed around them with trays of lidded brushed-steel serving dishes.

By the time they had gone backward and forward through the menu and exhausted its conversation, Guyer realized that he'd been trumped. The maître d', rather than having them stand around the entrance to the dining room, had marooned them on this island table, with only butter curls and glasses of water for sustenance. Now, if Guyer decided to bribe for his dinner, he had to walk all the way through the room to do it. Inside, he smoldered. In the twenty minutes that followed, he looked at his watch at least six times. Then Maggie said, "Excuse me just one minute. There's a phone call I need to make." He realized, from her voice and the way she moved, that she was enraged and that she thought *she* was the problem. After a few minutes—Guyer finished his water—she returned. Now she didn't seem angry at all. She began a long, meandering story about her Uncle Phil, who'd been torpedoed on a merchant ship during World War II and had spent nine days in a life raft with a man who'd been in the wholesale lamb business before the war, and about how when he mustered out in '45 he became a millionaire in the wholesale lamb business himself, based on hours and hours of tutelage in the South Pacific. As she told the story she kept glancing toward the front of the room, where the tyrannical maître d' stood guardian at his rope. Had she, Guyer wondered, gone and tipped the man herself? He was mortified at the thought. Ten minutes later he had his answer. Maggie began waving wildly at a man who stopped momentarily at the rope, peered around the dining room, then stepped over and came toward them. He wore soiled white pants, a white jacket with orange-red stains on it, and a square white cap. He had a flat white carton in his hands as he worked his way toward them. When he arrived, he set the carton down between them. Maggie said, "Angelo, I love you for life," reached into her jacket pocket, and handed him a twenty. He looked around him, laughed silently for a second or two, then left. Maggie flipped the top of the carton up. "Now," she said, "I ordered half with pepperoni and mushrooms, and half with just cheese, we can share any way you like."

In the cab going home he kept falling asleep, waking up when his head jerked downward. The day seemed to have begun hours and hours ago, with his early-morning calls from Arconada and the telephone man. Well, he would sleep tonight. Tomorrow, fly out to Wisconsin. Get the Delatte thing squared away and running: sooner over, sooner he would be free of it. He started to worry about Mains's probe, but he was too tired to worry. Maggie. Something warm came off her, nameless, not worked at, it was just there, and it didn't want anything. She'd told him a joke on the way back to her apartment. An ant and an elephant made love all night. In the morning, the elephant was dead. When the ant saw that, he said, "Just my luck. One night of passion and now I have to spend the rest of my life digging a grave." Guyer had smiled, Maggie stopped walking, grabbed him by the arm, leaned into him and said, "C'mon you sonofabitch, *laugh*." At her door, they'd briefly kissed good night. Her surface was tough. She could, he knew, take care of herself. But her lips had surprised him, they were that warm and that soft.

[112]

HE COULDN'T GET a direct flight to Milwaukee, so he flew to Chicago on a half-empty 747 and rented a medium-size Ford at O'Hare. Instead of 94 and 294, the Interstate, he took 90 northwest to Rockford, then north to Madison, cutting over toward Waukesha on what had been the main road before they built 94 East. Wisconsin Route 18 went through the towns: Cambridge, Jefferson, Roston, and Alata. Guyer drove forty-five and fifty, taking it easy. It was late in the afternoon, gray cloud cover moving in from the northern plains. The towns were old and sturdy, with two-story houses, mostly wood painted white, set square to the road in large, orderly yards. The streets were lined with big maples and oaks, mostly bare now, with here and there a few red leaves hanging on. Each town had a Rexall and a Woolworth. Guyer had caught the homeward flow of school buses, and had to wait behind them every ten minutes or so, while a bunch of kids in Windbreakers or wool jackets disembarked. Every town had a brick high school, prominently named Lincoln or Washington or Madison. Behind chain link fencing were the football fields, white goal posts on either end, teams at practice in scruffy uniforms, the defense wearing faded red overshirts. Guyer liked it. Under the gray prairie sky, immense and flowing, and in the failing afternoon light, the towns looked private and solid and safe.

He found the mall, having asked directions at a Shell station on the strip heading into Waukesha, and pulled into the parking lot of a McDonald's across the highway. He parked with his back to the traffic, and spent a long time with his eyes on the rearview mirror. He watched cars come in, people enter the restaurant, eat or pick up takeout orders, and leave. He wasn't looking for anything in particular, just watching. Strange, he thought, if you acted as though you suspected something, sometimes an element in the scene would stir in such a way as to make suspicion justified. But nothing happened. After half an hour he backed slowly around, left the lot, and drove five miles away from the mall, checking behind him all the way. Then he turned left across traffic into a gas station, filled his tank, washed his face and finger-combed his hair in the men's room, and drove back to the mall.

Inside, it was a colossal cruciform box, shops spread endlessly up and down its arms, a German Expressionist pun on a medieval bazaar. There were video-game arcades, boutiques, glitter T-shirt stores, kitchen and bath shops, a J.C. Penney, and a store made entirely of greeting cards divided into subsections labeled *Contemporary, Apology,* and *Get Well*. It seemed to Guyer a slap in the face to the sense of refuge he'd felt in the

[116]

towns but—he damned himself for a cynic—the people strolling through the long halls looked happy enough, if a little dazed. Except for the teen-agers, who seemed to move in it with great naturalness and ease. To them it was apparently just another thing in life that was there, and they used it.

After a ten-minute search he found The Shoe Tree. The window display was made up of various footwear hanging from the branches of Lucite trees. There was a running shoe, a basketball sneaker, a work boot, a galosh, a carpet slipper, a moccasin, a rubber hunting boot, and even a shoe—a shiny black brogan with laces tied up neatly in a bow. Across the top of the window was a printed sign in red block lettering: ASK US ABOUT OUR WEEKLY SHOE TREE SPECIALS! Inside the store a woman in a chair was bending forward and pressing her fingers against the front of a spike-heeled shoe, as though to locate her toes. Opposite her a man sat on a low fitting-stool with his hands resting on his thighs, elbows turned out. Waiting for the customer, his gaze wandered toward the window. It was a European face, with tiny lines at the corners of the eyes that gave the face a sense of amusement, and delicate features. Yet this face wore tortoiseshell glasses and the light brown hair was neatly brushed. The man had on a gray cotton work jacket with two pens clipped to the breast pocket. Guyer looked away. The man turned back to the woman sitting across from him. There were two other people in the store, a teen-age girl who wore a jacket like the owner's, and a woman shopper studying a rack of vinyl boots.

Guyer entered the store and wandered slowly among the displays, picking up a shoe every now and then and glancing at the price. There was a mirror at floor level, set at an angle so that the customer could comfortably see full length. In the mirror the man folded a shoe back into tissue paper in a red and gray box, then he and the woman stood. Chatting amiably, they moved to a small cashier's desk and took customer and salesman positions on either side of it. The woman handed over a credit card and he worked the slide on his charge-card machine after ringing up the sale. The woman left. The man approached him.

"Help you?" he said.

Up close he was older, gray flecks in the brown hair, the lines in the face slightly deeper than Delatte's. He was one of those men who stay young-looking for a long time, Guyer guessed him to be in his early forties.

"That's on sale this week," he said, Guyer looked down at a tassled loafer in his right hand. He returned it to the slanted shelf, hooking its heel on a plastic ridge.

"You're Bill Elden?" Guyer said.

"Yup. Have we met?" He had, Guyer felt it, merchant's friendliness. He was affable and pleasant on the surface, territorial and protective down inside. He was a man who would fight to defend his turf.

"Only on the phone," Guyer said.

"Oh?" The face seemed to close slightly. He began to realize that this was something other than a shoe buyer.

"Funny thing," Guyer said, "but the resemblance is uncanny."

"Say again?" Elden now looked puzzled. Then, after a moment, the mist cleared. "Why hell yes! The telephone call, from Los Angeles!"

"I'm Ted Collier," Guyer said, smiling and extending a hand. They shook.

Elden grinned to himself. "I didn't know whether to take it all that serious. Nobody I know ever heard of Tony Shaw."

Guyer nodded his understanding. "Tony actually has a hell of a following, but it's mostly people who come

[118]

to Vegas. The feeling in the business is that he's one of those artists who reach the top late. A little national exposure, one Carson appearance . . ."

"And he looks like me," Elden said, mostly to himself. Inside his head, Guyer knew, *he* was getting the national exposure, *he* was on Carson.

"Yes, he does."

"What sort of a singer is he?"

"He reminds some people of Tony Bennett."

"Well, I like Tony Bennett." Something made Elden glance over his shoulder. "Sharon?" he said. The teenage girl looked up from a daydream. The woman who'd been looking at vinyl boots had sat down and was taking off her shoe.

"Can we have a cup of coffee?" Guyer said.

"Sure we can." He turned to the teen-ager. "I'm goin' over to the Cottage House for coffee. You'll take care of things here?"

"Yes, Mr. Elden," the girl said, polite but bored. Guyer could feel the entire heavy day of high school riding behind the words.

After they went out the door, Elden shook his head. "Sharon's a decent kid, but her heart isn't in it. Neighbor's daughter, y'know. You'd think I'd've learned by now." Then he added, "This okay?"

"Fine."

The Cottage House had a bay window that extended into the mall aisle, and a white picket fence, bolted to the concrete wall, that ran its length. It sat diagonally to The Shoe Tree. Guyer bet himself a steak that Elden would sit facing the window. He wasn't going to let that store out of his sight.

A waitress brought coffee without being asked. "Afternoon, Mr. Elden," she said. "Do you take cream?" she said to Guyer. He shook his head no. Elden put two lumps of sugar in his coffee, then raised

[119]

them to the surface with a spoon and watched them dissolve. Guyer sipped and said, "Not bad." Elden nodded absently.

"What company did you say you were with?" he asked.

"Well I said Ted Collier Productions . . ." Elden looked up, responding to a hesitant note in Guyer's voice. "But I guess I should really come clean. What I said on the phone, and just now, that's all pretty much, well, what would you call it." The last part of the sentence he seemed to be addressing to himself.

"How about horse manure?"

"I'd say that's accurate."

Elden chuckled dryly. "By God I knew it."

"What did you know?"

"Well, we are out here in Waukesha, but we read *People* magazine and we watch television. And I bought a big stack of those fan magazines, right here in the mall, and not one single word about any Tony Shaw."

"Which led you to conclude . . ."

"Why it led me to conclude that it was monkey business. That is, until you walked in here today. After the phone call I figured some gyp artist was gonna try and sell me something. But you're not selling anything, Mr. Collier. I can always tell when somebody is selling something. I think you're buying."

"That's right," Guyer said. "There's no Tony Shaw, no celebrity look-alike game show, but . . ." he said, and let it hang.

Elden looked at him archly over the rim of his coffee cup as he drank. He wasn't going to bite that particular worm.

"It's true," Guyer continued, "that you look like somebody."

"Who?"

Guyer shook his head no.

"Secret, hunh." Elden was laughing at him. That was fine with Guyer.

"Yes it is." He returned Elden's ironic grin with one of his own. To a passerby it might have appeared that they were telling each other jokes over coffee.

Elden leaned forward in a parody of conspiracy and said in a stage whisper, "Is it the CIA?"

Guyer laughed. "No, not the CIA."

"Ahh, the *KGB!*"

"Nyet."

"Well now"—he drew a hard pack of Salem Lights out of his shirt pocket and lit one with a disposable lighter—"what do I have that anybody'd want to buy? Not the house, not the car, not the *wife,*" he blew smoke through his nose for dramatic emphasis, "so it's got to be the franchise." He leaned back with a smile of satisfaction. "Do I have it, Mr. Collier?"

Guyer said nothing.

"You say I look like somebody. I'll hazard a guess that what I look like is a man who wants to make some money by selling something he has that somebody else wants. Now you, Mr. Collier, if your name is Mr. Collier, are a private detective of some kind. And I'll hazard another guess, that you represent the Sol-Aire Shoe Corporation of Los Angeles. Am I right?"

"Can I call you Bill?"

"Sure."

"Bill, you're wrong."

"Am I." He wasn't convinced.

"It has nothing to do with the franchise."

For a few moments they both just sat there. Then Elden gave a nervous little laugh and said, "Hey, what is this?"

Guyer nodded. He was getting there. "It's this. If you fly to Brazil, to Rio de Janeiro, then fly back to New York, spend one or two days there, there's somebody that will pay you to do that."

Elden sat dead still and stared. Guyer looked directly into his eyes, leaned forward, and, smiling in a certain way, quickly raised then lowered his eyebrows. It was a gesture that, between two men, meant the smiler probably *had* gone to bed with the lady in question, but of course he wasn't actually going to say so out loud. It meant that the world was naughty. And that Guyer was too. And that he knew Elden was.

"You're serious," Elden said.

"Yes." He watched Elden's face as the idea percolated.

"Would you run that by me again?"

"Stay at some nice hotel in Rio, on the beach. Take a flight up to New York. Another hotel. You'll probably be met at the plane, maybe have lunch, go somewhere to a meeting. Then fly home."

"This is crooked, isn't it."

"No. It's not in any way illegal."

"Because if that's what you've got in mind, forget it."

"You'll fly Rio–New York using a Canadian passport in another name. Does that bother you?"

"Well, I don't know . . ."

"You'll be paid ten thousand dollars."

"Say?"

"Ten thousand."

"Goddamn," Elden said, shaking his head. It was a comment about the world, the times. It wasn't pro or con, it was a bystander's reaction. Guyer, needing something to do, made whirlpools in his coffee with the spoon. Strange, he thought, but in small ways he was Elden and Elden was him, the business fretting, sluggish employees, the little coffee shop where the waitress knew your name. Elden continued, "Well, I don't know *what* to say about that."

Guyer looked up. "Say yes," he said. He was surprised that, somewhere deep down, the words *say no* formed. Then dissolved.

"I just might." Elden was challenging. He meant that he was as much a man as Guyer was.

Guyer closed him: "Can you get away from the store? From home?" It was only very slightly insinuating.

"Hell yes."

"Then okay."

They both, instinctively, drank some coffee. The mutual gesture drained off the tension that had been there seconds earlier. "Just for discussion's sake," Guyer said, "what would you tell people you're doing?"

Elden thought for a moment. "There's NAISR conventions." He pronounced it *nacer*. "That's the N-A-I-S-R, our association. They're always having some sort of meeting."

Guyer habitually took acronyms apart. *National Association,* he thought, *s for shoes, i for independent.* "You'd have to tell people about the convention when you got back." He thought for a moment. "You have a passport?"

"I thought you said something about a Canadian passport."

"That's coming back. You fly down there as yourself."

"Oh. Well then no, I don't."

"Probably a regional office in Milwaukee. Take a day or so."

"I can do that. When is this?"

"Next Friday. The 28th. You'd be in Rio that night. One thing we could do is have a letter sent to you from New York, from one of the big national chains, asking you to come and interview for a sales management job. Now the way you'd react to that, here, you probably don't want the job, but if they're willing to pop for a fancy hotel and a few dinners, what the hell, you might as well go and listen to what they've got to say. How does that sound?"

"You can produce a letter from a national chain?" Elden was, for the first time, truly impressed.

"Not a real one," Guyer said. "Stationery from a job printer, that's all." He shrugged and smiled.

"Oh."

"But you're comfortable with that? A job offer?"

"It wouldn't be the first time. I talked to a man last year."

"Great. Then all you'd really have to do is reproduce that conversation. Once you get to New York, if you want to call your wife or something, just say what hotel you're at. You'll only be in Brazil for twenty-four hours. For the rest of the time you can tell the truth, pretty much."

"Okay. What sort of people would I meet in New York?"

"Not very interesting people. Somebody's employees."

Elden thought for a bit, then shook his head and smiled to himself. "Tell you one thing," he said, "life's the damnedest thing."

"Yes it is. How do you want the money?"

"How?"

"Bearer bonds? Cash?"

Elden thought for a while. Stubbed out his cigarette. "How about Krugerrands?"

"Hmm. You can if you want. Where in Waukesha would you want to be cashing in ten thousand dollars in Krugerrands?"

"You have a point there. All right, cash. Delivered to the store, of course."

Guyer smiled. What could you do to somebody, he thought, by delivering ten thousand dollars in cash to his wife on a Wednesday afternoon. "Of course to the store," he said. "It'll come small-package delivery. In a shoebox." He waited to see if Elden found that funny. He didn't. "You understand," he continued, "that if something should come up and you're not on that flight out of Rio, we'll have somebody stop by and pick up the cash." It wasn't a threat, the way he said it, just an arrangement.

"Sure."

"So it's set."

"Yes, I guess it is." The look on Elden's face said that he couldn't quite believe that he'd agreed to do it.

Guyer took the passport out, checked around the restaurant to make sure nobody was looking at them, said, "Just slip this in your pocket, you can take a look at it later," and handed it over. Elden dropped it casually in the side pocket of his work jacket. "Now you start using that when you register at a hotel. The name is Gerard. You fly to New York, then to Brazil, as yourself. Taxi into Rio, just like a tourist, then find a nice big hotel and register there. This time of year you won't need a reservation. Just keep in mind that it's *Gerard* who's staying at the hotel. Okay?" Elden nodded. "Now, along with the money you'll receive airplane tickets, two hundred dollars for your night in Rio, and an itinerary. Be all for the best if you memorized that and threw it away. We'll book all the flights for you, you'll be on a 3:30 out of Kennedy, on Varig, for Rio, so we'll get you out of Milwaukee on the earliest possible flight on the 28th, we can't afford to get screwed up by airline delays. When you're done in New York, that's Monday at the latest, go out to Kennedy and fly back to Milwaukee as yourself, we'll include an open ticket for that trip. Keep in mind that when you arrive back in New York from Brazil, the page will be for *Mr. Gerard*. Okay, questions?"

"You'll write it all out for me on the itinerary?"

"Yes."

He thought for a few seconds. "What if somebody looks in that package?"

"What if they do?"

"They'll see all that cash money and airplane tickets, and . . ."

"And?"

"Well . . ."

"It isn't illegal to send cash through the mails. It's just a way business is done, sometimes."

"Not out here it isn't."

"Are you sure?"

"Now that I think about it, maybe not, last year the school board . . ." He let it hang.

Guyer finished his coffee. "Best thing, of course, is to relax and enjoy yourself. You work hard, this is a few days off and you get paid for it. Rio de Janeiro is a very open sort of a place, free and easy, if you have a day-dream or two you've never quite gotten around to trying out, nobody's going to know, or care."

"Hadn't really thought about that side of it."

Guyer took a card out of his pocket. There was the name Ted Collier and an accommodation address and telephone number in Los Angeles. "If you have a problem, try me at the office. More than likely you'll get my service, but I'll get back to you. Just be sure and leave a number." Elden took the card, read it, then put it away. "Last thing is the payment," Guyer said. "The first package will have five thousand dollars and all the other material I mentioned. The last five thousand should arrive on the Friday after you return from New York. You understand why we have to do it that way."

Elden nodded. "Makes sense."

Guyer breathed a little easier. It wasn't unusual for people to agree to do all sorts of things, then balk at the split fee. He leaned back in the booth.

"Money sure will help," Elden said. "Nobody's really sure what kind of Christmas we're going to have this year. That Ford assembly plant shut down three weeks ago, people here just freeze up when that happens, 'n' the retailers are the first ones to feel it. They can wait a month for shoes, y'know, but they've got to go to the supermarket today."

"I know," Guyer said. He stood, Elden moved to follow, Guyer stopped him with a brief motion of the hand. "I have a plane to catch," he said, "no reason for you to hurry." He extended a hand. "Deal?"

"Deal," Elden said. They shook hands.

"One thing, probably best not to talk about this. You'll be tempted, it's only human, but it's better just between us. That okay?"

"Yessir."

"Well then, good to meet you." Guyer took two dollar bills out of his pocket and dropped them on the table. "My coffee today," he said. Elden picked the dollars up and gave them back.

"Next time," he said.

"Okay," Guyer said, and smiled and walked out into the mall aisle.

There was a brightly lit chain drugstore several doors down and across from The Shoe Tree. Guyer circled to get there, went to a display area near the cash register, and ran his finger along a shelf of bottled vitamins. He had a good line of sight into Elden's store. As he pretended to shop he watched people walking up and down the aisle. There weren't all that many, not for the sixty or so retail outlets contained in the mall. A business here, he realized, could die a slow death. He watched Elden as he strode purposefully back into The Shoe Tree. He walked like a man who'd just gotten lucky. He spoke to Sharon for a moment, more than likely to find out if she'd managed to sell the lady shopper something, then moved about the empty store neatening up the shoes on the racks. When after ten minutes he hadn't gone near the telephone, Guyer left the mall.

In the parking lot it was almost night. The cloud cover had broken slightly, leaving cracks of dark blue light. Guyer inhaled deeply. All day—first in the airport, then in the plane, then in the car with the heater running, and finally in the mall—he had been breathing processed air. *Airplane air,* he called it, and it inevitably made him sleepy. He wondered momentarily if there wasn't perhaps just a little less oxygen in it, nudging the public gently toward an obedient, slightly passive state of mind. *Oh, yes,* he told himself, *and the Russians are chlorinating our water.* He climbed into the car, worked his way through various backtracking drills, then headed south through the night toward Chicago.

It was 1:38 when he walked down the endless red carpet of the passenger-egress ramp at Kennedy. He felt grimy and tired and used up. Outside, he stood for a moment in the white glare of the vapor lights lining the curb. It was midweek, late night, and the airport was dead, a long line of cabs parked at the curb, drivers standing around with their hands in their pockets. He turned abruptly and went back inside the terminal, found a bank of payphones, and dialed Maggie's number. After three rings he got an answering service and hung up without leaving a message. So she had a date, so the hell with it, go home, shower, sleep, start again tomorrow. He went back out and got into the first cab in the line, gave his usual close-to-home address, and settled back in the seat.

"Got a preference?" said the driver, inclining his head back toward the passenger seat without actually turning his body.

"How about the tunnel."

"This time of night, should be okay."

They moved out along the service road, entered the Van Wyck Expressway. "Tell you what," said Guyer, "why don't you go Triborough, then take Second Avenue to Fourteenth."

"A little longer," said the driver.

"That's okay."

"Once we're in the city, I could do better on Park."

"I know. Take Second anyhow."

The driver shrugged assent. Maggie's apartment was on Second, in the Seventies. He didn't actually intend to stop there, as far as he knew, he just wanted to go past in the cab. Probably, he thought, a last vestige of high school cruising come back to haunt him. The driver switched expressways, moving artfully through the late traffic, and got on the Grand Central in order to hit the Triborough Bridge at 125th Street. "Looka this," he said, eyes on the rearview mirror. "I got a shoe-fly."

"What?"

"Shoe-fly. Inspectors from the hack bureau in an unmarked Dodge."

"Sure they're on you?"

"Who knows, them ball breakers, nothin' to do but make my life miserable. You see in the mirror? Back about eight cars, in the slow lane?"

"You have something to worry about?"

"Nah. But hey look, you're my witness I threw the flag and didn't try to make no price, okay?"

"Okay."

After that they drove in silence. The driver checked his tail every twenty seconds or so, using his door mirror. They crossed the bridge doing a polite forty. The two best Manhattan views were from the 59th Street Bridge and from the Triborough. He had to have *something* before he got home. He slumped against the door and watched the miracle: towers of lights bulked together above a strip of black water, the East River.

[129]

Magic castles, he thought, glittering, seductive. The city from a distance sang the old but honorable song—you can fuck me if you can climb me.

The cab turned off the East River Drive at 96th, went west to Second Avenue, then headed south at twenty-six miles an hour in order to hit the timed lights. The traffic, therefore, moved in a pack. The leading cars sped up in order to retain position, slowed for the end of the red light, then accelerated as the green came on. Maggie's apartment house was in the middle of the block. Richard List was just leaving the canopied entrance and turning north and Guyer got a direct look at his face, if only for an instant, before the cab flashed by. Guyer started to tell the driver to stop, then didn't. Instead, he closed his eyes, retained the image, and examined it. The set of the face was arrogant, purposive, concentrated. And, his limp exaggerated by the pace, he was moving fast.

Foley

EDNA FOLEY LOCKED the driver's door on her Chevy Nova, dropped the keys into a compartment in her purse, zipped the compartment closed, and snapped the purse together. She had locked the other door before she got out of the car. She glanced at her watch. She did not, she could see, have to hurry. The Number 41 Trailways bus to Manhattan would leave in eleven minutes, at 8:04. That gave her time to walk briskly into the terminal, cross to Gate 5, and board the bus in time to get her usual seat. Most of the passengers were familiar, daily commuters who had nodded to each other for years, though the occasional interloper, unaware that seats were invisibly assigned, was not unknown.

She was glad that Frank took a later bus. Even in a town like Totowa, a rather anonymous suburb in northern New Jersey, people gossiped if you gave them a chance. Leaving the 41 each night with Frank, then parting as they reached their cars, was not especially remarkable. But to arrive with him every morning would stir up talk. She was, out in the world, a respectable widow of fifty-three who worked as a computer operator for a small company in Manhattan. She appeared slightly stout, in a comfortable sort of way, and a beautician friend once a month brought her hair back to its original light-brown shade. Her face, thought "pretty" at one time, was now at best "attractive," its best features a pale smooth skin and a mouth not drawn downward by time or circumstance.

Her husband had died four years earlier. A merchant seaman, away from home most of the time, he had contracted a viral infection while his ship was at São Tomé, an island nation off the South Atlantic coast of Africa. At first the problem did not seem that serious. When it became clear that he required hospitalization, he was put ashore at Dakar, where he died. She had received a letter in French from a Senegalese doctor, and a telephone call from an assistant manager of the shipping company. The letter had been translated through the assistance of a librarian at the Totowa public library. At the inception of widowhood, Edna Foley had a small house, a small benefit payment from her husband's union, and a job as a computer operator at the Prudential Insurance office in nearby Passaic.

She used the life insurance money to pay off the mortgage on the house. Then, face set and new suit bought, she set out to find a job that paid more than she was currently earning. Through an employment agency in the East Fifties she was selected for an interview with Metro Data Research. The owner met her in a coffee shop on Madison Avenue and explained that she would have to undergo a "substantive security clearance" before an offer could be made. She agreed, she had nothing to hide. Mr. Guyer she liked. She found him quiet, watchful, well-spoken. He assured her that the office was a pleasant working space but that he'd prefer her not to visit there until the security check was completed. The salary was extremely high. Extremely. He explained to her that it was so because they ran no benefit programs for their employees, outside the necessary federal and state contributions. And she would not be able to talk about what she did, since the work was of a private security nature. At the time, she believed that Metro Data Research was some form of credit reporting bureau.

For three weeks following the interview she was uncomfortably self-conscious. Mr. Guyer's representative had clearly been in Totowa. She could, she felt, sense it in the attitudes of the manager of her bank, one of the checkers at the local supermarket, and in her neighbors' glances. Her sister telephoned from Trenton to say that "a blond man with a cane" wanted to interview her. What was going on? Edna told her to tell the truth, there was virtually nothing in her life that was unusual or suspicious.

Since her husband's death there had been a few dates, with much drinking of rye and ginger ale and subsequent gropery. They'd turned her off completely. She missed companionship, but having a husband at sea eight months of the year had taught her self-sufficiency, and not so much self-denial as a turning away from the entire subject of the bedroom. She was a Catholic and went to mass more or less regularly. She had, early in marriage, wanted to have children but that was not possible. Thus she persevered and believed life to be principally a matter of perseverance.

The job, when she got it, was perfect. The hours were long but the work was steady and even, which suited her temperament. Unfilled office time at Metro Data would have been meaningless, since there was nobody to have coffee with, and she disliked office byplay anyhow. Nobody at the office especially supervised her, she knew her work and they gave her responsibility, which she felt she deserved. It was her task to run scanning machines that automatically encoded photographs and names into a computer, and, during heavy periods of input, she hired and personally supervised, at a rented office a few blocks away, girls from a nearby parochial school to hand-ready photographs for the scanner. She had once suggested that they use temporary personnel from an agency, but Mr. Guyer had said he preferred to put work in the way of the girls from St. Anne's. She had rather liked him for that, though she suspected that he was not in fact a Catholic. For the rest of the time, Kevin helped her part of every day and, when the stream of photos became a flood, Mr. Guyer and Mr. List chipped right in and worked alongside her.

For four years life was reasonably good. The daily commute into Manhattan tired her and got her home rather late, but the salary allowed her to build a savings account at the Totowa bank and, every now and again, to go to the racetrack, then out for dinner with a few of her lady friends. She spoiled her sister's two children at Christmas and birthday time, and dressed better than she ever had before. Once in a while she would agree to go out with somebody's brother or cousin, but she found that men who were single at fifty came in only two categories. Some were so shy that conversation was painful, and being with them was agony. Others affected expensive rings and groomed moustaches and they, speaking in a vocabulary not really their own, made her feel cheap, and cheaply desired. So she watched television in the evenings, and one or two glasses of wine made her ready for sleep.

Then she met Frank. He'd appeared on the 6:35 back to Totowa on a regular basis and she had noticed him almost immediately. He was tall, lean, and well-kept—perhaps, she thought, two or three years older than she. He was bald, but she found that rather appealing, it made his head seem strong and sculpted, and his remaining hair was black and neatly cut. He wore expensive sweaters and an old tweed sport jacket. After three weeks of riding the same bus, he took the seat next to her one evening and struck up a conversation. He owned, it turned out, a small antique store on Third Avenue. But he could no longer tolerate the stresses and strains of Manhattan life and had rented a garden apartment in Totowa to see if he liked it well enough to buy a home in the area. He was soft-spoken and intelligent, a nightly practitioner of the *New York Times* crossword puzzle.

After the first conversation they moved to a friendly hello basis and found themselves walking together to the parking lot at the Totowa bus station. She found out more about him. His antique store specialized in round oak tables, corner cupboards and breakfronts, obtained at estate auctions in central Pennsylvania, which were then stripped of paint and lacquer in a workroom above the store. She told him, as she had been instructed to do, that she worked for a market research company. As time went by they filled in their lives. He came from Minnesota originally, and early in life had wanted to be a college professor. He had served overseas immediately following World War II—which led her to compute his age at about fifty-five. His dream of teaching history at a small college had never worked out, but he read avidly and spoke with passion about the settling of the American West. She found him, throughout these conversations, to be a very romantic and idealistic man.

He walked her to her car one night in April and mentioned that he'd purchased tickets to a play at a repertory theatre in the area, would she care to attend with him? They went to see *Major Barbara,* which she thoroughly enjoyed. They shared egg foo yung and chicken chow mein at a local Chinese restaurant afterward. He saw her to the door and said good night. She realized, just inside the vestibule, that she had expected him to kiss her good night and that, if he had offered to, she would have welcomed it.

There were other plays. Once or twice a foreign film. A dinner at a tiny Italian restaurant in New York one night after work. She dreamed he embraced her. They now sat together on the bus each evening. When she stayed home two days with the flu, he telephoned on the second day to make sure she was all right, and asked if there was anything she needed. The next time they were out together, they kissed briefly before parting. She noticed that more and more often they used each other's names when they spoke.

At last the assertive side of her nature made its presence felt and she invited him for dinner on a Sunday night. He wore a soft flannel shirt and brought with him a bottle of French wine and a small bouquet of yellow tea roses wrapped in crinkly green paper. She put the roses in her best cut-glass vase. She had thought the dinner through carefully. She wanted to cook well for him, but did not want to overburden either of them with food. She settled, finally, on a roast chicken, unstuffed, though she made a good stuffing, fresh peas and a salad, with cookies from the bakery near the Metro Data office for dessert, and coffee. He offered to make a vinegar and oil dressing for the salad, she was surprised how professionally he did it. They drank his bottle of wine before and during dinner, then started on the one she'd bought. He complimented her on the food, but ate sparingly.

They sat in the living room after dinner and shared several glasses of wine. There was a strong sense of comfort in the room, with only one of her lamps turned on and the radio playing quietly. He asked if she would care to dance, and she said yes. They danced an easy fox-trot at first and then they danced close and then they kissed. "Shall we stay here?" he asked. The question's ambiguity gave her room to back away, and she appreciated that, but she did not want to back away, so she answered that perhaps they ought to go upstairs.

It had been a long while alone for her and though he was gentle, the first time was still tense and difficult. A lot like something that had to be got through in order to reach another place. Afterward they lay apart quietly, on fresh sheets, the quilt neatly folded back. She was at that moment a little at sea, anxious because things had not gone terribly well, yet relieved that that particular issue no longer stood between them. Did she, he asked, have a candle? She rose from bed, put on her best bathrobe, and brought one from downstairs. He lighted it. The bedroom was now lit softly and they commenced to make love again. This time was different. He whispered to her that her body was "like a woman in a Reubens painting, rosy and soft and full." Her face grew hot when he said it. She discovered that he was a sensual man, and the second lovemaking was entirely unlike the first. Some of the things they did together she knew about but had never done before. Slightly hesitant at first, she found herself deeply stirred, moved, and far more willing than she would have believed herself to be.

It was well after midnight when he left. Her body felt as though she were ready to fall into a dead sleep, but her mind was excited and kept her awake and she was snappish and cross at work the following Monday. As she reached the bus terminal on the Manhattan side, after work Monday evening, she felt real panic. She feared he would enter the bus and leer at her, or ignore her completely. When he appeared, however, he was the same as always. Somehow he managed to acknowledge that things had changed between them, while maintaining a public attitude no different than before. She was relieved. Their hands touched briefly as they parted in the parking lot. He called that night and asked if she would like to see *Camelot* the following Wednesday.

She knew that her love affair, outside the sacrament of marriage, should be confessed at Sunday mass, yet when the moment came, she could not do it. She felt protective of what she had and believed in her heart that what they had done was not a sin—wicked, perhaps, but not evil. It was a long, warm spring, then a cool and rainy summer. They were together each Wednesday and Saturday evening. Wednesdays they went out, Saturdays they stayed home. He never slept the night. Though the neighbors were surely aware of what was going on, certain gestures to propriety had to be made and he was in this, as in all other things, courtly and considerate.

Their lovemaking continued to be experimental and passionate, the word *pleasure* took on deeper meanings for her. One Saturday afternoon they drove in to New York and visited the Metropolitan Museum of Art, where they discovered an exhibition of Reubens paintings. She stood before a particularly voluptuous nude and prayed he did not find her so fleshy and rotund as all that, but he squeezed her arm in a special way to let her know how much she pleased him. The following Saturday they drove a large truck to Arensberg, Pennsylvania, and Frank bought several oak bed-frames and chairs at a well-attended auction. There was an immense old corner cupboard for sale, and Frank bid on it but was outlasted by a woman with eyeglasses on a silver chain. After the auction he approached the woman and told her he had a customer who would make an offer well above the price she had just paid. She agreed not to sell it until she heard from him, and he went to the truck and returned with a Polaroid camera, photographing the cupboard from several angles.

That night they stayed in a motel near Summit, New Jersey. They ate dinner in a small restaurant near the motel and drank rather more wine than usual. Back in the room, they hung a towel over the bedside lamp to soften the light and made love for a long time. He was, that evening, especially excited and avid, tracing her body with his fingers while telling her how she never ceased to stimulate his appetite. Would she, he asked, pose for him? He gestured toward the Polaroid on the dresser top. She laughed and waved him away, such things were for young girls in magazines. But he seemed to take her resistance as a form of flirtation, and he coaxed and kidded her for quite some time, until she realized that this was something he very much desired. Finally she consented, more in fear of bad feelings between them than for any other reason. It helped that they were not in her bedroom. There was something about being in a motel that made certain excesses agreeable. Though she did not much enjoy it herself—she found it distancing and not warm—she managed to enjoy his enjoyment, and was relieved that he did not demand of her revealing postures. He asked her to be "elegant" and "haughty" and to display her "naughty smile" and she did the best she could and was glad when it was over and they could be close again. He showed her the pictures. In the hard light of the flashbulb in the motel room, she thought she looked like a naked woman of fifty-three with a smile more self-conscious than naughty. She wished that he would offer to destroy the photos, but he did not. He apparently intended to keep them. If that makes him happy, she thought, then so be it. She was certain he would never show the photographs to anyone. He was, after all, a gentleman.

*   *   *

On the morning following a turnaround flight to another city, Guyer always woke up feeling edgy and disconnected. When he opened his eyes, he saw that the television was running with the sound off and that he'd kicked the covers into a snarled mound at the foot of the bed. His eyes felt hot and sandy, and he was tired in a way that sleep wouldn't help. He picked at the upcoming day, but it promised nothing that would sweep him out of bed. He worked himself upright, got his feet on the floor, shuffled to the bathroom like an old man, then stood in the shower and tried to blast it all away with hot water. But it wouldn't blast. Maggie hadn't answered her phone at 1:40. List came out of her building about a half hour later. What it wasn't: courtship, friendly call, coincidence. Especially not the last. The incident, the strange look on Richard's face, was like a brick wall in his mind, he couldn't get around it or over it and a torrent of hot water wouldn't rinse it away. Worst of all was that he knew he could not ask List in a natural and straightforward way what the hell he'd been doing there last night. He'd have to come around the other way, make lying an easy option, then label the lie *item #3* and file it with the other two events. The last thing in the world he needed right now, he thought, was to build a case on the one person he most needed to trust.

Six months after they'd started the business, he'd asked a man named Corpora, a private detective who handled his security arrangements, to do a work-up on List. Corpora hadn't found out much. He'd said, "Do you really need this guy?" Guyer answered that he did, he needed him for the computer part, and he needed someone to handle the black side of the business while he handled what he thought of as the gray side. Corpora

[142]

had said, "You know what he is?" Guyer knew. Corpora had shrugged, then asked rhetorically, "What is he bringing with him?"

List wasn't at the coffee shop. Guyer drank more coffee than usual, which made the post-jet jitters worse. As he crossed Madison Avenue, a car turning in from 80th Street crept toward him, attempting to force its way through a stream of pedestrians. Guyer gave the driver, dressed like a delivery man, a look that made him brake hard. He entered the building, pounded up the stairs, breathing hard by the time he reached the reception desk. Kevin bid him the usual stiff good morning. There was a fat maroon book on the edge of his work area.

"This go up to Edna?"

"Yes, sir."

"I'll run it up for you. Mr. List in yet?"

"Yes, sir. We came in at the same time this morning. 8:02." Kevin's white shirt was blinding.

Walking up the stairs, Guyer looked at the book in his hand. It was *The Bearpaw,* the college yearbook from Baylor University in Waco, Texas. What the hell was it doing arriving in October? Absently, he let it fall open.

LaVon Smith goes up for two against Tulane

Randle and Purvess accept Christian Citizenship Award

Jerry Milner starts early at Alpha Lambda Homecoming Blast

Anybody here seen a canoe?

List was at his desk with his head sunk on his hands, a manila folder full of papers spread open before him.

"Hello, Richard."

"Morning, Captain."

"Late night?"

List nodded yes without looking up. Guyer dropped off the yearbook at Edna's in-basket and said good morning. She responded politely without missing a beat. He thought she was looking very well lately. On the screen was an accounting program. He started to ask why she was running it, then stopped. There would be a perfectly sensible reason, and he would accomplish no more than an interruption of her work rhythm. He walked back over to List.

"Up to a meeting?"

List nodded yes. Guyer went to his desk and waited, thumbing through a small pile of mail. There was a *Mr. Businessman* letter from a mailing bureau, stern in tone, warning of the danger implicit in permitting profits to be eaten by the hidden costs of addressing and sending mail. There was a request for a contribution to a fund for the arts, with a cartoon of a Valkyrie holding a shield, captioned *She needs your help!* There were two offers of reduced-rate subscriptions to commercial journals, both letters computer-written, so that the company name appeared in the address at the top of the page and twice again in the body of the pitch.

"Anything interesting?" List lowered himself carefully into the leather chair beside Guyer's desk.

"Nothing much. Coffee?"

"Yes."

Guyer went over to the pot and poured out two cups.

"How was Wisconsin?" List said. His face was paler than usual, and his eyes were bleary. He ran a hand through the hair that fell down on his forehead.

"Not too bad. He'll go."

"What's the store like?"

"Oh, about what you'd expect. Suburban shopping mall."

List snorted contempt. "Malled beyond recognition."

Guyer didn't smile. It wasn't the day for jokes. "How's your coffee?" he asked.

List looked at him sideways. They both knew how the coffee was. Guyer rubbed the base of his palm against his forehead. He said, faintly interrogatory, "Richard?"

"Uh-oh."

"Everything okay?"

List stared at him in silence for a few seconds. Guyer looked right back at him. "Have I been bad?"

"Oh Jesus," Guyer said, voice full of resignation and fatigue. Maybe, he thought, there isn't a straight answer left anywhere in the world.

List was simultaneously conciliatory and offended: "One goes out. One sees one's friends. One is hung over." The sound of the word *friends* was like tapping a crystal glass with a butter knife.

"Your friends don't concern me."

"Naturally not." His smile had a mean edge, by way of saying that such friends as he had concerned everybody, whether or not they chose to admit it.

Start over, Guyer said to himself—he was already on the defensive as List repelled attacks on the two areas he cared absolutely nothing about—sex and drinking. He leaned back in the chair, trying for a nonverbal truce. "Why can't we make better coffee?"

"There's a service," List said.

"I don't want them up here."

"Well then . . ."

Guyer nodded. Bad coffee was their fate.

"What's on for today?" List asked.

"We have to do the housekeeping that gets the Delatte business on its way. Some cash, airplane tick-ets, an itinerary."

"Cash from what account?"

"I don't know. Look around, see what we have. We

front five thousand plus whatever it takes for a few airline tickets. You better start writing." List drew a ballpoint pen from his inside pocket and clicked it a few times, took a blank sheet of paper from a stack on the desk. "Make sure," he went on, "that you include an extra two hundred for Elden's night in Rio. That bills back to our fee, okay? I just sort of threw that in. By the time we have to pay the second five, that'll be November, Benauti's first payment will've come through the system. Airline tickets the same way. Now, the tickets. With me?"

"Yep."

"First, Milwaukee–New York, that's Kennedy, as early as possible on the morning of the 28th. If they have one of the those 5:00 A.M. salesman's delights, take it, 'cause he's *got* to be in Rio the night of the 28th. Next, Varig to Rio de Janeiro, that afternoon. Then he comes back out on the 29th, that's Varig also, leaving 3:30 P.M., Brazilian time, from Galeãeo airport. Now he's under Benauti's control. Finally, an open ticket from New York back to Milwaukee."

List laughed briefly.

"What's funny?"

"Why the hell didn't you have him pay for his own hotel?"

Guyer shook his head. "I don't know. It wasn't logical but it felt right. Anything else bother you in there?"

List ran the pen across the paper. "Yes."

"What?"

"I have to book him on Varig under the substitute passport."

"Right. That's Gerard. G-e-r-a-r-d."

"First initial?"

"Shit."

"That's *S*?"

"I gave it to him."

"Hmm. It would hardly be class to call him and ask."

"Make it *J*. It doesn't matter."

"*J* it is. Now, next problem will cost money."

"What?"

"Paying cash for a one-way ticket to Brazil for a passenger traveling alone. That's a boo-boo."

"Drugs?"

"They always take a lively interest in who's going where, but I was thinking Brazil, actually, the famous country without the famous extradition treaty."

"What are they going to do?"

"What *I'd* do, if I were a Brazilian customs type, and I happened to know about the circumstances, I'd take myself a nice long snoop through the luggage, expecting perhaps a gratuity. In this instance, what I might very likely find is a Canadian passport under another name, and a one-way ticket out the next day under that alias. Now I'll only know about the circumstances if some security person at the originating airline does a Telex, which he really might do given the profile we're considering."

"Okay, okay. Buy him a round trip to Brazil under the name Elden, put the return ticket in a drawer and we'll cash it in later. How's that?"

"Good. Next?"

"Do up an itinerary for him. Do it in such a way that you remind him to register at the hotel in Brazil under the Gerard name, but be discreet. I told him to destroy it once he's got it memorized, but I can just about guarantee that he won't do it. He'll be afraid of making a mistake."

"I'll do what I can. How does it move?"

"Put it all in a box and send it express by a private carrier, to The Shoe Tree address, that's in the computer."

"Why express?"

"I want him to have money in his hands before regret has a chance to set in. Let him spend some of it right away. I don't want him having second thoughts. He came on like a man of the world, but . . ."

"It's out today. Now, I have something for you. Cost you a refill."

Guyer took their cups over to the coffeepot and refilled them.

"Guess where I was last night," List said.

Guyer blinked. Would it be this easy? "Tell me."

"Monte Carlo."

"Oh."

"You're disappointed?"

"No."

"I found Jack Langer, gave him the X rays. He said he'd get payment started today, and he wanted me to give you this." He took a blue ticket from his pocket and handed it to Guyer. The ticket was for a seat at Oceanside Arena, out in Queens, where every Saturday night they had a local professional boxing card. The date on the ticket was October 29.

"End of next week," Guyer said. "He say what he wanted?"

"Not to me," List said. There was a pause, Guyer stared at the ticket as though it would tell him something. "I don't think he much cares for me," List went on, "my type, that is. The feeling was mutual, by the way. Who is he?"

"Jack's a mercenary."

"You know him?"

"I've seen him, here and there, over the years. He's a contract type, I don't think he was ever a fulltime Company man. He was over in Angola, that mess. The Cubans captured him, along with everybody else, so the story goes, and they made him watch while they executed Daniel Gearhart, the kid from Baltimore, who was already so shot up they had to sit him in front of the firing squad in a wheelchair."

"Viva Fidel."

"Yeah. Anyhow, that's Langer. There's a lot of stories about him. Some of them probably true."

"So you're going."

"Yeah. I guess so. Could be work, and we can use the work."

"You don't seem thrilled about it."

Guyer shrugged, drank coffee, closed his eyes, and leaned back in his chair. List started numbering the stops he would have to make in geographical order: the Varig office on Fifth, then a bank on Madison where the tellers didn't turn white when asked for a large cash withdrawal, finally United for the New York flight. "I paid Maggie," Guyer said absently.

"Mmm," List said.

Guyer tilted his chair back to the upright position and rubbed his eyes. "You seem blown away," List said, looking at him critically.

"Yeah," Guyer agreed. Then: "She seemed to enjoy doing it."

"I suspect she likes the drama of it," List said, doodling on his paper. He drew daisies: a ring of semi-circles for the outline, a blotch in the middle, a curving line for a stalk. "In the deepest, darkest alleys of New York, Maggie the spy works her artful wiles. She is young, you'll find."

Guyer didn't answer. List doodled awhile, finally said, "Well then . . ." and struggled to his feet. "I'll be back sometime after lunch." He moved to the desk where the checkbooks were kept, looked through a number of them, selected one, grabbed his cane from where it rested on his desk and left the office. He raised one arm, turned his palm facing Guyer, and made a *ciào* hand motion without turning around.

* * *

It was a cold, bright day and List enjoyed walking and cabbing around midtown. He wore a chocolate-brown trench coat and an ivory-colored wool scarf and dark sunglasses in dark frames. He drew a lot of attention, stumping along on the cane at a good pace, from men and women, and he enjoyed the looks. Staying to the sunny side of Fifth Avenue, he smiled back at everybody who checked him out. He felt like a prince, perhaps an exiled prince from a tiny country, and nothing, not even the fact that Guyer was surveilling him, could ruin his sense of celebrity and mystery and well-being. It was a forest-green Volvo, Guyer in the passenger seat, with a driver that List hadn't seen before. It passed him as he was moving down the avenue toward the Varig office, between 47th and 48th. Then came toward him, going west on 47th, as he walked east on the side street toward the bank on Madison. List felt joyously bitter, triumphantly betrayed. Like a *real* exiled prince. It always happened, the suspicion, the mistrust, this time it had taken quite a while. So long, this time, he had forgotten about it. Clever, he thought, for it to wait like that before it jumped from the shadows. He felt damaged and used and elated, elated because it confirmed the worst and the worst was what he believed in. As he walked, the joy and despair lit up his face and everybody looked at him as he went by.

SATURDAY NIGHT GUYER took a cab out to the Oceanside Arena in the Ridgewood section of Queens, just across the 59th Street Bridge and a little way past Long Island City. It had been a fairly good week, on the surface, a week when money came. Business had taught him the truth of primitive rites and ceremonies: it was all predicated on illogical gods. Sometimes, no matter what you did, money didn't come. Other times, no matter what you did, money came. The rhythm and sequence of it seemed set apart from reason and had absolutely nothing to do with expectations. Last Thursday a package had gone off to Elden without problems and no nervous phone calls followed, so that was in progress as he rode toward the arena. Elden was in some hotel in New York, apparently the Brazil turnaround and the meeting at Kennedy had all gone according to schedule. If it hadn't, he would surely have heard from Benauti. Benauti's payment had reached them through the brokerage house and so had Langer's and, to his astonishment, Novotny had met the Thursday deadline. In that way it had been a good week. It had been a bad week, below the surface, with Richard. Something was really very wrong. All week long List had seethed with suppressed hostility, his brittle sarcasm rising to a pitch that made the office seem to vibrate when he was in it. The late arrivals, long lunch hours, and early disappearances became a relief instead of an annoyance. Yet the thought of replacing him summoned up such unspeakable complications that Guyer found himself unable to think about it. He would try to ride it out. The attempt to turn a blind eye to trouble made Guyer surly, grim, and distant, and that in turn made the office even worse, so that Edna and Kevin walked on eggshells and wondered why work-life had all of a sudden gone tense and threatening. Meanwhile, Guyer had made no attempt to contact Maggie. He wanted to. But the possibility that she was somehow involved with List, in something that he couldn't be told about, kept him away from the phone. By the end of the week Guyer had begun to look forward to the meeting at the arena. Perhaps a new project—a challenge, a large fee in the offing, everybody needing to work together—would dispel the black cloud that had settled over the office.

Guyer arrived ten minutes before the first fight. The arena was located on a narrow avenue with an elevated subway running above it, in one of those old, lost working-class neighborhoods that seem to run for miles in Queens and Brooklyn. It had at one time been an Irish enclave, and the bars still had the closed, private look of local sanctuaries where wives and mothers and troubles weren't welcomed. The houses were red-brick three- and four-story walkups, the walls colored brown by years of grime and smoke. Many of the street-level storefronts were empty. On the sidewalk a few doors down from the arena entrance, a spray of broken glass glistened in the streetlight. Oceanside Arena was for club fights, that was clear right away. The big money was downtown at the Garden where you got on television, but if you didn't fight on the Olympic teams and get interviewed by Howard Cosell, this was the only road that went there.

Inside the arena there was a haze of blue smoke hanging still in the spotlights above the ring, Guyer could taste the cigar in it. The place was full. Two fighters had just entered the ring wearing shiny robes long past being new and towels over their heads with ends tucked into the shoulders of the robes. Both were moving nervously, dancing side to side, shaking their gloved hands loose, surrounded by old men in sweaters. Guyer's seat was one in, on a row halfway down the aisle. Langer was already there. He looked up as Guyer appeared and said, "Hey," and stuck out a hand. They shook. Langer stepped out and Guyer sat down.

"Starts in a couple minutes," Langer said, jaw moving up and down. He was a constant gum chewer, Guyer could smell it when he spoke. He was above five feet five and he wore everything big: thick, curly sideburns of sandy hair, thick black frames on his glasses, and a fat gleaming silver identification bracelet, the expansion-band kind, that said *Jack*. He wore a white shirt with the top two buttons undone and a cardigan sweater in wide brown and gold stripes, with sleeves of sweater and shirt pushed up to just short of the elbow.

Langer, Guyer knew, had killed a great many people. In Asia, Africa, and South America as a paramilitary hired gun and, rumor had it, in Europe and the Middle East as a hired counterinsurgency specialist of the street-level class. He was said to be a member of Catena, principally a European organization composed

[155]

of soldiers of fortune: typically ex-officers from the French Foreign Legion, Greeks who had left when the Colonels were deposed, Portuguese from the days of Salazar, Spaniards of Franco's time, and Algerians who had been in the OAS. Most of them had known to leave well enough alone when the chief of station for the CIA in Angola had recruited a mercenary force to fight with the FNLA against the Cubans. Most of the people who *were* recruited signed up on Monday, flew to Kinshasa the next day, fought on Wednesday and died on Thursday. Langer had been swept up in Luanda with the rest, but he had walked. Nobody knew why. Part of the Langer myth was that he had been in Angola representing a different part of the CIA, one that had better relations with Cuba.

"How 'bout a beer?" Langer said. A man stood in the aisle with large paper cups in a cut-down box.

"Sure." He started to reach across Langer with a five-dollar bill.

Langer pushed his hand away gently. "You get the next one."

"Okay," Guyer said. When Langer reached out to exchange money for beer, Guyer saw the leather edge of a holster peek out from beneath the cardigan.

They drank beer, for a minute or so, in ritual silence. Then Langer said, "How you been?"

"Pretty good."

"Yeah? That's okay." Langer had a slight southern accent—Guyer thought he was from West Virginia—which grew deeper when he got excited or drunk. But Guyer had also heard him speak without any accent whatsoever.

"How about yourself?" Guyer asked.

"Hell, it never changes with me," Langer said, shaking his head.

"In New York these days?"

"D.C."

[156]

"Hunh."

"Yep."

"How is it?"

"Aw shit, Guyer, you know how it is. Buncha G-12 fairies runnin' the country into the ground."

"Yeah."

The ring announcer spoke in the old tradition, crooning the first parts of his words, then landing sharply on the second syllables. "Good evening ladies and gentlemen. Oceanside Arena and East Bay Promotions are proud to present an eight-bout card of boh-xing, Andy Pregacido the promoter." He paused, looked at a card in his hand. "Our first event of the evening features light heavyweights, uh, light heavyweights. Six rounds. In this corner, weighing one hundred and seventy-four pounds, from Bedford-Stuyvesant, in Brook-lyn, Ellll-awrence Whitley. Whitley." There was scattered applause. "And in this corner, now fighting out of Jamaica Park, Long Island, lately from Miii-ami, Florida, weighing in tonight at one hundred and seventy-three pounds, Wil-fredo, Buster, Fwen-tess. Fwentess. Your referee is Jack Leisler. Judges, sanctioned by the state of New York Boxing Commission, Arthur Gomez and Herb Russo. Counting for the knockdowns, Arthur Feiner. And nowww, ladies and gentlemen, please rise for your national an-them."

It was a scratchy record, played through a fuzzy PA system. Langer and Guyer held their hands over their hearts. When it ended and they went to sit down, a deep voice said, " 'Scuse me," and they both moved out into the aisle to let a very tall black man in a fur jacket enter the row. He sat in the seat to Guyer's right.

The fighters were instructed by the referee and went back to their corners to take off their robes. The black, Whitley, was extremely broad-shouldered with sharply defined muscles. His eyes were narrowed by severe scar tissue at the corners. Fuentes had a rubbery hairless body with sloping shoulders and a bushy Afro haircut. He looked to be two or three inches shorter than his opponent. The crowd was silent after the bell rang for the first round. The only sounds were the squeak of rubber soles on the resined canvas surface as the fighters moved, the hissing of breath as they jabbed, and now and then a punch that landed on ribs or shoulders.

"Who do you like here?" Langer said.

"The Cuban looks like he can hit. But the other guy, Whitley, has the reach. I think maybe Whitley."

Thirty seconds went by, both fighters bouncing and circling, very classic, jabbing, trying to hook off the jab. Whitley's cut-man yelled, "Get off. Get off." Fuentes threw a right lead, Whitley stepped inside it and they tied each other up, punching offhandedly at each others' kidneys. "Step out," said the referee.

"First round never proves much," said Langer, working his gum.

"No, you're right," Guyer said.

The crowd noise grew slightly. Somebody yelled in Spanish.

"You come out with everybody else?" Langer continued to look at the ring.

"Yeah. In '77."

"Goddamn shame," Langer said.

"Way it goes."

"That don't make it right. More'n eight hundred people fired on one day. Good people. The best." Langer shook his head.

"Well," Guyer said evenly, "they had all the space-age tech coming on line. Telephone microwave interception. Computer theft by reading vibrations with a laser beam. Spy satellites. All expensive stuff. And they must've figured that what they called *Humint,* human intelligence, was history."

"Bull*shit,*" Langer said.

"Maybe."

"Damn government's problem is that it's all accountants and lawyers."

There was a ripple of noise from the crowd. As the round ended, Fuentes had come up from below with a left hand that landed audibly under Whitley's heart. Then the bell sounded.

"Who do you give it to?" Langer asked.

"Pretty even. Maybe 10–9 for Fuentes."

"Prob'ly. Hey, that List is a character."

"He's okay."

"Was he ever in the Company?"

"Contract employee."

"Like me. No benefits, no pensions, no nothin'. Just bleed a little and thank you very much. Last few years, they don't use Americans no more. Foreign nationals." Langer said it with contempt.

"Well, seems like you're doing okay now."

Langer grunted, meaning that he was, but it was no thanks to anybody in the bureaucracy.

The bell sounded for the second round. The crowd was heating up. Fuentes came out firing body shots, quite a few of them landed. Whitley carried his hands high, protecting his tender eyes. As Fuentes went underneath, Whitley backed up and tried to come over the top with his left, but Fuentes shifted his shoulders and tucked his head in and the taller fighter couldn't get at him. Langer finished his beer and put the empty cup on the floor.

"How's that thing of yours?"

"Surviving," Guyer said.

"Private work's the way to go now. Half the goddamn corporations in the country swing. Guy gets on there, he's got a good thing going. And some of them are pretty good. There's one computer company has a section called Commercial Analysis Department, and they're supposed to be topnotch. Come to that, we don't do so bad ourselves."

"We?"

"Hell, I thought you knew. I'm with Mains, Gulbenyan and Associates. I'm an associate."

Guyer glanced sideways to see if there was irony intended. There wasn't. "Congratulations," he said. "I hadn't heard."

"Good thing too," Langer said forcefully. "I was gettin' tired of bouncing all over the goddamn globe doing everybody else's dirty laundry."

"So you're pretty much in D.C."

"Pretty much."

They watched for a minute in silence. The round ended with a flurry from Fuentes, Whitley trying to cover up on the ropes, then holding on.

"I don't want to talk out of school," Langer said, "but a thing like you got might be right up Mains's alley."

"Oh?"

"Yes, sir. Might be just the right move."

"Why is that?"

"Well, the way I see it, the wave of the future is on the conglomerate side. The little guy don't stand a chance, not really. Now the whole security industry is spread out all over the place. You got the big boys in the commercial area, your Pinkerton and Burns and Wackenhut. Then there's the intelligence area, where your firms do the same things for the private sector that the CIA does for the government. Now in that area we're just about the best there is. And we're growing. Jesus, there's over four thousand private security outfits in the States alone, there just ain't room for everybody."

"Not unless you've got a specialty."

"But you see that's just what I'm sayin'. I bet you're doin' okay, y'know, as far as it goes. But last year Mains, Gulbenyan bought this little credit info company in San Diego, and they took that sonofabitch and they put in the money and the management, and put them in the way of the big contracts, the real stuff that comes out of D.C., and pretty soon that thing grew like wildfire. Real money, Guyer."

"Great."

He felt Langer turn to make sure he wasn't being facetious, but his eyes stayed on the boxers.

"You bet it's great," Langer said. "It's the horsepower. You get yourself in a position like that and you'll find out. And it's nothing to fear for you. They always keep the top guy, see, just like when a straight conglomerate buys out some little company. So he's got the money from the buy, *and* he's still got his daily place to go. Can't miss. I've seen it work."

"Makes a lot of sense."

"Well then what say I talk to Mains? He knows an opportunity when he sees one. I figure you have the technical abilities, like that little job you just did for me, all you really need is the big push. I could put in the word, about how Guyer's got a great thing going and he ought to take a look."

Guyer paused for a moment, as though he actually were considering it. "I appreciate the thought, Jack," he said, picking his words carefully, "but we should probably just limp along like we are." He paused again. "That's not to say we wouldn't welcome a subcontract situation."

"Well, I guess that's up to you," Langer said after a beat. But Guyer could tell he was angry. His jaw muscle rippled as he chewed his gum. "Now will you look at this," he said, nodding his head toward the ring.

Fuentes was pressing at the start of the third round, he had Whitley backed into a corner and was working him over hard. Whitley returned punches sporadically, waiting until Fuentes finished a flurry, then firing off one or two tight uppercuts. Suddenly the referee separated the fighters and sent Whitley to a neutral corner, where he hung his arms at his side and breathed deeply, his body shining with sweat. The expression on Fuentes's face was one of total disgust. A thin stream of blood from his eyebrow curved around both sides of the eye and ran down his cheek and the side of his nose. The referee gingerly placed a thumb on either side of the wound and squinted against the ring lights, then waved for the doctor. The gash was ugly, ran from the eyebrow down the lid, and blood was pulsing from it. The doctor leaned over from outside the ropes, looked for a second, then waved his open hand back and forth, indicating that the fighter was finished. Fuentes protested, the referee just shook his head and walked away. Whitley raised his hands in triumph, his second slipped the shiny robe over his shoulders, and he went over and touched Fuentes on the arm in consolation. The bell rang several times and the announcer stepped through the ropes, waited for the microphone to descend on its cord, announced the time of the TKO, and declared Whitley the winner. There were a few random boos from the crowd.

"Damn shame," Langer said.

"Yeah," said Guyer, though he didn't feel it was.

Langer turned halfway around in his seat so that they faced each other. "So, Guyer, you willing to think about it? It'd be all to your advantage."

"I don't think so."

"Then that's your answer. No."

"That's it."

Langer nodded. " 'Kay. Everybody's got a right to an opinion." He stood up, stretched, winked at Guyer, and moved up the aisle. Guyer got the impression he was going off to buy another beer. He waited until the middle of the following bout but Langer didn't reappear so he left.

*　*　*

The embassy stood just off Fifth Avenue in the Seventies, in a six-story gray stone building with elegant ironwork grilles covering the windows. Three men came out of the embassy, they were wearing topcoats, buttoned up, and one of them was blowing on his hands to warm them up. Two of the men were pale in complexion, with glossy black hair combed flat and carefully parted, sideburns just long enough to expand slightly at the base. The other man, who walked in the middle, had brown hair and delicate features, suggesting vaguely European origins.

They walked quickly—it was Sunday morning and not many people were about—and the two men on the flank appeared lean and alert. Midway down the block they reached the entrance to an underground garage, turned, and walked down the ramp. Parked back to the wall of the garage was a black Fleetwood Cadillac, long and smartly polished. The three men stood before the car for a moment, then one of the lean ones walked to a windowed office and returned, followed by a young man in a grimy coverall. The young man had a bad complexion and long hair tied back with a rubber band. The lean man handed him a set of car keys, then the three men in overcoats, as though they wished to have a private conversation, walked to the far wall and stood in a group. The man in the coverall found the door key, fitted it to the lock, and opened the door. Leaving the door open, he inserted the ignition key, paused for a moment, then started the car. The engine turned over immediately. He slid halfway out, then one of the men by the wall called, "Slam the door, please." He spoke in a slight accent and pronounced each word carefully. The man in the coverall moved back into the seat and slammed the door hard. Then he opened it and stood by the car. The three men approached him and the one who had spoken handed him a hundred-dollar bill, which he slipped into a pocket in the coverall. Then he went back to the office and shut the door. The two lean men sat in front, the one who had spoken, behind the wheel. The other man sat in the backseat. Both of the men in the front seat unbuttoned their overcoats, and the driver adjusted the rearview mirror. He did not turn on the heater or the radio. Cautiously, the Cadillac crept up the ramp, then turned into traffic and headed east. They reached 72nd Street and First Avenue, then the Cadillac entered a long, sweeping curve onto an overpass that would take them over the East River Drive, then down into three lanes of cars traveling north on the Drive. Traffic below was heavy, the highway bore cars going out to Long Island via the Triborough Bridge and also to the North Bronx and the Connecticut parkways beyond.

Behind the Cadillac a panel truck turned onto the overpass. The driver was a bald man in his fifties. He owned the panel truck, which he used for small-package delivery service to and from the airports on behalf of several freight forwarding companies, and he was going home to Long Island after a twelve-hour work shift. He was tired, and he was driving slowly, about three car-lengths behind the Cadillac. The white flash inside the car in front of him was brilliant, it lit the back window for a second, then disappeared. The Cadillac's right front fender struck the retaining wall of the overpass, then it veered to the left, and the truck driver hit his brakes. The Cadillac crossed into the other lane, bumped the opposite retaining wall and, because of the slight uphill grade of the overpass, rolled backward to rest against the retaining wall in the right-hand lane.

The truck driver climbed halfway out of the cab and stopped. He did not understand what he'd seen. There was no fire, the Cadillac simply sat where it had come to rest. The car hadn't been traveling very fast, and the damage to the bodywork from the two collisions was minor. But nobody got out. A car appeared in the opposite lane, the driver saw the Cadillac turned sideways, and stopped hard with a slight skid. Traffic behind the truck had come to a halt, and horns were beginning to honk impatiently. The truck driver walked to the Cadillac, then bent over to look in the driver's window. He was braced for what he might see, although it hadn't been much of an accident. But he couldn't see anything at all because the windows were black. He grabbed the door handle, then drew his hand back violently and swore. He'd burned his palm. He blew on it for a moment, then wound his other hand inside the front of his sweat shirt and, using it like a potholder, opened the door. A black tree stump toppled sideways toward him until it lay half out of the car. He jumped backward and stared. The thing was crackled and charred like a log that had burned for a long time and then gone out. Then the smell hit him and he twisted away. The blood drained from his face. Two other drivers were coming toward him and he waved at them wildly to go back, although the motion of his hand made the burn hurt badly. Behind him, from the open door, black flakes of upholstery and overcoat were lifted and swirled by the wind.

Monday. 9:20 P.M. The coffee shop. *Why not?* he thought to himself, *really why not?* If you stripped away all the stuff you were supposed to—that was basic, given—then beneath the *emotion*, the *subjectivity*, *bias*, *prejudice*, *hidden premise*, the dreaded anathemas of intelligence, what clear motive remained for turning Mains down? Langer hadn't lied, they would pay, they would keep him, for a while anyhow, until they had what they wanted, then they'd put in a management type. And they'd get rid of List. Certainly that. But what the hell good was he anyhow? Lately, not much. They'd be the worst *kinds* of fools to let Edna or Kevin go, people who worked like they did weren't so easy to come by. And they, Mains, Gulbenyan, and the rest, were no kinds of fools at all and Guyer knew it. So then why? *Really.*

Because.

Because of what Mains had done to him. Because of what Mains had made him see, the image of it, and because he lived with that. Mains was himself under orders, of course, but Guyer suspected he had done it with relish, because he suspected a streak of something in Guyer, because that was just the way Mains was. It was Guyer who would have said, if anybody had thought to ask him, that sometimes you give the rules a little twist, sometimes you make a small space for somebody to crawl through. And it was Mains who would have said no. Let it happen. So it is written and so it shall be. He *gloried* in the broken glass and smoking ruins that came of decisions made in distant rooms, it *proved* something to him. It proved, Guyer believed, that the world was finally no better than he was and that made him not so bad.

And therefore he would not lay one finger on something that belonged to Guyer. And the reasons were *only* emotional. Let him suffer—perhaps just this one time in his life, perhaps there'd been other times—for reasons purely of the heart.

Guyer looked up from the table when somebody came through the door, but it wasn't List. He hardly showed up at the coffee shop anymore. It was cold this morning, the last day of October, and the place was almost empty. Guyer noticed a woman, alone, drinking a cup of tea, who glanced at him briefly. Her eyes were cool and gray, and she was tailored and perfect. He thought for a moment to make something more of it, but he knew he hadn't the finesse. So, a small sigh within, he drank his coffee and lowered his eyes to the Monday-morning newspapers.

The Wall Street Journal was headlining Japanese incursions into the California microelectronics market and he didn't want that. *The Christian Science Monitor* featured internecine struggles at NATO over purchase of the French Mirage-X3 fighter/bomber and he didn't want that either. So he fell back on the *Times*. Trouble again in Guatemala, the junta accused of murdering a Dutch journalist. An IRA car bomb had blown all the windows out of the British Embassy in Bonn. The nineteenth day without kidnapper demands for the missing shipping heiress in California. He turned the page. Reagan up a point in the polls on economic forecasts reported last week. Italian magazine claims new information casts light on Kennedy assassination. Argentinian diplomats die in car-bomb incident. That one was datelined New York and he read it.

The pain in his stomach blocked out everything else. He thought it was a heart attack and for many seconds believed he was about to die. When he opened his eyes, the waitress was looking at him, and he cleared his throat and pretended to go back to his reading, but the print swam. The pain receded. It was replaced by the thought that he had always known this would happen, some day, some time. There were rules against it happening. Unwritten rules but powerful, an imaginary line that wasn't to be crossed. But, of course, now somebody had crossed it. And, of course, somebody had broken the rules. Now there would have to be new rules. But there was one thing that wouldn't change, and that was the fact that he'd just murdered William Elden, owner of a shoe store in Waukesha, Wisconsin.

(NY) Police report that three men were killed Sunday morning when an Argentine Embassy vehicle was destroyed by an explosion on the East River Drive overpass at 72nd Street and 1st Avenue. Two of the dead have been identified as Enrique Vargas Tormann, 44, an Argentinian economic attaché, and Luis Cabral, 36, embassy security guard. A spokesman at the Argentine Embassy had no comment on the incident. Police report that the third man in the car has been identified by a reliable source as Raoul Delatte, a French national. State Department sources who declined to be quoted have informed *The Times* that Delatte was known to have been associated with the intelligence services of several Middle East nations.

Police report that the substance used in the bombing was a "Napalm-like explosive" though the precise nature of the device remains uncertain.

Guyer put two dollars on the table to pay for his coffee, then spread out a handful of change and selected a quarter. Carefully he got to his feet and walked toward the back of the coffee shop. In the hallway by the rest rooms there was a pay telephone. He took the receiver off the hook and put in the quarter. A dial tone came on the line. He stood and listened to it for a long time, until the tone changed to a *beep* signal. He pressed the lever with his index finger and his quarter clanged into the change slot. He should go back to the office, he thought, he should think this through, he should not react, not in any way at all. The textbook answer was to freeze, go still, like an alarmed animal, until the mind had a chance to fight off the shock wave. He fingered the quarter out of the slot and dropped it in the phone a second time. This time he dialed. An operator came on the line with charges. He put in more quarters. The phone rang six times and then a woman answered. She had a high, querulous voice that whined with exhaustion, as though the speaker had been very ill for a long time.

"Is Ralph around?" he asked.

"No he's not."

"Can he be reached?"

"I can try."

"Right away?"

"I'll try."

"I'm at 213-8019, in Manhattan, it's a payphone. Would you please ask him to call me? The name is Guyer."

"Just a minute."

He could hear her put the phone down and go off into another room.

"What was the number?"

He repeated it.

"Spell the name."

"G-u-y-e-r. Please call him right away."

"Yes, yes. I'll call him." She hung up.

He touched his face and realized he was sweating profusely. He went into the men's room, opened the door of the stall, unrolled a piece of toilet paper, and wiped his face. He went and waited by the phone, watched the waitress clean up the table where he'd been sitting. The phone rang.

"Yes?" he said.

"Guyer?" It was Corpora.

"Yes."

"You want to see me?"

"As soon as possible."

"You know the IRT stop at 181st Street?"

"Yeah."

"I'll be there. How long will it take you from where you are?"

"Fifteen minutes if I can get a cab."

"Take the subway, if you can get to the West Side, it's faster."

"Okay. Where will you be?"

"On the platform, toward the front of the train. There's a bench there."

"I'll be there," Guyer said, and hung up.

He left the restaurant, waved a cab down, and a few minutes later was at the subway station at 79th Street and Broadway. The train was almost empty, but Guyer stood at midcar and stared at the tunnel walls racing by in a blur. If he kept moving, he thought, there was something following him that wouldn't catch up. He had never before in his life needed so badly to act, to go someplace, to do something. He knew that if he admitted for one moment that there was any possibility that Benauti was not responsible for this, his opponent, whoever that was, would have mated him in one move, would have, with a confusion of motives and possibilities, neutralized him completely.

He got off the train at the 181st Street stop. Corpora was sitting on a bench with his arms spread across the top and his legs crossed at the ankles. He had a toothpick in the center of his mouth. It was hard to tell Corpora's age—Guyer would have put him at about thirty-five—because he was extremely fat. He looked to weigh over three hundred pounds. Yet his face was handsome, not at all the face of a fat man, and his curly blond hair was carefully combed. He was wearing a bright red shirt buttoned to the top, a brown suit that hung on him like a tent, and aviator sunglasses. At one time he had been a licensed private investigator, a highrolling one who had handled celebrity divorces and disappearances. There'd been a magazine article about him, and he'd had more clients than he could manage, no matter what he charged. He lived in a large house at the end of Long Island and was a great frequenter of nightclubs and racetracks. But he had been subpoenaed before a grand jury, had declined to testify, and had spent ninety days in jail. After that his license was revoked on a technicality and his bonding company had terminated his coverage. Those circumstances had in turn changed the nature of his clientele.

He nodded to Guyer as he approached. Guyer sat next to him on the bench and they waited until the noise of the train pulling out had subsided.

"Hello," Guyer said. "Thanks for being here on short notice."

"Don't worry about it," Corpora said. "You look like you saw a ghost."

"Can you take something right away?"

"Of course. Can you pay for it?"

"Yes. What'll it take?"

"That we'll have to see. Figure five yards a day for starts, unless it's gonna give me some huge fuckin' problem, in which case it'll take more."

"Okay."

Corpora nodded slowly. Something in his presence made Guyer relax slightly. Corpora changed his position. Sitting upright, he reached in his back pocket and handed Guyer a clean white handkerchief folded into a square. "Wipe your face, my friend."

"Thanks," Guyer said. He dabbed at his brow and made to give the handkerchief back. Corpora waved him off, then produced a small battered spiral notebook and a short stub of pencil. He leafed through pages of dense black script, methodically licking his index finger each time he turned a page, until he found an unused space.

"Go," he said.

"The name is Benauti," Guyer said, and spelled it.

Suddenly there was loud hooting and shouting that echoed off the tile walls of the subway station, and a very tall teen-ager with a pearl earring loomed above them. "Hey my man," he called back to his friends, "we got a *whale* down here."

Guyer and Corpora looked up. Corpora raised his sunglasses by pushing up the bridge with his index finger. His eyes were the color of cold stones. "Go away," he said.

The kid whooped with laughter, but he moved away quickly and his friends followed. Corpora dropped the glasses and turned to Guyer. "You were saying?"

"Benauti."

"He have a first name?"

"I don't know it."

"Description."

"Male. Over forty. About five feet six or seven. Slim build. Olive complexion. Thinning hair, brushed back. Pronounced semitic nose. Speaks with an accent."

"And he wears?"

"Well, continental suits. Expensive overcoat, wool I think, knee-length, sort of a greenish-brown color."

"Domicile?"

"Don't know."

"Nationality."

"French Tunisian. Said to be, anyhow."

"Like an Arab?"

"Partly."

"Hunh. How about occupation?"

"Go-between. Agent, representative."

"But no trade or anything."

"I don't know."

"Sexual preference?"

"Don't know."

"Now, all the places you ever met with him or talked to him on the phone. Whatever you know."

"We had dinner at a place called La Coquille, a French restaurant. That was my choice. We met on the observation deck of the Empire State Building, that was his choice. He's called from payphones, taken one call in a bar someplace, and he's used a post-office box."

"Nothing."

"Also, he's been at the Monte Carlo."

"Still nothing. He pick up from the PO box himself?"

"I don't know."

"But he's got the brains to use a messenger service, like to send a kid over with a key and have the mail returned to a hotel desk."

"I would think so."

Corpora tapped the notebook with the end of the pencil. Guyer said, "It isn't very much, is it."

Corpora didn't acknowledge him at all, just kept tapping. Finally he said, "Now you want me to find this guy, that's right, isn't it? I mean, I'm not checking a credit application, right?"

"Yeah."

"What can you give me? I don't need to know the family secrets. I don't *want* to know the family secrets. But I need, uh, like the gist."

"It was a double-cross."

"Unh-huh, and this Benauti, what part does he play in it? He's the boss? The accountant? The coffee kid? What?"

"The salesman."

"I see. And did something happen? A deed? Or is it you heard something or somebody had a feeling?"

"A deed."

"When?"

"Yesterday."

"So maybe he's long gone. You would be, I would be, but we don't know that for sure. Does he have reason to believe you found out what he did? Or could he be sitting where he always was thinking he got away with it?"

"He knows we know."

"He come in as a client?"

"Yes."

"How did he pay you?"

"Brokerage account."

"Still owe?"

"Yes."

"My, my." Corpora shook his head.

"It's all very arm's-length," Guyer sighed.

"Now, my friend, don't be sad. I find almost anybody, given time."

"I know."

"So good, you told me what you know, now tell me what you think."

Guyer hesitated a moment, walking himself through the pattern before he said anything. "Something like this," he said. "There's a certain X, and he's very, very hot. Everybody wants him, people will pay large sums to have him delivered. So Benauti comes to us and asks us to fix it so X can be observed to be doing certain things. We come up with a factor Y who will do what he wants while X can stay hidden. Now the double-cross: Y is eliminated, in such a way that X is *thought* to have been eliminated. That frees X. For a while, anyhow. Enough so that he can wheel and deal to a point where he can come up undead at a later date. That's the hub of it. I'm left with more questions than answers. For instance, he may have had help from inside, from my office. For another instance, I suspect there's a group backing X in this attempt. Who they might be I can only guess."

A train roared into the station and Guyer stopped talking. They both looked up at the train. The doors opened with a hiss, stood open though nobody got on or off, then closed. The train idled for thirty seconds, then departed. The teen-agers were in the last car. The tall one shouted something at Corpora through the open window, but they couldn't hear it.

"What you really need," Corpora spoke slowly, "is

to find this character and to talk to him. Talk to him in such a way that he tells you the truth. You understand what I'm saying?"

"Yes."

"Okay. You have maybe one chance. You're in business, I'm in business, I'm not gonna mince words with you. If he's left New York, he's gone. You can forget it. If he has the sense to hide, if he knows enough to go off to some little neighborhood in The Bronx or Brooklyn and rent an apartment and just sit tight, again we're not going to find him. What you've given me so far is less than useless. There's no place to start, no place he's got to go, no place to stake out. Guys in hiding will come up for air, which is to say money or sex, but in what you told me there isn't hook one. Your one chance is that he's flopping around *trying* to get out. We can get him for you if that's the case, but only if you can get us a photo. Your description is half the people in New York, y'know. You should know that the slim chance could cost you between eight and ten grand, no guarantees. It comes down to how badly you want him. Maybe you don't want him ten-grand worth, in which case you go wherever you go and I go to the racetrack and sometime you buy me a lunch for showing up here. So? Tell me something."

"Do it."

"Okay. By the way, does he carry?"

"I don't know."

"He wear a drape jacket, something like that?"

"No. Narrow cut. Fancy. Tight."

"So the next thing is we meet again. You bring me a picture and we'll go to work. Call me when you're ready. I have your office number and your home number if I need to get in touch with you."

They waited a few minutes for a train, then rode together as far as 72nd Street, where Guyer got off.

List

GUYER CAME UP from the subway at 72nd and Broadway. There was a clock in the window of the Off-Track Betting office on the south corner of 72nd Street that said 11:26. He checked his watch. The OTB clock was five minutes off. He wanted coffee. He walked half a block to a kosher dairy restaurant and bought a cardboard container of coffee. He said black but they gave him a cream and sugar. He threw it in a garbage can. He didn't want to go back to that restaurant, so he kept on walking and found a convenience grocery. He got a large coffee black, threw the lid away, drank some as he crossed West End Avenue.

Riverside Drive started here on a broad curve. He watched a bearded man come out of the park with a bull mastiff on a leash. The mastiff had a spiked collar, which supposedly made the dog kill-proof. Guyer walked a little way down the path into Riverside Park. He wanted to see the Hudson River and the Jersey shore. He registered two tall kids with team jackets on a hill to his right. They were carrying umbrella canes from which the fabric had been stripped. It passed through his mind to provoke them, part of his imagination dawdled on the ensuing action, and the result. He sat down on a bench and sipped at his coffee. When the sun came out of the clouds, it sparkled on the blue river. He checked his watch again. 11:44. He felt cold, pulled his raincoat tighter, watched the play of the light on the river as the clouds moved overhead.

It was 1974, late June. The unending SAGSE meetings were boring, such picking and probing at tiny details garnered by agents in bars and bedrooms. Barcelona was blistering in the summer sun, the beaches were impossible from ten in the morning until three in the afternoon and jammed with busloads of German tourists after that. So he stayed home that summer, in a small apartment with no air-conditioning. There had been an affair with an embassy code clerk that ended badly with a scene at her apartment. He had sought a promotion the previous spring but didn't get it, losing out to an unctuous office politician who said all the right things to all the right wives. When the chance came for a special off-station assignment in North Africa, he volunteered.

For the CIA it was the year of Kurdistan. The Company seemed drawn to operations involving disaffected hill tribes: six years earlier it had been the Hmong, the Meo, the Montagnards, now it was the Kurds. Kurdistan was a cultural entity, though not a national one and that was the heart of the problem. Kurdish tribesmen lived in Turkey, northern Syria, Iraq, and Iran. The

Shah in 1974 sought to provoke his western neighbors by stirring up mischief among the Iraqi Kurds. In this he was aided by CIA and military advisers. The Iraqi Kurds received weapons and training from Iranian and American specialists, then received rockets and Napalm from Iraqi war planes. The center of the Kurdish revolution was the Pesh Merga (Facers of Death), whose political infrastructure was based in northeastern Iran, in Rezaiyeh and Mahabad near the shores of Lake Urmia, guests of the Shah.

That much Guyer, in a general way, already knew. When he flew down to Algeciras and met Francis Mains at a small hotel facing the Mediterranean, he got the details. There were many operations running in support of the Iraqi Kurds, he was to be fieldman in charge of one of them. There was a man named Rashid Khyal, known as "the Poet of Kurdish Nationalism," in whom agency analysts placed great faith. His potential impact, it was felt, might rival that of Pablo Neruda on Chile. Khyal was a symbol to the political infrastructure of the Kurdish rebellion—he sang the truth of what was in their hearts, and his following among the tribes was broad and devoted. The CIA had sent in a propaganda and public relations specialist to help Khyal become an effective spokesman, for the Kurds, to the world at large. They had seen the impact of Russian emigré writers and poets, they knew what could be accomplished in the theatre of world opinion.

Because Khyal was perceived to be such a valuable asset, the agency had him hidden in the small town of Oulma, near Agadir in southern Morocco. The specialist, named Carr, was on the ground and working. Guyer's predecessor had had to be evacuated after being stricken with hepatitis. It was Guyer's job to keep both Carr and Khyal secure. Since Iraq belonged to the Soviet sphere of influence, her cause in suppression of the Kurds was supported by the KGB and the intelligence services of the Eastern Bloc. Mains expected no serious trouble, Oulma was so far off the beaten track, they could do their work in peace. Guyer was to check in by radio once a day with Mains, who would be staying up the coast in Casablanca. That night Guyer was flown into Agadir. Carr met him at the airport and drove him to Oulma in an old Fiat.

They were based in a strange blue hotel on the central square. The exterior stucco brick had been painted, a very long time ago, with a blue wash, and the damp walls of the interior were a faded sky-blue. After dusk there was a desert chill. The mercury vapor lamps in the square buzzed all night long and clouds of moths danced in the hard light. There was a desk at the end of the corridor, and a group of men sat there until dawn smoking cigarettes and talking quietly. Guyer's window looked out on a cafe where, at night, fifty men sat outdoors wrapped in jellabas, drinking tea and watching a flickering black and white television mounted above the bead curtain of the doorway.

Their day was tightly organized. At 8:00 A.M. they had tea together in the hotel dining room. A huge Moroccan entered the dining room each morning with fried cakes, distant cousins of the doughnut, strung on a long, thin palm leaf. That was breakfast. Then Carr and Khyal worked together until noon, mostly on Khyal's English and on Farsi transliterations of Khyal's Kurmanji calls for freedom and self-determination. After a lunch of flatbread and vegetables—it was really too hot to eat much—the three of them gathered and talked. Khyal had been a high school English teacher in Rezaiyeh, and his English was not too bad, if a little archaic, as he'd learned it from British grammars written around 1915. He referred to SAVAK as "a bad lot of fellows." This, Carr pointed out to Guyer in private, was a double error: an error of diction, and an error of thought. The Iranians hated the Kurds, so did the

[182]

Turks. But Turkey and Iran were important U.S. allies, so Khyal's invective had to be aimed carefully at the Iraqis.

Carr was a peculiar man. He was pale, with thin blond hair and a domed forehead. He chain-smoked Pall Malls all day long and sweated inside the blue suit that he wore constantly. But he worked hard at his job, which was to prepare Khyal to speak to the world: at the United Nations, on television—*Face the Nation, Meet the Press*—wherever a spokesman might be needed. Five nights a week Khyal was assigned to write a press release on various events that Carr made up. A cowardly Iraqi attack on a mountain village containing only women and children. A glorious ambush staged by Kurdish freedom fighters in which an Iraqi tank, a Soviet T-41, was destroyed. A commemorative on the occasion of the birthday of the Shah's father, Reza I, in whose name Khyal's home city of Rezaiyeh had been renamed. "Would you be pleased," Khyal said in this connection, "if your city of New York had been renamed New Nixon?" Carr flinched when Khyal said such things. His nails were already bitten to the quick. Sometimes in the afternoon, when the white stone square shimmered in the heat and the only sound was the droning of flies, they would play games. *Liberal Correspondent from* The New York Times. *Conservative Columnist from* Commentary. They would meet in Carr's room, where Khyal's student press releases were tacked up on the walls with pushpins, and Carr would take the part of the interviewer. Guyer listened for an hour one day while Carr tried to teach Khyal the meaning of the expression *gossip column*. Khyal was horrified at the idea.

Guyer tried hard to play the part of security man. He allowed them only one walk per day, tried to vary the time and the direction, but the town only had six streets. The people of Oulma stared at them wherever they went. Carr in his blue suit, cigarette held between the index and third fingers of his right hand. Guyer wearing a lightweight jacket that ill concealed the heavy, uncomfortable .45 strapped beneath his shirt. But most of all they stared at Khyal, who had reddish tints in his hair and blue eyes, and wore traditional baggy pants gathered at the ankle and an embroidered skullcap. Beyond that, Khyal had the look of a poet. Though he was well into his thirties, his face was baby-fat and soft, and he wore steel-rimmed spectacles through which he peered intently at whatever interested him: a donkey laden with cardboard cartons, a stall of green and red peppers in the marketplace, a veiled woman. Often, as they walked, he would recite poetry in Kurmanji, then attempt English translations for Carr and Guyer. There were two kinds of poems: Some were pastoral scenes where the sun's early-morning flame struck gold off the western mountainside, goats grazed amid the dew, and the lover longed for his beloved; others began, "Arise, my silent brothers!" On one occasion he asked Guyer, "Is azure the proper color for a lake?"

As the weeks went by, Khyal grew impatient. Carr fed him an endless supply of magazines and newspapers that arrived in the mail, shattering all of Guyer's instincts about security. Khyal kept a list of things he wanted to do and people he wanted to meet when he got to America. Over the usual dinner of couscous and chicken he asked them questions based on the day's reading: "What is the fame of Jimmy Carson?" Carr would answer, "*Johnny* Carson. His fame is humor. And he speaks nightly with famous people." Khyal would sigh with understanding, then nod in a certain way that Guyer came to understand meant that he found poet's magic everywhere, in every fact about the world. Neither Guyer nor Khyal could communicate with the people who ran the hotel, that was left to Carr, who spoke reasonable French. Though the three spoke nine languages between them, not one of them had any Arabic. Sometimes Khyal would come to Guyer's room at night and they would watch the black and white television across the square and wonder what was being said. There was only one program and it never changed: a man in a suit seated at a desk who spoke into the camera by the hour.

Every night at midnight he made contact with Mains on the radio. It was an open conversation, with a vague attempt at maintenance of informal code. Guyer was *Boston*, Carr was *Portland*, Khyal was *Atlanta*, and Mains was *Tampa*, not at all the customary CIA encryption, which used combinations of null syllables. From a security standpoint the operation was so flimsy that it reminded Guyer of something out of a World War II movie. One night the transmission did not come through. Guyer worked the dial carefully but received only static. He stayed in the room, waiting, a blanket wrapped around him against the cold. He stared at the damp blue walls, lit by a sixty-watt bulb in a ceiling fixture. At a few minutes after four Mains came on the frequency. His voice, quiet but rich with authority, sounded wrong to Guyer. Atlanta was to spend the following afternoon at the cafe across the square. At an outside table. Alone. There was no way Guyer could question the instructions. He could only ask for retransmission and confirmation, which he did, but the results were the same. After lunch he told Khyal what he had to do. Carr looked at him for a moment, then looked away. Dutifully, Khyal left the hotel, walked across the square and found a table in the shade. At midday the cafe was deserted and Khyal sat alone, drinking mint tea and reading an American magazine. Guyer watched him from the window. The heat made him sleepy. Time and again a fly would try to land on his face and he would flip at it with the back of his hand. Two hours went by, and nothing happened. Once, Khyal glanced up at the window, but Guyer made a gesture signaling that he should not do this. A few minutes later a man in a white jellaba walked slowly across the square toward the cafe, he had his hood up against the glare of the sun and Guyer could not see his face. He sat briefly at a table, then got up as though he meant to go into the cafe. As he passed behind Khyal he placed his left hand on Khyal's forehead and forced his head back across the top of the chair so that his face was to the sky then, with a small knife in his right hand, cut his throat. He took a step back, waited one beat, then ran around the corner and disappeared. Khyal never moved. His head hung backward, eyes and mouth wide open, arms slack at his sides, flies gathering where the collar of his shirt grew bright red in the sunlight.

On the beach, a few hours later, Mains told him things he hadn't known. Iran and Iraq had made peace, under the auspices of OPEC at a meeting of the cartel in Algeria. Iranian support of the Kurds had disintegrated, the Pesh Merga abandoned to their fate in the mountains, Kurdish refugees in Iran sent back across the border into Iraq. U.S. involvement had ceased, their operations were now in the hands of Iraqi and Iranian security agencies.

Guyer got up from the park bench. He thrust his hands deep into the pockets of his raincoat and watched his feet as he walked. He had thought, rushing off to his meeting with Corpora, that he could outdistance the dead, burnt feeling inside him but, he realized, he'd been wrong, it had him, loss produces inertia, he could not evade it. *The office*, he thought, *the office*.

[186]

But he knew immediately that he couldn't hide there, either. There was only one obligation at the office, and that was to come up with Benauti's photo, and there was only one person who had the skill to do that, and Richard List was the last person he wanted to see today. He was desperate to be rid of the cold, heavy thing riding in his chest, but he didn't want to tell List about it because there was the possibility that he was responsible for it. *I hate betrayal.* He blinked when he thought it. The statement seemed so flat for the weight of feeling it carried. As an intelligence officer, he'd seen the spectrum of human behavior—sacrifice, duplicity, sadism, numbness, fanatic ambition, and psychoses without name or number—but it was betrayal, a word from melodrama, that cut him deepest.

He came up short against Broadway. A stream of people. Packs of cars heading downtown. For one instant of time he questioned his ability to physically cross this street. Then a cab stopped and he got in. He hadn't waved or anything, the driver apparently saw him standing there and decided that he was a fare. And so he was. He mumbled an address, the cab tore into traffic.

The driver's hack license said his name was St. Hilaire. He wore a lime-green shirt and Guyer thought he might be Haitian. He drove erratically. Sometimes carefully, normally. Then, as though remembering that New York cabdrivers were supposed to jockey for position and knife through available openings, he would alternately speed up and stand on the brakes. The traffic was heavy and clogged and slow. The sun moved in and out, at times there was a sudden sprinkle of rain. The cab entered the park at 72nd and Central Park West, moved south on the road through the park, then exited into a mass of crawling traffic on Central Park South. It took two lights to make it through the Fifth Avenue intersection. There was a band on the corner;

conga drums, tambourines, and a trumpet. *There are so many ways to do it,* he thought. *Phosphorus gel packed up into the cushions of the front and rear seat, an electric-spark detonator, a wire running from the seat under the floor mats to the odometer.* He stared out the window, they'd reached Lexington Avenue, discount drugstores and anonymous lunch restaurants serving the daytime business district. He knew that if he measured the distance from the garage where the embassy car was parked to the flash point on the overpass, the measurement would fall evenly on the tenth of a mile, because he had seen those devices and that was how they were calibrated.

The cab stopped. He paid and walked the one block north. There was a different doorman on duty, an old man with a game leg and longish white hair. He gave his name, the doorman called upstairs. *If not,* he thought, *I will go to the movies.* "Go ahead," the doorman said. He rode the elevator, rang the doorbell. The peephole opened and closed. The door swung wide. Clearly, she'd been asleep. Her hair was flat on one side of her head. He started to say something, but she was already walking away from him, her nightgown diaphanous. She reached an arm up and gestured for him to follow her. The living room was a mess. There were crumbs on a table, an open box of Cheerios, newspapers spread out, underpants drying on a yellow towel spread over the radiator. By the time he reached her bedroom, she was already in the bed, the nightgown flung on a chair, only her head visible with bedclothes wrapped around it like a shawl. He took off his jacket. There was no place to put it, so he laid it on the thick carpet. He started to loosen his tie.

"I think I ought to say—" he started.

"*I* think you ought to say *nothin'*," she cut him off. "Do what you like," she said, "just don't *say* things."

He undressed. When he was naked, she raised the

sheet and blanket so they stood high, like a tent, and he climbed in. Gently, he put his hand on her side. Her skin was very warm, and smooth to the touch. He closed his eyes. In darkness the place where his hand rested became the only place in the world.

After they made love, she got out of bed and went into the kitchen. She reappeared a few minutes later, walking carefully, a steaming white mug in each hand. "Take this from me," she said. She went around and got into the bed carefully so as not to rock the mattress, then took one of the cups from him. It was very dark tea, loaded with sugar, and it tasted delicious. "Breakfast," she said, sitting up to sip at it.

"Thank you," he said.

"Is it the way you like it?"

"Yes."

After a while he said, "Is Maggie short for Margaret?"

"No," she said. "Ethel."

He grinned.

"My mother's favorite aunt," she said.

"Hey, Ethel," he said.

"Don't you dare tease me," she said.

Together they made the afternoon disappear. She took a long, hot bath. He sat on the edge of the tub and she sang a slow version of "Fly Me to the Moon," looking in his eyes the whole way. Her singing was really bad. She put a blue washcloth over her face and made bizarre noises. He hadn't any idea of what she was supposed to be and she wouldn't tell him. When she'd dried off, they ate toast and then cake for dessert. It was safe in the apartment. Nothing was allowed in that cut or shattered and there was the temptation to stay until life outside dried up and blew away in the wind. But a little after four the guilt began to gnaw at him, so he tied his tie and left. At her door they kissed good-bye, which meant, he was sure, both godspeed and hurry back, although nobody said anything like that.

Back on the street, Manhattan rushing by like the sea, he found a payphone in a coffee shop, called the office, and was put through to List.

"Did you see the *Times*?" he asked.

"Yes I did," List said.

"About Delatte?"

"Yes."

"So you know what happened. You know they killed him."

"Yes," List said again, after a pause. His voice was hesitant. It was as though he were waiting for Guyer to tell him what to feel.

"Well?"

"Well what?" Resentful. Put-upon. Nervous. Why?

"Did you have a reaction? Or is it just Monday."

There was no answer for several seconds, just the slight hiss of an open line. Then List said, slowly, "That's the end of the business." That stopped Guyer cold. List went on, still moving a word at a time: "We thought something had happened to you. When you didn't call."

"I'm okay. I had to get away."

"But I'm right about the end of the business. I mean . . ."

"I don't know. Maybe. Maybe not." Guyer wondered why List was so anxious to shut it down. "What I mean to do now is to have Benauti tracked, and found. After that, we'll have to see where we are."

"Can that be done?"

"If you'll help, there's a chance, a possibility."

"What can I do?"

"I need a picture of Benauti. Can you put that together?"

"A composite?"

[190]

"Yes."

"I can try. We're not really set up for that. It'll take a great deal of sorting. I'll try if you want me to."

"I want you to. I'll be there in about a half an hour. Send Edna and Kevin home."

"Okay. I'm really sorry about Elden."

"See you later," Guyer said, and started to hang up.

"Captain?" List said.

"Yes?"

"Buy a lot of magazines."

In the office, they took off their jackets and made coffee. Guyer went downstairs an hour later and brought back a large bagful of roast beef sandwiches. They pushed two desks together and worked amid coffee cups and sandwich wrappings and pages torn from the magazines. Guyer had returned with thirty-eight—everything from *Penthouse* to *Road & Track*. They spent a fruitless hour trying to align, verbally, their recollected images of Benauti. Two people rarely agree what somebody looks like: a fact that makes detectives and prosecutors old before their time. They turned the radio up loud, which they couldn't do while Edna was on the premises, and worked through a variety of stations until they found a program of forties dance bands coming in from New Jersey. It felt like old times. Not completely, because Guyer had walled off part of himself, and List remained defensive and distant, but enough so that the work moved, inch by inch, forward. Having decided to work separately, turning pages and snipping photos where a single feature reminded them of Benauti, they immediately violated the decision, one or the other saying, "How about this?"

When it got to be 9:20 and they'd made no progress at all, they agreed that part of the problem was that Benauti's facial character, as they'd both observed it, reflected fear and suspicion and hostility. People having their pictures taken for magazines tended to look triumphant or happy or studiedly casual and they, like everybody else, made faces in front of cameras that they never made at any other time in their lives. List pointed out that the computer, which understood only light and shadow, was better at this than they were. Eventually the magazines were destroyed and their pages shoved off the desk onto the floor, suggesting a metamagazine that covered everything of interest to everybody, from coin collecting to eggplant recipes to clothes-for-winter and player of the year. What remained was a stack of cutout photos, large and small, face and full length, color and black and white. From these, they attempted to collate a face. After arguing back and forth for thirty minutes, they had the thinning, brushed-back hair from a pilot in an advertisement that said, "This year, fly El Al." The dark eyes from an Italian stevedore in a travel magazine. The nose of a popular television actor. And the mouth and chin of a political fund-raiser featured in a news magazine. Working carefully with scissors and paste, they assembled a face on a piece of white paper. It looked totally absurd. The scale was wrong, it was four different colors and resembled only a surreal painting. But List waved off the problem. The computer, he said, could make those adjustments. So they moved to their customary positions at the console. List ran several A/P Factor programs until the composite began to take on the look of a human, but the resultant face was lifeless and strange and looked nothing at all like Benauti. The computer didn't like it either. When List asked it to produce a series of matching faces, it put up a series of six and stopped. Guyer swore. List widened the numerical range, his face slightly crooked with concentration. Finally, the screen began to run long sequences of photos. But they were still a long way away from duplicating Benauti. List backtracked, working by numbers and recompositing the face by using a manual overdrive that replaced the usual program: in effect keypunching and programming simultaneously.

By 11:30 it became clear that the problem was in the lower face. List maintained that Benauti's mouth and chin were from his French parentage and the remainder of his face from the Tunisian side. It was also true, they both acknowledged, that Benauti's particular personality was projected by that part of his face. Listening, he would often open his mouth slightly and move his head to a three-quarter position. Then they got lucky. Having discovered the trait, they almost immediately found a face with it and List factored the characteristic into his running program. Guyer began to have the eerie sensation that the computer was somehow *trying,* very slowly figuring out what they wanted and striving to get it for them from its data banks. Guyer said something about that when, after looking at three hundred faces, they took a break to eat sandwiches and drink coffee. List wasn't surprised, said that animism was the predominant religion among serious computer people. Guyer went to the men's room and splashed cold water on his forehead. In the mirror his own face looked back at him as though it were on a screen, red-eyed, pale, and tired. They resettled themselves and started to run photos; by now their seven-digit identification code had wandered far afield from what the computer had assigned their original composite. Half an hour later they had it. When the photo came up, they both yelled "Stop" simultaneously and List punched the *hold* button with his index finger. For a minute or so they both stared in silence. It was a kind of miracle. List tapped in the identification request.

RUNNING SUBJ 522 157 8212
SOURCE EDMUND WINSTON PORTRAIT
STUDIO 2/23/80

4/6/80 IN
0 FILE
14 WESTON PLACE
BOSTON MASS 0 CODE
SUBJ: JORDAN I SHABLE

List said, "What might have been." The reference was obvious to Guyer. It was Benauti, but a Benauti of another destiny. The face was slightly heavier than Benauti's, but the true difference lay in the implicit signals in the face and posture. This was a man of business, of wealth and circumstance, a man deeply satisfied with what life had given him, even though, the expression implied, life had to be savagely kicked in the ass before it coughed up its gifts.

"Pompous old bastard," List continued. "Bet his daughters got together and bought him a portrait-sitting for his fortieth birthday."

"It's him, though," Guyer said, squinting at the screen.

"Indeed it is. See that last name? Bet you a nickle it's been anglicized from Shabul, or something like it. Syrian or Lebanese, I'd say. Poppa probably worked with his hands but he had the sense to name his son Jordan. Will you look at the *set* of those shoulders? The man with the most sheep in the village. The patriarch." It was true, Guyer thought. The chin was held high, the eyes were proud and fierce.

"Run a hundred copies," he said.

Guyer came awake suddenly. He had been dreaming about the interior of a combination lock. The face was removed, and he watched the dialing mechanism circle slowly past the steel cylinder bars coated with an oily film. He saw each tumbler fall into place. He watched

[194]

the dial spin, then reverse and spin again, and his anxiety grew and grew until the discomfort became acute. As each set of revolutions was completed and the metal-on-metal snick sounded, the fear deepened. He knew, in the dream, that when the combination was fulfilled, the locking bar would spring from the round body and he would scream out loud. He sat up quickly. The telephone was ringing. He groped for it, knocked the receiver off the cradle, then managed to bring it to his ear. Instinctively he checked his watch at the same moment. 2:34.

"What," he said.

"It's me, Maggie."

"You okay?" He pressed his left hand to his chest. His heart was still beating hard from the dream.

"Sort of. Yeah, I'm okay. You were sound asleep."

"Doesn't matter."

"I wasn't really sure about calling. Then I decided I better. I mean, maybe it doesn't have anything to do with you . . . ."

"I'm awake. What is it?"

"Richard was just here."

"Oh?"

"I didn't let him in. I don't know how the hell he got past John downstairs, but there was no phone call or anything. He called me a whore."

As his senses returned he could hear her fighting for control. She was upset, trying to play it cool. There was a nervous flutter in her voice, as though she wanted to laugh or cry. "Start from the beginning," he said.

"I was watching *The Late Show*. Some dumb thing. I'd rolled the TV into my bedroom and I was half-asleep. All of a sudden there's a bang on the door. Jesus Christ," she laughed, very tight, "I jumped out of my skin. Then again, and again. My first thought was call the cops, and I had the phone in my hand. Then I heard somebody yell something in the hall. And I thought what if this is somebody I know, and they're drunk or stoned or something and they're trying to get help. So *dumb*," she laughed again, "I actually imagined somebody lying on the floor of the hall and they couldn't ring the bell so they were pounding on the bottom of the door. I figured one look through the peephole and then I'd call the cops or an ambulance or whatever. I get about ten feet from the door, in the living room, and somebody on the other side of the door yells 'Whore!' in this strange voice. Like when the voice can't get out? It sounded like they were saying *poor,* but that didn't make any sense, and then he said it again and I realized what it was. And all I could think was, Oh Jesus the *neighbors*. So I opened the peephole, just a crack, because by now I'm getting very scared, and I'm afraid he'll shoot me through it. And it's Richard. He's red in the face and looks all crazy and just as I open the peephole he swings his cane around and hits the door again. I screamed. I think I yelled, *Get out of here*, but he was already moving. He opened the fire door, to the back stairs, and disappeared. I was shaking. I called downstairs but they didn't know anything. They just said, *Should I call the police?* but I told them to forget it. Then I called you. I'm sorry I woke you up. I'm okay now. It was just so strange."

"You want me to come over? I can be there in ten minutes."

"No, you don't have to, I'm okay now. I just needed to talk to somebody. I mean, you're welcome, you can if you want to, but I'm okay."

"You're sure."

"Yeah. It's all right now."

"If anything else happens tonight, anything at all, call 911. Right away, don't think about it. There a chain on the door?"

"Yeah. It's on."

"Try and get some sleep. I'll call tomorrow around noon."

"I'm sorry I woke you."

"Don't be. I'm glad you did."

"What's going to happen?"

Guyer rubbed his hand over his face. "I don't know. But I think Richard and I better have a talk. Right away. There's been some kind of . . . I'll call you tomorrow, okay?"

"Okay. Thanks."

They said good night simultaneously. Guyer flopped back on the bed and stared at the dark ceiling. He cursed himself for avoiding the problem, hoping it would go away. His heart was still beating hard, the bad dream and the phone call and what had happened that morning were all mixed together. He felt sick. The more he stared at the ceiling, the angrier he got. It was a delayed reaction, in a sense, to Elden's death. All day long he had been consumed by *tactics,* but now the feelings came at him really hard. Lying there, he almost hyperventilated. Khyal had trusted him, Elden had trusted him. Now something was after Maggie and that went too far. Suddenly he stood up. He couldn't lie there anymore. Upright, he was a little dizzy. He staggered into the bathroom, ran the water warm and scooped handfuls over his face, letting it drip back onto the porcelain. Still wet, he opened the medicine chest and took out a brown plastic pill bottle. He wasn't going to wait until morning for anything. It would all be resolved tonight. He adjusted the tap water to cold, took one of the green capsules, and washed it down with cupped handfuls of water. He held a towel against his face for a minute. The prescription had been filled at a pharmacy in McLean, Virginia, and dated from his last year of service. It was time-release Dexedrine.

He sat on the edge of the bed and waited for the pill to work. He picked up the phone and dialed List's home number. It rang ten times. No answer. Well, that figured. He was probably in the bars. What made them think they could get away with all of the games they were running on him? Did he give off some kind of passive scent? A signal that he wouldn't hit back? Well he'd see about changing that. He found his clothes where he'd flung them and got dressed. He had a pretty good idea where List would be. That'd be *conversation* number one. Then he'd see about Benauti, and whoever was running him. Somebody was playing chess with him and that somebody figured he'd sit quiet and play his next move. They might be surprised when he picked up the board and rammed it down their throat. He glanced at the dresser top and the stack of photos. Now he really meant to set Corpora free, let him hunt. It didn't matter what it cost. He'd pay whatever it was and borrow the rest if he had to. He wrestled into his raincoat, paused to count the money in his pocket, over a hundred dollars. The magazines had cost him close to a hundred, maybe more. He couldn't remember. He set the locks and slammed the door and rang for the elevator.

In the street it was cold and damp and deserted. There were lots of cabs. He stepped to the curb, and one of them cut across traffic and stopped hard in front of him, the body rocking on its suspension. Guyer climbed in. "I'm going to several places, there'll be some waiting time. I'll pay the meter and fifty bucks on top of that. Okay?"

The driver said nothing, just punched the meter into action. Guyer gave him List's address—maybe he'd come home, maybe he just wasn't answering his phone —the driver hit the gas and circled the block to head uptown. It had rained earlier, the streets were still wet, as they passed other cars the windshield was sprayed. List lived in the East Fifties near Bloomingdale's, in a three-story brownstone. He had half the second floor.

Guyer had always wondered how he was able to afford it. Perhaps, he thought, he'd find that out tonight also. By the time they reached List's address, Guyer could feel the blood pounding at his temples as the Dexedrine began to work. He set his teeth together hard and resisted an impulse to talk to the driver.

"This it? You said 122 East?" The driver was leaning back over the seat. He was in his twenties, a thin cigar stuck in the corner of his mouth, long black hair carefully combed back on the sides. The name on the license was Italian.

Guyer got out, stood in the street, and looked up at the windows on the second floor. There were low lights on in the apartment. He walked up the steps to the front door, which was glass backed by thick wire mesh. There were two bells beside the door, Guyer tried the upper one. He waited. No answer. Tried it again, a long, insistent ring. There was no sound from within. He counted to sixty, then returned to the cab. He didn't know the names of the bars he wanted, but assumed that List would stay close to home. He told the driver to go to Third and drive north slowly. The first one he saw was called The Palm Hut. Blue neon script sign in the window, a stab at 1930s ambience. He went inside, it was very dark and very quiet—no women inside, only men—and crowded. So many people, so little noise, he found that part of it a little spooky. He sensed a few looks, walking toward the bar, heads turned briefly toward him, then away. The bartender raised his eyebrows a fraction and said, "Yes?" The tone of his voice implied that Guyer was going to ask a question rather than order a drink.

"Looking for a friend."

"Mmm," said the bartender. He walked to the other end of the bar.

Guyer moved among the crowd. They glanced at him without acknowledgment, eyes lingering for an instant then moving away. He sensed an invisible wall around him, sensed that his progress was carefully observed. The telepathy in the crowd was almost tangible and, wherever he wanted to go, a narrow aisle opened for him. He circled through the room, there was no sign of List. He arrived back at the door, swung it wide, and walked out into the street. Just as he crossed the threshold a sharp, civilized voice somewhere behind him said, "Good evening."

The driver knew the bar. When Guyer climbed back in the cab, his tone was different. "Now where?" he said.

"North," Guyer said, "nice and slow."

Joel's, three blocks away, had a higher noise and action level than The Palm Hut. There was a jukebox playing Christopher Cross's song "I Really Don't Know Anymore." The patrons were younger, and there were scarves and hats and sunglasses and the occasional shirt open up the front and tied in a knot. Because of the costumes Guyer had to look harder. Somebody behind him rested a hand on his shoulder. Guyer shrugged it off without turning around. There was a short fat man, in a black-satin coach's jacket open to reveal he was shirtless beneath, singing along with the jukebox. As Guyer went by him he extended his arms in a crooner's pose and, where the lyric broke, made a kissing pantomime with his mouth. Guyer worked back and forth through the crowd. No List.

Not at Firenze either. Polished oak floor and a buffet table full of hors d'oeuvres in the center of the room. The rich smell of the food sickened Guyer. They stopped and started. Down Second Avenue, back up First. Guyer looked at his watch. The time was moving toward 4:00, when the bars would close. It was a fool's errand, he decided. List could be anywhere. He could have been home, not answering the door. Or trust him, Guyer thought, to find a bar nobody else knew about.

He could be at a party, an all-night movie, someone else's apartment, or at any one of a thousand places all over Manhattan. The driver stopped for a *Daily News* at a kiosk, and read the sports page while Guyer was out of the cab. At Gallimaufry there was a colossal mirror behind the bar, in a thick gilt frame, cupids embracing on top, lit on either side by a pair of soft yellow globes. Guyer got a good look at himself. His face was red from the Dexedrine. His hair was tousled, raincoat rumpled and dirty. "Three more," he said to the driver when he came out. There wasn't much time, and the drug had twisted Guyer's stomach into knots. His skin felt dry and itchy, his mouth tasted like ether. The cab crawled up 49th Street, between Third and Lexington. Mostly expensive restaurants, small brick commercial buildings left over from the forties, and garbage cans set out on the sidewalk waiting for the 4:00 A.M. pickup. The street was deserted except for a prowling cat. Midblock, a large door painted bright red. In the center, in block capitals, VANITY FAIR. The name clicked deep in Guyer's memory.

"Here," he said.

"Hunh?"

"Right *here*. The red door."

"Take it easy. This okay?"

He walked quickly across the sidewalk. The door was heavy and opened slowly. Inside, it was very dark and packed with bodies. There was hard-rock music blasting from giant speakers, the thumping bass level hurt his ears. Guyer took some time to let his eyes adjust. Some of the men were wearing rouge and eyeliner. He shouldered through the press of bodies but could find no place to get an overall view of the room. People pushed back against him and he fought for balance on the glossy black linoleum under foot. Red and blue spotlights swept nervously through the crowd, turning skin odd colors and making it difficult to focus vision. The mixed smells of cologne and liquor were overwhelming.

Guyer saw him. Back toward the entrance door, thirty feet away. He was slightly stooped, in the midst of an intense conversation with a short man in a double-breasted overcoat with a satin collar. List was bent over to hear what he was saying. The man in the overcoat had brown hair brushed down on his forehead in the Roman style, and gold-rimmed glasses. As he talked he extended his index finger, thumb straight up, and rolled his hand in a tight circle by his right cheek. The gesture was for emphasis, for describing a logical series of events, each rolling by in turn. List was concentrating on hearing what the man said.

"Richard." He realized he had yelled as loud as he could, his voice violent and challenging and thick with rage. Heads turned. The man with List spun toward him. List's reaction was slower, he simply raised his head and looked around, the red and blue light flashing on his face. Guyer shoved hard against the bodies packed around him. Somebody said, "Really!" in a theatrical mockery of irritation. Stiff, oiled hair scraped across his cheek. Unable to control himself, he opened a space before him by shoving people aside. List turned and started to limp away quickly, toward a green-lit EXIT sign above the front door. Guyer tried to move faster. Now there were voices around him slurred with real anger. Somebody pushed back at him. Somebody grabbed his raincoat. The sound level began to swing into a gear of inquiry, people suddenly aware that something was *happening,* and asking their neighbors what was going on. List was receding fast, body canting over each time he thrust his weight on the cane. The man in the double-breasted overcoat suddenly appeared in front of him. Eyes narrow, mouth set. Guyer tried to move him out of the way, but the man shoved back by slamming his open palms into Guyer's shoulders. Guyer

grabbed for his coat. One wrist was knocked aside, the other hand felt shirt material. He started to pull at it, then somebody hit him in the back of the head with an open, but stiffened, hand. The sound of the slap was a loud crack. A voice at his shoulder said, "Good heavens." Guyer lurched forward with the impact, slipped to one knee, felt something give where he held the shirt, heard a ripping noise immediately followed by a furious grunt: "*Scheiss.*" Somebody in back of him kicked him between the shoulder blades and he went sprawling on his belly on the linoleum floor. The kick knocked the wind out of him for a moment and when he returned to himself he found he'd curled up protectively with his arms covering his head and face. He came up out of it fast. They'd made a small space for him and he was able to get to his feet. A point of pain where he'd been kicked began to throb, no more than an inch from his spine. A man dressed like a sultan broke through the crowd. He was huge, with a shaved head, wearing one gold hoop in his ear. He jerked his thumb savagely back over his shoulder and said, "Eighty-six." A way parted to the door, Guyer moved toward it. Both List and the man in the overcoat had vanished.

On the sidewalk, he realized there was a piece of material clenched in his right fist. It was fine-spun cotton, cream-colored. He walked slowly to the cab, his back hurting with every step. Carefully, he climbed into the backseat. The driver laid his newpaper down, turned off the dome light, and started the engine. "Looks like you got what you came for," he said.

Guyer gave his home address.

Corpora

MONDAY NIGHT Edna Foley and Frank stood by her car in the bus depot parking lot and talked about Thanksgiving. It was the last day of October, a cold, wet evening, and Frank blew on his hands and rubbed them together. He was wearing a plaid cashmere scarf she'd bought for him in September. He wore it casually, like a student, and she wanted to reach out and run her hand down it, but that was something she couldn't do in the public lot. Thanksgiving was a small problem. She was invited to her sister's, in Trenton, and she wanted him to come along. He was reluctant, perhaps shy, and urged her to go and be with her family. The idea of his being home alone on a holiday bothered her, but turning down her sister's annual invitation was easier said than done, and she didn't want to put herself in the position of making explanations or, worse, telling lies.

Secretly she very much wanted him to come with her, she had a fantasy about it. Thanksgiving, in her mind, was always a cold sunny day, cheerful despite the bare trees and dead lawns. While the turkey cooked and her nephews played catch in the backyard, she imagined Frank and her brother-in-law, sales manager for a truck dealership in Camden, watching the afternoon football games, drinking a beer or two, and chatting amiably. At five there would be the dinner, the pies, the pointless urgings to have one more piece, the relaxed torpor afterward, and a nice, slow drive home. There would be kitchen conversation with her sister, Frank much admired and praised. It was a small fantasy but a compelling one. On the other hand, she'd promised herself never to press him, never to presume on his courtesy and put him in situations where he really didn't want to be. He was an independent man and she liked that. Still, she thought, it's only Thanksgiving, three or four hours. Finally they left it up in the air, at least he didn't say no. He reminded her that they were going to the movies on Wednesday night, looked at her in the way that had come to substitute for touching, and went off to his car.

At home she took a chicken pot pie out of the freezer and started it heating for dinner. She made these herself, cutting up cooked chicken, adding peas and carrots, then freezing the mixture in a white sauce in small aluminum pie plates she bought at the supermarket. Waiting for the pie to heat, she turned on the news and poured herself a glass of wine. Her thoughts idled along with the pace of the news, none of the disasters or political moves of that day falling close enough to home to concern her much. Things would be better, she thought, if the office would straighten up. Life there was not smooth lately, there were undertones of stress and conflict and the mood was definitely sour. It didn't help that there was nobody she could talk to about it.

[208]

She attended to work, scrupulously, minded her own business, and pretended not to notice. She only hoped that it didn't signal some drastic turn of events, she'd never had much of a taste for sudden changes. The timer buzzed, and she went into the kitchen to eat dinner. When she was done, she had her bath and changed into a sweater and an old pair of slacks and carpet slippers. The idea of being in bathrobe and nightgown at 7:30 in the evening was physically appealing—she *was* tired, it *had* been a long day—but somehow morally improper: a notion developed over years of living alone during marriage and subsequent widowhood. Spending evenings in a bathrobe implied, to her, growing old. She was not yet ready for that. She settled in to watch television, tried hard to follow a lecture on Byzantine art on the PBS station, felt a snooze coming on, gave it up and switched over to Fonzie. A little after eight the door chimes rang.

This was unusual, callers who didn't phone ahead were not part of her life. "Yes?" she called, loud enough to be heard outside.

"Mrs. Foley?" came back through the door, faint but polite. That was sufficient to get her to open the door a crack. There was a tall black man in a fur coat at her door, and that scared her. He was accompanied by a rather short white man who was chewing gum. She was about to slam the door in their faces when she realized that they had made no move to force their way inside, but stood respectfully back in the porch light. She then understood that they were policemen. What else could they be? Plainclothes police on television dressed casually, it must be so in New Jersey as well. There was also the sense, and it reenforced her notion about police, that these men were partners. That, too, had its television analogy. She compromised, looked out through the narrow opening, ready to slam the door shut at any instant, and said, "Yes? What do you want?" She real-

[209]

ized that her hand was touching her throat and, self-consciously, lowered it to her side.

It was the short man who spoke, jaw shifting rhythmically. "Mrs. Foley, may we come in?" His tone was respectful, and the gum made him seem relaxed and casual. The way the question was put gave her every opportunity to decline, and both men continued standing quietly, well away from the door. So she did the gracious thing, said yes, and stood aside.

"Thank you," they both said. When they were in the house she shut the door and stood with arms folded. She suddenly felt much less sure of herself.

"What is it?" she asked.

"It's about Metro Data Research. Where you work. May we sit down?"

She felt simultaneously safe—they obviously weren't there for robbery, or worse—but anxious in a different area. Her intuition told her that this, some species of federal or state inquiry, was the answer to the difficulties at the office. More, it had always been in the back of her mind that what the company did was in a border area of legality and that some day she might have to confront official questions about it. Her loyalty rose to the surface. She prepared herself to stall, feign ignorance, tell lies, whatever was required. "Of course," she said. "Please sit down. What kind of officers are you?"

The short man sat on one end of the couch, the other in an easy chair. The former drew a white envelope from his inside pocket. She noticed he was wearing a madras sport coat, much too thin for the cold evening. "We're not officers," he said.

"You're not?" She heard her voice quaver. *Stop it,* she told herself.

"No."

Still, there wasn't a threat. Looking at the envelope —by his holding it out it had become the center of the room—she believed she was about to be served a summons. She searched her mind for a reason. A civil suit? Her husband's death—a will, a pension, something to do with the union?

The short man balanced the envelope, weighing it. "These are Polaroid photographs, Mrs. Foley. I won't embarrass you by taking them out of the envelope unless you insist. Will you take my word for it?"

Her stomach wrenched. The memory of the motel room in Pennsylvania rolled over her. Another fear was waiting behind that reaction. Frank. Had they hurt him? Had they stolen them? She took a step back toward the door. "What do you want?" she said. Her voice was breathless and frightened, she could feel her heart pounding.

The short man answered her quickly. "Only a little information about your work. That's all we want."

"How did you get those?"

He shrugged.

She stood and stared at him, realized that she had started to shake uncontrollably, and that she couldn't stop it. "Calm down, Mrs. Foley," the short man said. It was an order, and she was amazed to discover herself responding to it. "Probably better if you sit down and take a deep breath." His voice was concerned, he wanted to get her through this, she realized, the solicitude calmed her further. She went to the nearest chair, sat on the edge of it. He nodded his approval. Put the envelope away, took out a package of Sight Savers, removed his glasses, and began to clean the lenses with a circular motion. His eyes, without the glasses, blinked and narrowed. "This is business, Mrs. Foley," he said in a soft, apologetic voice. "A few facts, no more, and we'll be on our way. We don't want to ruin your evening. Okay? We haven't hurt anybody, we're not going to hurt anybody. It's just our job to find out one or two things."

She canted her head over, honestly puzzled. What on earth would she know to cause anybody to go to all this trouble to find it out? Seeing her confusion, he added, "About the way the computer works." Set against the fear inside her, it seemed so little to ask. She quieted down immediately. She also remembered something Mr. Guyer had once said: *If anybody ever tried to force you to tell them something about us, about what we do, just tell them the truth. When you're absolutely sure that you are safe, call me and tell me what happened.* Remembering that, she nodded assent.

The black man drew a small cassette-recorder from his pocket and pressed the record key. He looked around him for a table, then balanced it on the arm of the chair. Then he took out a small notebook, turned the cover back, and leaned toward her. "Now the first thing," he said, his voice deep, tone unaccented, "is the encryption code. If there are several, we'll need to have them in series." He looked up and raised his eyebrows and smiled encouragingly.

She tried. She opened her mouth to tell him what he wanted to know, but her mind was a blank. There was a long silence. The short man said, with barely the faintest edge of irritation, "Now, Mrs. Foley . . ." But the other man waved him off. She realized he understood exactly what had happened. "Start another way," he said. "How do you get up to work from the bus terminal?"

Carefully, he took her through the routine of going to work, going from detail to detail, what bus went north, who made the office coffee, until she'd settled in to a routine of response. When he asked for the encryption code a second time, she was able to tell him, visually imagining her fingers pressing the keys. There were several codes used for the various operations of the computer, and he questioned her about them for a long time. Some questions she could not answer. She did not know, for instance, if when the encryption was completed, a signal was made outside the office. The idea that a telephone might ring in an apartment someplace when the office computer was set in motion was novel but, she realized, not at all hard to achieve. If such things happened, she said, she didn't know anything about them. Carefully, he went back over office procedures that seemed meaningless to her, but it was easier to respond than to question. After a while, he covered the ground they had first gone over, and she realized that if she had lied about the numerical codes, it would have been impossible to remember the lies. The man's voice was relaxed and had a sweet tone to it, but he had laid several traps for her and she was thankful that she had not been caught in them. When he was done, he turned off the recorder and closed the notebook. "Thank you," he said, "you've been very patient."

The two of them stood simultaneously. The short man put the envelope on the coffee table. "There aren't any copies," he said, though that possibility hadn't yet occurred to her. He apologized again for ruining her evening, and seemed genuinely sorry. He said, "It's just a job we do, Mrs. Foley. We're working people, like you are." They said good night, and left.

For a long time she sat still. The house seemed alien to her. The only sign of their visit was a plain white envelope on the coffee table. She had no desire to look inside it, no desire to touch it. Laverne and Shirley were still on the television. She shut her eyes, the one feeling she had was a deep fatigue. She got up, used the bathroom, walked aimlessly around the house. She was cold, found a heavy sweater in a drawer, and put it on. Her only desire was not to do anything at all. She should call Mr. Guyer, but the idea of going back over every-

[213]

thing that had happened, and explaining *why* it had happened, or trying to lie to him about why, defeated her. She felt drained and had no will to act in any way at all.

She recognized, deep down, that she had brought this upon herself. The job involved her with a secret intelligence operation of some sort, she had always known that, and her major response to it had been that it was none of her business. She had followed their directions, had never told anyone, Frank included, about the true nature of her job, and in turn had accepted very good financial compensation. A question about going to work the following day drifted into her mind. She couldn't do it. She would, she was sure, blurt out the whole story, or they would draw it from her. She was ashamed about the pictures, not because they were immoral but because, to the world at large, she was fifty-three years old and carried herself with dignity and was not the sort of woman who would approve of such things. She was afraid they would laugh at her behind her back. Perhaps not Mr. Guyer, but surely Mr. List. *So this is how you really are.* That's what they would think, even though that wasn't true.

The headache began in her right temple, a sharp throb that moved to a place behind her right eye. Holding her hand against her eye, she went to the medicine cabinet and took two Bufferin, drinking from the plastic cup that held her toothbrush. She would stay home tomorrow, Tuesday, because now she really was ill. She wandered into her bedroom, undressed, put on a night-gown, and got into bed. Turned off the bedside lamp, then turned it back on. She wasn't yet ready for darkness. If she fell asleep with the light on it didn't really matter. It was quiet outside. It started to rain, she could hear the light patter on the eaves. Downstairs the television was still on, she'd forgotten to turn it off. It would be best, she thought, if she took the rest of the week off and went in the following Monday. She needed time to collect herself, to decide what to do. They'd been good to her at work. But then she'd been a very dependable and hard-working employee. She wasn't sure exactly what she owed them. If she unraveled the whole story, what would happen then? Could this go further? Where? How would it involve her? She had been blackmailed, that's what the word meant, the experience she had just had. What if she had refused to say anything? Would they have circulated the photos, to her neighbors, her employers, her family? Even though they had nothing to gain by it? That would be, she thought, pointless cruelty. In the movies it never reached that stage, the story never closed in that way, and that was her only reference point where blackmail was concerned. Usually, police caught the blackmailer. Or, in another sort of story, the person being blackmailed murdered the criminals and a detective later solved the mystery. The ride into New York every morning took too long. It tired her out so that she needed the entire weekend to recover. There must be jobs available closer to where she lived. She could sleep an hour later, and would get home earlier. The secrecy of her work, she had to admit it, she had found just a little glamorous, exotic. In some ways she had become a different person, more important than she'd ever been. It had, perhaps, given her something special, something attractive, something that had provoked the interest of a person like Frank.

There was a telephone beside the bed. She reached for it, then drew her hand back. Everything inside her told her to be cautious. She didn't want to weep all over him: alone, she was maintaining. But she knew the minute she heard his voice, concerned and sympathetic, she would split wide open. She also hesitated because

[215]

her need for him was touched with anger. He had made her pose for those pictures, and he had kept them, but she was the one who was compromised. As she went over it she realized that she had no picture of him at all, though he was forever promising one. He probably didn't even know his house had been entered and searched, the two men were that slick. She had to tell him. As she lay there, rain falling outside, the television yammering downstairs, the need grew and grew. They'd have to see it through together, he'd have to know, if not exactly what she did at work, then at least the general nature of it. It might be wrong to go against what Mr. Guyer had told her, it might be wrong to lean on Frank, but she could not bear the whole burden alone. This time, when she reached for the phone, she dialed Frank's number. It rang four times, then changed to a ring of a different tone and rang three more times. A recorded voice came on the line: "The number you have reached has been disconnected by order of the subscriber. Please stay on the line if you require further assistance." Eventually a live operator answered. The possibility that the line was out of order was tested, but it wasn't so. The operator checked her records and, now growing slightly annoyed, said that the phone *had* been disconnected by order of the subscriber. No forwarding number was available. If further information was needed, the business office was open in the morning. She hung up. The house was cold. She got out of bed, put a sweater on, crawled back beneath the covers, and turned off the light by the side of her bed. She knew that sooner or later, if she lay quietly with her eyes closed, she would go to sleep. It was the fault of the captain, she thought, when Larry had first gotten ill it should have been seen to, there should have been a doctor on board, he never should have been allowed to die like that, alone, far away, nobody by his side.

[216]

*　*　*

Guyer got home at 4:00. He was terribly thirsty and drank three big glasses of cold water at the kitchen sink. The water tasted chemical, but he gulped at it. The inside of his nose was hot and dry. It irritated him and he tried to put a little warm water up in his nostrils but that actually made it worse when it dried. He took off his clothes and climbed slowly into bed. His back really hurt. His eyes were wide open in the darkness. The Dexedrine wouldn't wear off for a long time, the only alternative was a counteracting drug. He didn't want to do that, but was thankful there wasn't anything in the house because he would have been tempted. He kept looking at his watch but the minutes crawled. Finally he thought *the hell with it* and called Corpora. Mrs. Corpora answered, voice thin and raspy with sleep. "Mister," she said, "do you know what *time* it is?" She started to say something else but the phone made a noise as it was snatched away. Corpora said, "Yeah?" Guyer told him he had a composite photo of Benauti. He wanted to get it to him as soon as possible. Corpora suggested 6:00 A.M. He would come in from Long Island on the early train and meet Guyer at Pennsylvania Station. He gave Guyer directions to a quick-service lunch counter on the lower level and hung up.

Guyer knew that by staying in bed with his eyes closed, and consciously trying to relax his body, he was getting forty percent of the benefit of actual sleep. So he made himself do it. Once, he fell into a very light doze but the combination-lock dream returned and woke him up. After that he stayed awake and checked his watch until 5:00. Then he got up, dressed, wrapped the stack of photos in a sheet of newspaper, and crisscrossed it with a rubber band. He flagged a cab downstairs and reached Penn Station at 5:45. Corpora was fifteen minutes late getting to the counter. He was wearing a bright yellow shirt, open at the neck, and a tan light-weight suit. He seemed unaffected by the weather. He had the sunglasses on, and a toothpick in his mouth. He looked fresh and pink and newly shaved.

Guyer had wanted coffee, the taste of it would have raised his spirits, but he was afraid of what the caffeine would do to his system, still racing from the pill he'd taken. So when Corpora arrived, he was drinking a ginger ale through a straw and eating powdered dough-nuts.

"How are those?" Corpora asked by way of greeting.

"Good," Guyer said.

Corpora ordered a half dozen and a pot of coffee. "The coffee here is good," he said. "You always drink that stuff in the morning?"

"No. Sometime today I have to get some real sleep."

"You look lousy."

"Yeah. I know."

Corpora's doughnuts arrived. He carefully unfolded a paper napkin and tucked it in the collar of his shirt, patting it flat across his chest. He picked up a doughnut and ate it leaning forward, letting the powdered sugar fall back onto the paper plate. Each time he finished chewing, he delicately licked the ends of his fingers. " 'Kay," he said, "watcha got for me."

Guyer undid the rubber band and slid a photo out. The computer reproduced photos on special paper with a brand name in blue script repeated across the back.

Corpora stared for a moment. "This the real guy?"

"Look-alike."

"Hunh. But this is what he *looks* like, this is the impression he gives?"

"No," Guyer said. He thought for a moment, hunting for List's line about Benauti. "No, it isn't what he looks like. He looks like after he's walked through a room there should be a snail-track on the wall."

"Ah so," Corpora said. " 'Cause going by this we'd just as like haul in the Omani vice-consul."

"Homemade job," Guyer said. "Best we could do with the time we had."

"Helluva lot better than nothing," Corpora said, holding the photo by one corner to keep it away from the powdered sugar. After a moment he said, "You want to spend some money?"

"That's what I said yesterday. Nothing's changed."

"I mean with this either you spend money or you don't."

"I know."

"Okay. Now what I think is that this guy is liable to be moving around. When they're nervous, they run. He could've gone down some hole in Brooklyn with a helper to go to the market once a day and if he did that nobody is ever going to find him. That's what I told you yesterday. But then I thought about it, and you'd be surprised at how people don't do that. Even if they think they're going to do that. They get someplace. And then that place don't *feel* right. So they figure they'll be safer someplace else. So they go there. And then *that* place don't feel right. Somebody looks at them cross-eyed, or they hear noises in the next room, or they think the motel maid is a FBI. They jump around, here to there to here, and they make mistakes. The one exception to all this is a guy who's at home on the ground. You and me could do this, but you tell me this guy's a foreigner. That's the key. You with me this far?"

"Yes."

"So what I do—and I thank you for making copies but I need many more than this—is I put out a picture. On a Telecopier. Quality reproduction, you can get a very good image."

"Put out to who?"

"Well I got people in every bus station, airport, train terminal, you name it. Car-rental agencies, whatever, in all the major cities."

"Jesus Christ!"

"What?"

"I can't afford that."

"Ten grand you can't afford?"

"For all that?"

"Look, I like everything simple. That's my secret. Everything in life simple, that way nobody gets confused. I don't pay anybody. I'm talking about the private security people who are already *in* those places. They're paid to hang around all day and look at people. And when they go off at 4:30 they got a relief who comes on and then that guy hangs around until 12:00 when the night man shows up. See, there are these profiles—hijackers, heisters, terrorists, whatever you got. So these guys are paid to watch the crowd go by, and they see something they recognize they watch and see what happens. So what I do is offer a reward. Spot this guy, you're ten grand richer. Now that makes for a more interesting day. Because you know, security work, well, what it is, is fucking boring. You spend your life waiting for some guy to show up and do something. And mostly he never shows up or if he does, he doesn't do anything. Or if he does something, it isn't what you thought he was gonna do. Boring. So a ten-thousand-dollar reward is very motivating. I mean most guys never see it, but it makes for a better day, see?"

"Okay, that's ten."

"Then, there's guys who have to be on call if something happens. Now I'll go in and take him myself. You pay me for that and I'll do it, it isn't a problem. But the better way is to involve a few people, because that way it's not so likely to cause a scene in public. Now for the guys on call, that costs you nothing. It costs *me* something, but that's okay. But if we get a bingo, then these guys move and it costs you some money."

"How much?"

"Hard to say. I'm giving you rates to the trade as it is. And if I go over bid, I'm not going to eat the expense. Let's say this: With everything, my fee, extra people, reward, you're not going to get in it for more than twenty grand. If it's more, it won't be much more. Keep in mind that for top money you get your guy. If we strike out, then you pay me five grand for my trouble. And that, believe me, is to the trade. So?"

Guyer ate a doughnut and washed it down with the last of the ginger ale. Money wasn't the problem, not really. It was the gray area that lay beyond the money: if they got him, or if they didn't. "How much up front?" he said.

"For you? Couple grand, whatever's handy."

"Say I meet you at the bank about 10:30. Forty-sixth and Madison, northwest corner."

"I'll be there."

Guyer put a five on the counter for the food, and stood up. "See you then," he said. Corpora waved and drank coffee with his other hand.

He moved into the early-morning crowds around Penn Station. Home was too far away to go, the office wouldn't open until 8:00 or so, and he didn't want to be there anyhow. The twenty grand, assuming that Benauti was stupid enough to get himself caught, would take the account down very close to the bone. And what he really wanted that twenty grand for was to get on a plane. He had to spend the five, maybe not so much to actually find Benauti, more to let the world know that he was looking, high and low, with the best help that could be bought. What the State Department would call *a gesture of will*. The action presumed a future, for Guyer, for Metro Data Research, and that's

[221]

where the problem really lay. Because he'd had it. He fought the idea—it was reflexive in him to kick back against failure—but it flowed over the top of his defenses and settled in. He walked aimlessly, hands plunged in raincoat pockets, and gave himself the usual sermons: he was tired, exhaustion always painted the future black. He'd been tricked, but he could build new defenses against that. He hadn't lost the war, only a battle. He was at the bottom of a trough, now all he had to do was climb up the other side.

It was like tapping a steel wall with a pencil. He *was* tired, his eyes itched as though there were grit beneath the lids, his skin felt hot, a thick, woolly space divided him from the sensed world. There was one salvation only: the plane to nowhere. A place that wasn't especially a place, that was the point, the key to it. Somewhere flat, with wide, clean streets where everybody went to work five days a week, played on the sixth, rested the seventh, then started all over again. That was a vision, he knew, that would not change with sleep and recovery.

He found an open movie theatre, paid, and went in. It was close to Times Square and most of the people inside were asleep. His eyes stayed on the screen, a discipline to stay awake, but he didn't see the movie. He made himself get up at 10:00 in order to meet Corpora at the bank. Instinctively he stopped at a payphone and called the office. Kevin answered, told him that Edna had phoned, and that she wouldn't be in for the rest of the week. Mr. List had not appeared. There were no phone messages that demanded his attention. After hanging up, he felt a pang of conscience about Kevin. He was faithful, never failed, was always there. If there was any money left after the business wound down, he had to do something for Kevin. He'd taken him too much for granted. As for Mr. List not being in, he thought, that was probably permanent. He wondered if he'd ever find out what really happened.

Richard List was drifting slowly through a thick fog of Demerol. He felt peaceful, warm and free. Every once in a while he would catch a glimpse of a blurred, floating face and a bad feeling stirred and tried to reach out for him, but the Demerol would rise from the center of his body and smooth the white fog shut and then there was nothing to see, and nothing to feel bad about. Which left his mind free to pursue dozens of amusing thoughts. In Morphia, that perfect place, he was astonished by the sweetness of the images his mind made for him, and the best thing was simply to wait by the banks of the river and enjoy them as they flowed by.

He was in a bed at St. Vincent's Hospital. After a long evening of hard work, putting together the photo of Benauti, he'd felt pretty good. Better than he had in some time. Working with Guyer, burning up the computer, making it perform like the beautiful piece of electronics it was, felt like old times. He'd locked up the office and emerged at midnight. He was hungry. He'd nibbled on one or two of Guyer's horrid roast beef sandwiches, but now he had an appetite for real food. His most recent favorite place was in the Italian section of the Village, and there they had a veal piccata that would make a dead man sit up and sing arias. It was the veal, he thought, tender and white. They were getting it someplace special, and there was somebody in that kitchen who knew what to do with it. They had also a Lachryma Christi, grown on volcanic slopes, with a taste like no other wine in the world. Dry, severe, and full, all at the same instant, and the second glass was better than the first. He flagged a cab, told the driver how to find Propizio, and settled back to enjoy

[223]

the ride. Night Manhattan, lights and lovers—it was at least so in his mood—rolled past the cab windows for his pleasure.

The green Volvo followed him all the way downtown. In front of the restaurant he paid off the cab and got as far as the sidewalk when he heard a sharp whistle behind him. He turned around, naturally curious as to who would greet him in that way. He saw the car, and recognized it. He caught a glimpse of Guyer, sitting in the backseat this time, staring at him angrily through the window. He thought *what have I done?* There wasn't much time to think about that. He tried to protect himself as best he could, but with the bad leg it was a lost cause from the start. One of them kicked the cane out of his hand. He heard it clatter in the street. Then from the other side somebody hit him below the ribs and it hurt him so badly that he sang with pain and was embarrassed at the sound he'd made. The first one broke his nose, and with the tears filling his eyes, he didn't see anything after that. Just fell down on the cold pavement and tried to pretend they'd knocked him unconscious. That didn't work because each time they kicked him he cried out. Some people came out of the restaurant in the middle of it, saw what was happening, and went back inside. When it was over and the Volvo had driven away they called the police.

THEY TOOK BENAUTI on Wednesday, in the men's room of a Holiday Inn at a thruway plaza near Glens Falls, New York.

It had been planned for him to fly out Sunday evening, a few hours after the "Delatte" incident. He had prepaid a lease for a small efficiency apartment in Fort-de-France, on the island of Martinique. He had a French passport under a fictitious name, and because of the French nationality he would not require a *carte de séjour* for the island, a French possession. He had enough money to stay for a year if he had to. The schedule was set up this way: At 4:00 P.M. on Sunday he was to meet Delatte, and arrangements were on to get him safely to the airport and out on a flight before the heat was fully on. He had possession of the documents for his residence in Martinique, but Delatte kept the exit arrangements to himself. This was for insurance purposes and Benauti felt no resentment because of it, controllers habitually held something back. They did not trust him, he did not trust them, that was the normal state of affairs.

He was early for his meeting with Delatte. The pressure had been building in him since the final meeting with Guyer, and by Sunday it was almost unbearable. The reason they kept him in New York, he felt, was that he was an asset—something to be sacrificed if the operation fell apart. So he had spent the last two weeks in a hotel room, eating room-service food, hoping that nothing went wrong. Delatte, his face darkened several tones by a sunlamp, was hiding in an apartment in a twenty-story housing project on 118th Street in Spanish Harlem. Benauti entered the neighborhood a little after 3:00 P.M. and immediately went to the apartment. Going early had violated procedure—he'd intended to circle in cautiously—but he was terrified in the streets. In his expensive overcoat he was much too obvious, and he could feel the sharks gathering. From every corner, long cold stares confirmed his status as prime target. The building itself was a hell of blasting radios, fried garlic, and packs of roving teen-agers. He found the apartment, knocked on the door, but Delatte did not answer. He could hear a radio playing inside, but he supposed that was a ruse to deter predatory junkies. He waited by the apartment door because he did not know where else to go, and because Delatte might return any minute. He could not afford to miss the rendezvous. As people went in and out of other apartments on the floor, he smiled at them in what he hoped was an ingratiating manner and gestured toward the door to explain what he was doing there. Nobody smiled back. 4:00 P.M. passed. He was sweating. He decided, at 4:30, that Delatte had not heard his knock and beat hard on the door, calling out in French. There was no answer. Through a window at the end of the corridor he could see it was getting dark and he did not want to go out in the streets alone. He tried for the last time at 6:30. Kicking at the metal door and yelling as loud as he dared. Every sort of possible terror visited him. He was in the wrong building, on the wrong floor, at the wrong apartment. He tried to ask a passing woman about the tenant of the apartment, but she swept around him in a wide arc and clutched her handbag to her breast. The worst fear was that he had been abandoned on purpose, that he was being set up, to be arrested or murdered. A little before 7:00 he left the building. Someone yelled at him in Spanish. He saw a bus pulling to a stop outside the project and ran blindly toward it, not caring where it went. Inside, he sat behind the driver, his wet shirt drying in the cold air.

He got off the bus in the Seventies, on the East Side. He found a restaurant and went in and ate a dinner, anything to get off the streets. He'd had contact with the security forces of several countries and he imagined teletyped descriptions of him burning up the wires. He knew enough not to go anywhere near an airport or a train station, and he was afraid to go back to his hotel in case his worst fears were confirmed and he had been thrown to the wolves. He was, he realized, on his own, and would have to think his way out of the situation. He left the restaurant, hailed a cab, and told the driver he was a tourist, bored with staying in Manhattan, what would he suggest? The driver took him to a small hotel in Brooklyn Heights. Arriving, he sensed immediately that it was a place not much visited by the authorities, but there were a number of rough-looking people hanging about and he feared for his safety. He was carrying thousands of dollars in cash, and from the way they looked at him he felt certain that they knew it. Sunday night he stayed in the room with his door chained from the inside, lying naked beneath the covers, his sweated-through clothing hung on chairs and doorknobs. The hotel got noisier as the night went on, drunken laughter, loud radios. Somewhere down the hall glass shattered and a man yelled obscenities. He tried to sleep, but in the end he was too frightened and so stayed up with the lights on, staring out the cloudy window at a bricked-in courtyard. At dawn, he checked out.

He took a cab uptown, to Eighth Avenue in the Forties, and found a large, busy hotel. Here he had a shower, and ate a breakfast of eggs and toast in the coffee shop. He wanted badly to go for a walk, but decided it wasn't worth it to expose himself on the street. He slept the morning away, then sat down in the afternoon to think things through. The last two weeks of hotel living had made him claustrophobic, the walls were closing in on him, he didn't think he could stick with it much longer. He bought a newspaper and discovered that the project had gone off successfully. Why Delatte had abandoned him he did not know, but on consideration there were many possible scenarios, some of them benign. For one thing, Delatte was not operating independently. There was an organization, probably a national intelligence service, behind him. After one meeting at his hotel, he had gone down to the lobby to buy a newspaper and had seen Delatte talking to a man he thought he recognized from somewhere, though he could not remember where. He had gotten back on the elevator before they saw him. Whoever they were, they certainly had sufficient power to change Delatte's plans on short notice. He paced back and forth in his room, looked out the window, and picked over his options. There were two threats: Guyer and his people, and the American police. The former hadn't the resources to find him, not in a city of New York's size, and the latter, historically, tried hard at the beginning and then lost interest as new felonies were piled on old ones. Because of the particular way they had worked Guyer, he wondered if the authorities had even been informed —usually it was better to hide your mistakes. But, he reasoned, he could not take that for granted, he would have to act as though he were of interest to the police.

He decided to give it another day and then try for Fort-de-France. He would take a bus to Montreal and fly into the Caribbean from there, then short-hop to Martinique. The FBI had no jurisdiction in Canada. Perhaps they had informed the RCMP, but bulletins of information passing between national police services, he knew, were not of the first priority. It was a gamble, there was passport control at the border, but the Canadian-American frontier was not the nightmare one found elsewhere. Besides, there were hundreds of border crossings, and Canadians were traditionally less hostile and suspicious than American customs personnel. Public bus was the answer. It was the most anonymous, and somehow unlikely, method of travel. He thus avoided airports and, once in Canada, could speak French and blend in better. If he had to lie low and wait a few weeks to cool off, he would at least be away from Guyer's immediate area. He called Greyhound and learned there was a bus to Montreal at 10:04 A.M. on Wednesday morning. With less than forty-eight hours to spend in New York, he relaxed. His confidence returned. Sunday night had been terrifying, but here it was Monday afternoon and he was still a free man. He had money, he had a place to go. With Delatte free and again at large, there might be more work for him in the future. He had, after all, pulled it off. What stood between him and total freedom was a longish bus ride, but he could easily put up with that. He had, after all, been in much worse spots than this and survived.

They had him Wednesday morning, ten minutes after he entered the terminal. A security employee spotted him, a woman in her late forties who sat in the waiting room all day long with a battered suitcase parked by her feet. She had gotten the job after taking a course in security work she'd seen advertised in the back of a magazine. On Tuesday afternoon she'd received a copy of the photo *and* a personal telephone call from Corpora, who'd had a good deal of experience with people trying to flee the country. He had observed that if they were carrying cash, and they usually were, they never went to Mexico. Not if they had a brain in their head. They were smart enough to avoid airports, where agents of at least three different services were in evidence. They all believed that people riding long-distance bus lines were invisible. They all believed that the Canadian border was a soft penetration. And they were, all of them, absolutely correct. They simply didn't realize how many others made the same assumptions. The woman, carrying her suitcase, tracked Benauti to the ticket window, then to the platform from which the Montreal bus departed. She went to a public telephone, called Corpora's beeper number, and twenty seconds later got a call-back. Corpora had rented a room at a midtown motel and had a car and driver waiting downstairs. From the woman's description of Benauti's clothing and manner, matched up with Guyer's, he was fairly sure they had a hit. The woman was overjoyed. She had dental bills and a dying car, and ten thousand dollars would bail her out just fine. She signed off with professional abruptness but could not keep the excitement from her voice. When Corpora hung up, he grabbed a road atlas and a bus schedule from a huge pile of papers spread out on the bed, made two fast phone calls, hurried downstairs, and directed his driver toward La Guardia airport. As the car pulled away from the curb, he smiled. *Montreal,* he thought, *life should only be that easy.*

Benauti had planned not to get off the bus until he'd

left the country. He woke early Wednesday morning, a little too edgy for breakfast. But he knew he'd be hungry later. After he checked out and paid his bill, he walked south toward the bus terminal. On the way he spotted a convenience grocery and bought a large assortment of dried fruit: apricots, peaches, and figs. The boy behind the counter tried hard to please, and sealed the fruit in double layers of plastic wrap to keep it nice and fresh, then slid it into a paper bag and rolled the top over. That was all the luggage he had, the few clothes he'd bought while in New York were cheap and meant to be disposable. He'd had no intention of carrying a suitcase to Delatte's apartment. As an afterthought he bought a bottle of mineral water, thanked the boy, and headed for the bus terminal.

He bought a ticket and boarded the bus without difficulty, then chose a seat in the middle, next to the window. He'd felt very inconspicuous in the terminal, hidden among crowds of people moving about. When the bus pulled out of the underground tunnel and rode through the city streets, he breathed a sigh of relief. The bus itself made him feel secure: it was huge and sturdy, driven by diesels of great power that roared politely and altered pitch as the driver changed up through the gears. The windows were tinted to protect the passenger from the sun. Settled in the comfortable seat, listening to the engine purr, staring out at the city through thick green glass, he felt removed, enclosed, and safer than he had in a long time. Once the bus reached a thruway, Route 87 North, the motion became fluid and the hum of the engines threatened to send him to sleep. He ate some dried fruit, sipped at the bottle of mineral water, and watched the play of traffic on the thruway. After an hour he decided to take a nap. Took off his coat, folded it carefully, and set it on the seat beside him. It was an expensive coat, made of heavy wool, bought in Germany the previous winter. He closed his eyes, felt tension draining from him, and dozed.

He woke when the bus pulled in to a rest stop. His mouth tasted terrible and he needed to use the bus's rest room immediately. He stood, for a time, by the door, but the OCCUPIED sign did not move. Annoyed, he walked quickly from the bus toward the large restaurant-motel complex across from myriad lanes of gas pumps. The men's room was busy, toilets flushing, hand-dryers humming. He waited until a urinal came free, then stepped up to it. He was startled by the sound of loud, boisterous singing, and turned his head toward the source of the noise. It was a very fat man, standing in front of a urinal at the far end of the rank and singing at the top of his lungs, head thrown back, voice echoing off the white tiled walls. The fat man was singing a dirty song—he caught the words *monkey* and *flagpole*—and some of the men in the bathroom snickered, but most looked away, embarrassed. Benauti looked away also, this was inappropriate behavior and he had the unpleasant reaction experienced in the presence of people who are doing something strange in public. Something pushed hard against his left buttock, and he was half turned, angrily, to protest, when he froze, then sagged forward. He tried to put one hand on the wall to steady himself but his arm would not respond and became pinned between his body and the edge of the urinal. His senses were intact, but his muscles had turned to liquid. Immediately, helping hands caught his weight before he could slide to the floor. There were two men, they supported him from either side and walked him out of the rest room, past a gift shop, telephone booths, and vending machines that sold candy and road maps. One of the men said, "Pardon us, please, this man is ill." A path cleared, concerned eyes watching from both sides. Benauti knew he was being abducted. "Please call the police," he said, "please help me." But all that came out were garbled sounds, gibberish. People moved farther away. As the three of them left the restaurant, a car pulled up and the two men carefully slid him into the backseat, then climbed in after him. The fat man got in the front of the car, and they drove away from the plaza, down a long exit lane that merged with the thruway. Benauti realized that he was dying. His heart was fibrillating. It would beat two or three times very rapidly, then pause, then stutter again. He opened his mouth and tried to plead for help but nothing at all came out. The man sitting next to him picked up his arm, which flopped like a dead thing, rolled up his jacket and shirt sleeves, and injected him in the forearm with a hypodermic needle. A moment later his heart adjusted, and he could breathe again. A prayer of thanks entered his mind as he fell deeply asleep. Fifteen minutes later the bus left. Benauti's overcoat and his bag of dried fruit and bottle of mineral water left with it.

"Why so sad?" she said.

"Who said I was sad?"

"Just the way you lie there, not looking at anything."

He turned toward her. "Now I'm looking at you. Is that better?"

"It's a step."

She was lying on her side, facing him, covers pushed down to her waist even though it was cool in the bedroom. The window was open an inch and it was raining and blowing outside and making the curtains shift. She was smoking a mentholated cigarette, a pink ceramic ashtray resting on the sheet between them. She looked very young, hair plastered to her forehead, without makeup, face slightly flushed. He tried to remember

[235]

what she used to look like. He thought, *People never look the same to each other after they've made love.*

He'd been at her apartment since Tuesday. After he met Corpora at the bank and paid him, he'd walked and walked, finally found himself in front of her building. He telephoned from across the street. She wanted to see him. When they woke up late Wednesday morning, he'd called the office and again found only Kevin. He left Maggie's number—for Corpora only—and told Kevin he wouldn't be in for the rest of the day.

"You going to take me out for dinner tonight?" she said.

"Sure. What would you like?"

"What would *you* like?"

"Good BLT'd be nice." She popped him a good one on the left shoulder with her fist. It was a clumsy swing but it had some force to it. They'd attempted BLT's for their dinner the night before. She had fried the bacon so stiff that it shattered on the first bite. Even the toast turned out wrong. She had sent the doorman out for bacon, lettuce, tomatoes, mayonnaise, bread, potato chips, and beer and Guyer had tipped him a twenty on top of the bill. The BLT's had come to around fourteen dollars apiece, he figured.

Watching her face, he realized that she was playing, but he really had hurt her feelings. That he could do that surprised him. "I see," he said, "that you'd rather not have BLT's again."

"You behave," she said.

He looked at his watch. "Maybe we should wait an hour and then decide. It's 2:30. Little early for dinner, no?"

"Sometime when you're not lookin' I'm gonna hit that thing with a stick."

"As long as I can take it off first."

"You mean it actually comes off?"

He stripped the watch from his wrist and laid it on

the carpet by the bed. When he shifted back toward her, she was stubbing the cigarette out carefully, as though she were making a decision. Then she put the ashtray on the night table on her side of the bed. Now the space between them was clear. She propped herself up on one elbow and grinned at him for a second. "Bring that ear over here," she said.

He moved his body against hers. She moved away an inch. "Not the whole thing. I said the ear."

He inclined his head, she spoke very softly. "You like me."

"Yeah."

"A lot."

He reached around and drew a line with his index finger across her forehead, tucking her hair behind one ear and smoothing it down.

"You better watch out. I might decide to believe that."

He moved away from her and rested his head on his hand so their positions matched. They stared at each other. Just before it became uncomfortable she said, "That's really true, isn't it. That you feel that way. You're not tryin' to screw my head around."

"Nope."

"How come you feel like that?"

He silently shook his head that he didn't know why. She glanced away for an instant. When her eyes returned they were shining and her look changed suddenly, became shy, soft, and triumphant all at once. Then, as though she didn't want him to see everything he had seen, she hid by moving quickly against him, butting her head into his chest. He felt her make a sound against his skin. He wasn't sure what it meant and he tried to lift her head up, gently, so he could see her face. She shook her head no, that she didn't want to be moved, so he rested his hand on the side of her face. They stayed like that for a minute, then she reached up and pulled his head down next to hers. He moved his arms around her and started to stroke her back. "Wait a second," she whispered.

"Okay," he whispered.

"Pull up the blankets."

He did it. They were in a cave under the covers. "Why are we whispering?" he asked, kidding her a little.

"I don't know," she said. Then she said, "So they don't hear."

"Who?"

"Them."

"They can burn in hell," Guyer whispered.

"Oh *yeah,*" she said.

She was fast asleep, her mouth slightly open, teeth only just visible, and he listened to her breathing, long and slow. She slept with the pillow crushed in half between her forearm and head. Through the slit in the curtain he was conscious of the weather, dark and violent, rain drumming hard against the window glass. The silence made by the two sounds, her breathing and the rain, was something he had never heard before.

When the telephone rang he didn't move at all. Instead he watched her. Her eyes opened after the first ring. She blinked. It rang again. It was a small phone and the way it rang made it sound like it was far away. He waited for it to stop, aware that she was fully awake and had no intention of answering it. He counted the rings, and after number twelve he closed his eyes for a moment and then reached across her and picked it up.

"Yes?"

"Guyer?" It was Corpora.

"Yes."

"We got what you want."

Guyer was silent.

"You hear what I said?"

"Yes. Good."

"There's a private airfield, out past Port Jefferson, on Long Island Sound. Can you find it?"

"Yes."

"We're flying in from upstate. You be there in an hour." The voice didn't leave him room to say no.

"I'll be there."

"Not bad, hunh?"

"Very fast."

"About twenty-six hours, I figure. And it's in perfect condition. You follow? One of my people saw it, and we went and got it, and everything went very nicely. So now all we need is you."

"Okay."

"See you there," Corpora said, and hung up.

He climbed off the bed and got dressed, like a man who weighed a thousand pounds. Maggie watched him silently. Slowly he buttoned his shirt. He'd had to try to find Benauti, he realized, but he hadn't wanted to find him. He damned Corpora for his efficiency, Benauti for his clumsiness, himself for things he didn't want to name. He stepped into his trousers and pushed his shirttail down, zipped the fly, and buckled his belt.

"I was in bed with a guy a little while ago. You seen him anywhere?"

"He'll be back."

She raised her eyebrows. "Oh yeah?"

"Yeah."

"When's that?"

He stood still for a moment. Everything said *stay*. "I don't know," he said. Then went back to getting dressed. "The minute I can. I'll try to call."

She nodded to herself and made a dumb face. "He says he'll call."

"Hey," he said, his mouth a little twisted.

"Okay," she said. It was half a warning, half a truce, and all, for the moment, he was going to get.

He put on his raincoat, looked at her a last time, and left. He made sure the door would lock behind him, went down in the elevator and out into the street to look for a cab that wanted to go to Long Island.

Corpora was waiting for him at the edge of the deserted parking area and they walked together out toward the plane. It was just after 5:00 P.M., the daylight was fading fast and it was very cold. Guyer lowered his head and clenched his teeth to keep from shivering. The wind, blowing hard off Long Island Sound, made conversation difficult, and the walk across the field seemed to take a long time. The asphalt on the runway was cracked, with stubborn grass trying to grow up through the fissures. The airplane was idling, he could see the metal skin vibrate and blue smoke whip away from the exhaust manifolds in the stiff breeze. It was an old twin-engine Fairchild STOL, made to carry small amounts of freight over short distances. It could cruise at low airspeed, 40 mph, and land or take off almost anywhere. There was a man waiting for them by a set of portable steps in front of the open cargo door. He nodded at Guyer and waved him in. Climbing the steps, he was struck by a sudden perfect apprehension, a déjà vu, as though the scene were mirrored, at that moment, a hundred times in a hundred other places: bulky men in suits climbing aboard a small airplane, at dusk, on a runway lined by tall reeds thrashing in the November wind.

He saw Benauti as soon as he entered the plane. He was sitting directly opposite the door, his back propped against a collapsed cardboard box. His wrists and ankles each wore a set of plastic ring-locks. He appeared to be semicomatose: mouth hanging loose, eyes nearly closed, head jiggling slightly with the plane's vibration. Guyer waited while Corpora entered, then the other man followed, lifting the step unit up after him. He rolled the door closed, using both hands. It made a harsh metallic squeak, then shut with a loud bang. Guyer felt Corpora's heavy hand on his shoulder, guiding him toward the front of the plane. There were four seats in the cockpit, the second pair set behind the pilot and copilot. The pilot was a man in his thirties with olive skin and black curly hair, wearing a green tanker jacket. Guyer realized that they'd met before, but he couldn't remember where. They nodded to each other. The other man, who'd pulled up the steps, stooped to enter the cockpit. Guyer guessed him to be in his fifties. He was tall and beefy with white brush-cut hair and skin mottled dark red from the cold, or from alcohol. "This is Doc," Corpora said. They shook hands silently, the man looked Guyer over carefully, then sat in the copilot's seat.

"Where are we going?" Guyer asked.

The engine pitch rose sharply, the plane taxied down the runway. Corpora pointed with his index finger, moving his hand vertically. "Up," he said. The plane accelerated, Guyer snapped the seat belt around his waist. Abruptly they lifted off the ground, gained altitude, then banked gently and headed east above the lights of Long Island. Corpora tapped the man he called Doc on the shoulder and jerked his thumb toward the cargo hold. The man stood, picked up a small leather case, and walked toward the rear.

"Be a minute," Corpora said to Guyer.

Guyer stared out the window, his stomach tight. The lights below fell into the patterns of their subdivisions: some curving predictably, others in squared blocks. The curving ones all seemed to have amber streetlights.

"It was pretty sweet," Corpora said. He took off his sunglasses, folded them carefully, and tucked them into the breast pocket of his suit jacket. "Doc back there," he continued, "came up behind him in the men's room at a service plaza on the thruway and hit him in the ass with an inoculator." Corpora smiled grimly. "Boom good-bye," he said. "You know those air-driven things they use for mass inoculation?"

"Yeah."

"Well, all you get is an intradermal. Usual effect time for an ID is twenty minutes. So we had to use a very concentrated dose, then hit him in a vein once we got him in the car, that way the antidote beats the drug. Ephenarene. You know it?"

"No I don't."

"We damn near lost him."

"Where was he going?"

"Montreal by Greyhound."

"Makes sense."

"Yeah, except that fuckin' everybody does it."

"Where'd you pick him up?"

"Right in the waiting room of the bus terminal. We flew up to the first rest stop and rented a car. If he didn't get off, we were gonna try and get somebody on the bus with him. If not, we would have followed in the car. But I didn't want to go into Canada. We figured if he gets off, he goes to the can. So I had Doc waiting in a stall. We got lucky."

Guyer turned back to the window. Suddenly the lights below ended and there was total blackness beneath the plane. The wing-tip flashers lit off every two seconds. The plane, now freed of thermals rising off the landmass, ran smoother and the engine pitch dropped. Guyer felt the pilot throttle back. There was an occasional white wave-top faintly visible below. They were over the Atlantic. He was aware of a presence behind him, Doc stood awkwardly in the hatchway. He tapped Corpora on the shoulder. "Ready when you are," he said.

"Let's get it over with," Corpora said.

Stooping, they moved to the center of the plane. Guyer ran one hand along the metal stanchions to steady himself. Benauti's condition had altered violently—whatever Doc had given him had brought him back flush with reality. His eyes were wide open and alert and there was a fine film of sweat on his forehead, though it was very cold in the plane. The other two men moved away, Guyer squatted so that he was eye-level with Benauti.

For a time he didn't say anything, just waited patiently for Benauti to begin, but the man stared back at him. Guyer spoke as softly as he could, his voice barely rising above the noise level. "The easiest way is if you'll just begin at the beginning and take me through it one step at a time."

Benauti said nothing, his chest rose and fell as he breathed.

"If you'll start at the beginning, it'll all come."

Benauti stared.

"No? You want me to work for it?" He tried to read Benauti's eyes, they weren't exactly defiant, something else. He let the silence ride. "Threats, then. That what it needs?" Again, he waited.

"What is there to tell?" Benauti said.

"Start at the beginning. We have lots of time."

"What? What do you think I know?"

Guyer nodded casually. "Well, I'd really like to hear from you who ran it. You could say, of course, that it was a man in a mask, or a man who sat in darkness while a light was shone in your eyes. But you know that I wouldn't believe anything of that sort."

"A man in a mask!" The voice was rich with contempt.

Guyer waited.

"You want to hear that Raoul Delatte told me what to do? Hear it, then."

"And?"

"And that is what I know. The fact is what you have for all this."

Guyer nodded. "There were others," he said, off-handedly.

"Oh yes. *Sans doute.* Perhaps whole squads of KGB." He shrugged his shoulders violently. Guyer waited. Benauti closed his eyes for a moment. When he started again, his voice had calmed. "I take messages. From one man to another man." He looked hard at Guyer. "Is it your belief that I am important? Truly?"

Guyer shifted his position. "I'd like to find Delatte. How would you suggest I go about that?"

Benauti laughed, harsh and sudden. "You cannot know anything about him if you believe that *he* would tell *me* such things."

Guyer felt his poise slip a notch. "Tell you why I want to know. There was a perfectly decent man who died in order that Delatte could buy a month of time to maneuver in. I don't like that, because it was my hand that did it. Do you see?"

Benauti crowed. "So! A moralist! It is rare in this business."

"He wanted to live," Guyer said quietly.

"Did he." Benauti fairly screamed it, holding his cuffed wrists in front of Guyer's face.

Guyer just nodded yes. Benauti changed his voice so that he wheedled like a street-peddler. "Was he not paid?" Guyer was silent. "Were you not paid?"

"When Delatte first came to New York—" He was interrupted by a loud screech of metal and an icy blast of wind that almost knocked him over on top of Benauti. Simultaneously, he fought for balance and looked behind him. Corpora had shoved the cargo door open wide, so that the black night rushed past and the engine noise screamed.

He turned back to face Benauti. Watched him lick his lips and struggle for control, sweat now standing in beads on his forehead. "Please wait a little," he said. His chest was rising and falling rapidly.

[244]

Guyer counted to ten. It was hard to think amid the wind and noise. "When Delatte first came to New York, what did he tell you to do?"

"What I did. What you already know. I found first the blond man. Then you. We bargain." His tone implied that such details were common, trite, beneath consideration.

"Where was he hiding?"

"On 118th Street. In the poor district. But he is gone from there now."

"When? When did he first go there?"

"September, I think. Yes, September."

"Under what name?"

"He used the name Ricard."

"How many times did you see him there?"

"Just one time."

"After that?"

"I telephoned a number."

"What number?"

"I cannot remember."

"You spoke in French? Arabic?"

"English."

"You were to get out afterward. Alone?"

"No."

"Who was to help you?"

"Delatte."

"Did he?"

"No. He left me." He seemed to sag back a little. "Water, please."

Guyer looked at Corpora. "No water," he said. "There's a Pepsi. He want that?"

"Please," Benauti said.

Corpora went away toward the cockpit, and returned a moment later with the soda. He handed it to Guyer. Guyer peeled back the flip top and handed the can to Benauti, who drank deeply, holding the can in both hands because of the plastic cuffs.

"Is there more? More that you can tell me?"

Benauti shrugged, shook his head. Then mumbled something in another language. Guyer said, "What?"

Benauti stared at him, his eyes were strange, as though something inside him had closed up. "I say you one thing"—his voice was low and flat—"it is the wind you chase."

Guyer stood. His legs hurt from holding the uncomfortable position. Corpora moved next to him. "Well?" He had to speak loud, and close to Guyer's ear, to be heard above the noise from the open door.

"Not much," Guyer said. Corpora nodded sympathetically, mouth glum. "He's nothing," Guyer continued, "we can put him down at some airport someplace and he'll vanish into the night."

"C'mon. We'll go up front," Corpora said. He made a small motion to Doc.

"I'm serious," Guyer said. "The hell with him. We tried. You did your job, I did mine. We came up empty."

"Yeah," Corpora said. "Let's go up there and sit down."

"Look—" Guyer said.

Corpora cut him off, now speaking very close to his ear. "No, you look. I don't care about you. It's me I care about, and the people who work for me. You want to leave something lying around that can come back and hurt you, you do that *alone*. You don't involve me in something like that." He put a hand on Guyer's arm and said in a softer tone, "Okay? We'll just go up front now."

Guyer hesitated. Corpora's hand grew heavy on his arm. The message was clear. They went up to the cockpit together and sat in the passenger seats. Corpora picked at some dead skin near his thumbnail, then looked past the pilot at one of the green-lit dials. Guyer glanced down, the ocean was black below them. He heard, after a minute, two muted but distinct bangs, as though somebody in the cargo area had rapped a signal on the metal skin of the plane. The pilot looked over his shoulder, Corpora made a slight gesture with his head and the plane banked, the left wing lowered, then rose again after a few seconds. Guyer heard the grating noise as the cargo door was rolled shut. A few seconds later Doc appeared in the hatchway. He was lighting a pipe, his cheeks sucked in as he pulled at it, the match flame drawn down into the tobacco. After he got it lit, thick smoke rising from the bowl, he held out a handful of cloth squares. "Clothing labels," he said. Guyer looked away. Corpora said, "Put it with the other stuff. Take care of it later." Doc said "Mm-hm" around the pipestem and sat next to the pilot.

"Sorry, my friend," Corpora said, "but what must be . . ." His voice was gentle. Guyer felt a pulse beating hard near his temple and shifted his position so Corpora could not see it.

"What's our time in?" Corpora asked the pilot.

"Twenty minutes." He reached out and tapped the dial Corpora had looked at earlier.

"Bad gauge?" Corpora said.

"Yeah," the pilot said. "Not important."

Corpora gave a low grunt of irritation, then settled back in his seat. Guyer looked out the window. Lights reappeared below, houses, streets, streams of cars moving along the arterials. "A favor," he said.

"What?" Corpora said.

"I need to go to Washington, D.C."

Corpora asked the pilot if that was a problem. The pilot said it wasn't, they had plenty of fuel. Corpora and the pilot discussed which airfield to use. Doc suggested one in Virginia. Corpora said College Park, Maryland, was better because Guyer could rent a car there. For twenty minutes they talked—louder than necessary, their voices animated and urgent—about airfields, rental agencies, and access highways. Guyer listened, from a great distance. It was not for his benefit, not really, although that was the frame of the conversation. It was for themselves. It gave them something to do—arrangements, particulars, times, numbers, locations—some neutral area in which to dispute, so that a certain presence could be banished from the crowded cockpit. He tried to name it, his concentration itself a refuge. After a long time the best word he could find was embarrassment.

Mains

THERE IS A law in Washington, D.C., that no building may exceed the height of the Washington Monument, which rises thirteen stories. Given that limitation, Mains, Gulbenyan and Associates had situated themselves for maximum power effect. Their offices occupied the twelfth and thirteenth floors of a building located in the middle of the K Street corridor that runs, lined by linden and plane trees, straight into the heart of the government. The street was also host to the American Association of Manufacturers, the International Monetary Fund, and others equally influential though perhaps less well known. The building itself was a box made of bronze glass, which reflected the sky and thus glittered on sunny days and darkened on somber ones. The lobby—dark red marble floor and black Plexiglas walls—had at its mathematical center a stainless steel sculpture of a seagull in flight.

[251]

Guyer had spent Wednesday night in a motel on Route 1 in Maryland. After checking in, he drove to a nearby shopping plaza and bought razor and shaving cream, toothbrush and toothpaste. He spent a long time choosing between brands. In another store he bought underwear and socks, and an inexpensive white dress shirt. Returning to the motel, he parked the rental Ford precisely between the white lines in the space in front of his room. Inside, he closed the curtains, laid out his cosmetics on the edge of the sink, and shaved very carefully. Next he took a long shower, soaping and rinsing himself twice. When he was dry, he telephoned Maggie. Her answering service said she was out for the evening, he left a message he'd called, but did not leave a number for a return call. After that, he chained the door and lay on top of the bedspread. The night lasted a long time. There was only the sound of traffic going by on the highway, trucks changing gears, now and then the growl of a glass-pack muffler. As it grew later the traffic thinned to an occasional lone car or truck. At dawn the curtains over the windows grew slowly translucent, implying first daylight outside. For a time the highway was silent. Then the noise built slowly again as commuters began their day with a drive into Washington. When the clock on the motel dresser said 9:00 A.M., he got up and made instant coffee with the apparatus provided by the motel. Then he washed and dressed, throwing his old shirt, underpants, and socks into the wastepaper basket. He left the motel, and drove the Ford into the city. He found a parking lot a few blocks from the Mains, Gulbenyan address. He walked along K Street for a time, until he was ready. He watched the stream of people coming toward him, they all seemed modestly dressed, open-faced and slightly bland. He entered the lobby of the building and found a tenant directory on the wall by the elevators. Among the boards and commissions, trade councils and product associations, was MAINS, GULBENYAN AND ASSOCIATES.

He took the elevator to the twelfth floor and was directed to the thirteenth, where thick gray carpet ran to the edge of the elevator and a soft chime rang when the door opened. A receptionist appeared, he asked to see Francis Mains. She took his name, then left him alone in the reception area. Next to a leather couch was a pile of magazines in plastic binders: *U.S. News & World Report, Forbes,* and *Foreign Affairs.* It was very quiet in the small room, there were no windows, and the indirect lighting was subdued. The air was lightly scented, something fresh, soapy, unnameable, but he could detect a faint odor of ozone, which he knew came from the constant operation of electronics. It was a smell familiar to people who spent time in highly secured installations.

"Mr. Guyer?"

A young man in a brown Dacron suit had entered the room.

"Yes."

"If you'd come with me, sir, Mr. Mains can see you now."

The young man let him go through the door first, then followed him down a long hallway. The acoustical tile on the walls and ceiling was a pale blue color and their footsteps on the gray carpet made no sound at all. Guyer assumed there was, in fact, a lot going on in the hallway: sound and temperature monitors, invisible TV cameras, and metal-detectors. He could, somehow, feel them at work. All the doors leading off the corridor were without external handles and were color-coded in pastel tones of red and blue. The young man behind him said, "Sir," and they stopped by one of the doors. A moment later there was the sound of a chime and the door clicked open an inch. The young man knocked twice and, when there was no response, opened the door. Guyer entered. The office was quite dark, there were no windows, the lighting was turned down low, and it took a moment for his eyes to adjust. Mains was seated behind a small white table with a telephone on it, making notes on a yellow legal pad with a fountain pen. He looked up at Guyer and smiled. "A civilized conversation?"

"Yes," Guyer said.

"Then you can go, John," he said to the young man. The door closed with a slight hiss of compressed air and the click of a locking mechanism. Mains continued writing, the scratch of his pen audible. Guyer found a leather chair, about ten feet from the desk, and sat down.

"I was afraid," Mains said, still not looking up, pausing while he continued to write, "that you'd come up here meaning to blaze away at me with some great pistol. I don't much care if you kill me, but for God's sake please don't blow holes in the wall tiles. Those really are hard to replace."

"Not my intention," Guyer said.

"Well, thank heaven for that," he said, still writing. "The older I get the more I seem to lose tolerance for violent emotions." After a moment he said, "There, now that's done." He pushed the tablet away from him, capped the pen and placed it atop the tablet, then looked up at Guyer. He took off his glasses, folded them, and slid them into his breast pocket. He was a tiny man, no more than five feet four inches tall, frail and stooped. He had large ears, and his thin, steel-colored hair was divided carefully at a part and combed neatly flat. There were deep lines in his face, pouches below his eyes. Everything in his life seemed to be in his eyes: they were blue and cold, on the edge of laughter, amused by something nobody else would ever see.

"How do you find my nest?" he said, one eyebrow rising.

"Impressive."

[254]

"I suppose it is. Something you must see." He pressed a button somewhere beneath the table and part of the wall to Guyer's left was lit by a dim light. It was a kind of terrarium, set into the wall. There were mossy rocks arranged on sand, with flowering bushes above them, against a wall of old, cracked brick. A trickle of water dripped from a crevice in the brick wall and ran down the branches onto the rocks. Closed in by a glass panel, it made no sound. "Plastic," Mains said. "Every bit of it. With all the electronics we run here no plants will ever grow. Too many positive ions generated by the electricity. So . . . this."

"Realistic," Guyer said. "I wouldn't have known it was plastic."

"How we change," Mains mused. "When Anton and I started out, we had a different sort of picture in mind. The oldest kind of Washington cliché, a couple of bureaucrats, separated from the Fed, with a small but terribly elite consultancy. We saw it situated in a two-story brownstone in Georgetown, with a girl from Vassar talking through her nose on the telephone. I believe you know the sort of thing we had in mind. Terribly cerebral, best case/worst case scenarios, with all the ants over in Langley left to confront the plangent realities." He laughed briefly. "You see what comes of such fantasies." They sat silent for a moment, water running down the brick wall onto the rocks. "Manners, Francis. Would you like a coffee?"

"No."

"Tea? Lemonade."

"No, thanks."

"Well then. Let's chat about Mains, Gulbenyan and, ah, Metro Data Research."

"It's yours."

"It is?" He appeared honestly surprised.

"Of course it is."

"We'll pay you, you know."

"Yes, I know. I'll need that to tie up some things."

"A question. What made you see the light?"

Guyer hesitated a moment, thinking. "Well, it was a brilliant play."

Mains tapped a finger on his table. "How much of it can you see, from your perspective?"

"Quite a bit. I know you had Delatte all along. You knew that after what happened to Elden, the man we put in, I wouldn't stay in any longer. You probably guessed that all along we were afraid of something like that happening—we did not intend to furnish corpses. We were approached by people who wanted a stand-in victim in order to claim life insurance, but we always, before this, kept it from happening. We refused to become a slaughterhouse. Perhaps that was a weakness." He shrugged, then went on. "When we switched X-ray files, at Langer's request, we were taking out Delatte's X rays and putting in Elden's. You knew, somehow, that we would use Elden, and you somehow obtained his X rays. I don't know how you did that, not precisely, but it wouldn't have been that hard to do. After the car-bombing the only way the police could identify the third body was by dental X ray, and Elden's was waiting for them at the dentist's office. Somebody told the police that the third man in the car was Delatte, and that he'd been in New York and used the name Ricard, and that he'd once visited a dentist. When the police chased that down, they gave the story to the papers and you had a client officially dead. Which is what he must have wanted. We'd murdered, indirectly, and you knew we had no stomach for that and that you'd wind up with the company. Was it you who chose Benauti?"

"No. That was Delatte's idea."

Guyer shook his head in admiration. "We never connected him with Mains, Gulbenyan. Not somebody like that."

"I presume you found him."

"No. But when we saw the newspaper story we put two and two together. There's probably more to it than that, something involving Delatte on your end. Another operation for somebody else."

"Actually, you were meant to find Benauti. Given his nature, we thought that was a fair possibility. In a way it was the most elegant part, the messenger becomes the message."

"You can't have everything. I guess what I really want to know now is what you plan to do with the company."

"Nothing."

Guyer's surprise showed.

Mains watched him carefully for a moment. "The truth is, I had some trepidation about this meeting. Not to be indelicate, but you and I once had a little problem, back in the mists of time. I knew you wouldn't want to sell, and that if you did decide to, it would never be to me. But, alas, we simply had to have it."

"Why?"

"We're a corporation, Guyer, we grow or we die."

"How does *nothing* add up to growth?"

Mains sat back in his chair. He looked at Guyer for what seemed like a long time. "I am concerned," he spoke slowly, "that you may feel remorse about what's happened in the past few weeks. To be frank, your objectivity surprises me. I need to persuade myself that, in the future, you will not decide to attack me, or this company. You undoubtedly know, from the years you put into the intelligence business, that the most finely drawn schemes can be smashed in an instant when strong emotions come into play. Resentment, desire for revenge, any passion at all really, is liable to destroy something that took years of care and patience to create. To that end, to assure ourselves of your *continued* objectivity, restraint, we have a document. While not entirely damning—you might be able to escape its consequences—we think it sufficient to hold your silence. It will also go some way toward explaining phenomena of the last two weeks, that you believe I do not know about. Lastly, it makes clear why we'll let your company die a quiet death and, furthermore, why it has to die. What logicians call an elegant proof. But before we get to that, there are some things that need to be said. We're going to pay you a hundred thousand dollars for your company. That isn't anything at all, not really, in terms of acquisition in the private sector. The fact is, we could have it for nothing and you know it. We've established the vulnerability of your business and could, if we chose, prey upon it again and again. Certain associates of mine counsel precisely that, *taking it,* period. You believe in your heart that I am a venal and vicious old man and you are correct. Nonetheless, it is only my intercession that protects you from learning how very wicked this business can be. Combat in the upper levels of the private sector can be brutal, but it is child's play compared to the techniques that you and I have learned over the years. It is not my intention to destroy you. It may be your silent intention to destroy me, but you will not be able to do that without destroying yourself. In order to get the money, which is in cash, by the way, there will be some papers for you to sign at the reception desk. Read them if you like, but read them with the knowledge that a lawyer cannot help you here. They are pro forma. For cash considerations duly received you turn over all interest to us. You leave here with money and without a company. We expect you to be angry, but we also expect that you will act ultimately in your own self-interest, which is to forget what has happened and go on your way in the world. Now, if you like, you may call me bad names."

"Do you need our computer encryption?"

"We have it."

"From Richard List."

"No. From Edna Foley."

Guyer shook his head in sorrow.

"She was not suborned, if that's what's troubling you. She was blackmailed."

"I thought List had been bought, or pressured, somehow."

"He was not."

"It's a relief to know that," Guyer said.

"Hard to trust anybody, Guyer. And not just in this business. We all learn the lesson, sooner or later. I could introduce you to twenty people, without moving more than a block from this office, who've betrayed and backstabbed for years, with very profitable results."

"I believe you," Guyer said quietly.

Mains glanced at him sharply, but Guyer's face was expressionless. He cleared his throat, then took his glasses from his pocket and put them on. "Now," he said, "show and tell."

Guyer, wearing a rainproof hat and an old tweed overcoat, walked up and down the aisles of the convenience store. It was a small store, the kind that stayed open twenty-four hours a day where everything cost fifty cents more than it did at the supermarket. He seemed very tense; picked up a package of breakfast rolls, glanced around him, then put them back on the shelf. At the counter a young woman was counting out change from a small purse, poking her index finger among the coins to find the right denominations. The clerk at the cash register was very patient, apparently he had watched this many times before. He was an older man, bald, wearing a tired cardigan sweater that hung away from his body. He'd been on duty for a long time, and leaned on the counter with one elbow to take the weight off his legs. Guyer picked up a can of dog food and looked at the price. The young woman finished paying and said, "G'night now," settling her shoulder bag into place and cradling a grocery sack in the crook of her arm. A buzzer on the door sounded as she left. Guyer picked up a loaf of bread and moved to the counter, setting it beside the cash register. The clerk checked the price label. "That'll be a dollar sixty," he said. Guyer took a ten out of his coat pocket and laid it on the counter by the bread. The clerk hit buttons on the cash register and the cash drawer sprang open. "Out of ten," he said. Guyer brought the gun out of his overcoat pocket very quickly, in one motion pressing the barrel into the man's throat and forcing his chin up and head back. Holding the clerk in that position, he reached into the open cash drawer with his left hand, swept each compartment clean of bills, and stuffed the money into the pocket of his overcoat. Then he moved against the counter, forcing the clerk farther back and applying pressure so that the man now looked directly at the ceiling. The thrust of the barrel made him gag slightly and his eyes blinked rapidly. Guyer's left hand searched blindly beneath the cash register until he found the open shelf. When he brought the hand back, there was a small revolver in it. This went into the same pocket as the money. Abruptly he stepped back a pace, releasing the clerk. He turned his hand sideways, then swung backhand, clipping the clerk across the bridge of the nose with the trigger guard. The man clutched his face and sagged back against the wall. Guyer dropped his hand to his side, backed up a few feet, then turned and hurried out of the store. The film continued for a few seconds, grainy black and white, shot from a camera hidden in the wall above the cash register, its lens fixed to record transactions taking place at the checkout counter. The rest of the store was visible, the image flattened and distorted to maintain foreground integrity. A time and date setting ran in white numerals in the lower left-hand corner.

[260]

Mains pressed a button and a panel slid back to cover the screen set in the wall.

"How long have you had it?" Guyer said.

"We finished writing the program about fourteen months ago. Then it was simply a matter of stuffing enough data in to get results. Even with scanners, the hands-on labor was very demanding. We had to hire fifty people and work them ten hours a day. But the time did come, finally, when the retrieval rate began to make financial sense and then, alas, it was time to eliminate the competition."

"9930."

"Kevin."

"Mr. Guyer, good morning."

"Kevin, is everything okay? Anything strange at all?"

"No sir. I'm alone here. But it's been like that all week."

"Any word at all from Mr. List?"

"No sir."

"Okay. Get a pencil, Kevin. Write down all the items I'm going to give you. This is important. Do every single thing I tell you to do. If you hit a snag, you'll have to act on your own initiative, because it may be a long time before we talk again. But I have faith in you, you can do it, we both know that. Are you ready?"

"Yes, sir."

"Number one. And I want you to keep to this sequence if at all possible, okay?"

"Yes, sir. In sequence."

"On the table where we keep the coffee, upstairs, is a table knife. If that won't do, there may be a screwdriver in, ah, in my desk someplace. One of the drawers on the right-hand side. Anyhow, use the knife, or whatever you can find. You know the linoleum squares in the console area?"

"Yes."

"Okay. Now count in from the edge that faces you when you enter the office. Starting at the extreme left square, three in, toward the console, then four out, toward the opposite wall. I want you to dig that tile up off the floor. You're looking for a piece of white rubber with numbers press-printed into it. There should be about thirty-five numbers. Kevin, if it's not that tile, it's another. It's under there somewhere, just start digging. Don't worry about the floor. Turn the computer on at the switch, then press each number in turn. It starts with an encryption code so the screen will light up on the fifth number. Keep pressing, one at a time. Now, when you complete the sequence, if you've done it right, the screen will go black and the computer will turn itself off. You'll have erased every single item in the data bank. If it doesn't turn off, start again with the first number. Do you have that?"

"Yes sir. Three tiles in, four across, computer on, hit the numbers in sequence."

"That's the first thing. Do it when you get off the phone. Second, find the bankbooks, checkbooks, all the financial material. Throw it in an envelope. Mail it to this address: Mr. George Rand, Skyway Motel, Trenton, New Jersey. Write across the envelope *Please Hold for Arrival.* Got it?"

"Yes, sir."

"Okay. Next, I want you to call Howard Hulin at the brokerage office. Tell him to clear all our accounts, not to accept further payments. Forward all funds to the same address I just gave you, in Trenton. Now, when that's done, your work at the office is finished. Lock up behind you. You're owed salary, Kevin, and I'm going to try and provide some kind of severance pay in addition. There'll be a money order coming to your house, at least for the salary. It will take thirty days. As for the rest, I'll do the best I can. Okay so far?"

"I . . . yes, sir. Okay."

"Next, go to the post office, fill out a change of address card for Metro Data Research and all other resident companies. Look in the telephone book, find a large corporation, have everything sent to that address. It doesn't matter which one. Now, you'll have one last thing to do, but it's the most important one. You have Mr. List's address?"

"Yes, sir."

"Send him a postcard. Don't sign it. Just print the single word *go* on it. Got that? In the next few days I want you to call his phone number intermittently. If he answers, tell him everything I've told you, tell him also I'll find him sometime, if I can. Tell him I'm sorry. Can you do all this?"

"Yes I can, Mr. Guyer." His voice, over the long distance line, sounded strained and thick.

"Kevin, you're a fine young man. You'll do well at whatever you decide to do, I'm sorry we have to say good-bye like this but it can't be helped. Now listen well: If anybody comes around and asks you questions or tries to threaten you in any way, call the FBI immediately. Understand?"

"Yes, sir. I liked working for you, Mr. Guyer."

"I'm glad you did. You did a fine job, and I appreciate it. I have to hang up now, so good luck to you, Kevin."

"Good-bye, Mr. Guyer. And luck, too."

Guyer hung up, his throat so tight he could barely breathe.

The telephone booth was two blocks away from Mains's office. He'd practically run there, to buy time. He thought Mains might have people in New York, ready to take possession, he just hoped his surrender had been convincing enough to keep Mains from executing any sort of emergency plan. He'd said good-bye quickly, looking away, a beaten man already brooding over his failure. At least he'd tried hard for that effect. He'd signed the papers without reading them, while brown-Dacron-suit stood by politely. Then he'd taken the manila envelope, without looking inside, and left the office. He waited, watched the crowds move past him on the sidewalk until his composure returned, then called the next number on his list.

"Hello?" She sounded like he'd woken her up.

"Hello."

"Hey! Look what I found."

"How do you feel about packing?"

"Packing?"

"As in suitcases, airplanes."

"Oh that. Well it happens I'm very good at that."

"I'd like you to do it."

There was a pause, he could feel her thinking her way into it. When she answered, her voice was much lower. "Okay," she said. She meant it.

"What I have in mind is cleaning out the refrigerator and turning it off and leaving the door open."

"Oh."

"Clear?"

"Unh-huh. And that's okay too. Where are we going?"

"I'd rather not say on the telephone."

"Yeah but see, I belong to this sex called women, and that's the one that sometimes wears more than one thing a week. Get it?"

"One suitcase. For the beach. Where it's hot."

"Ahh. *Another* thing I'm good at. When are you coming?"

"I don't know. There's one more thing I have to do, then I'll be there. Maggie, I didn't mean, I didn't want everything to happen so abruptly, what I mean is—"

She cut him off. "Listen Babar, you just climb into

your striped balloon and fly on up here kinda quick and skip the explanations."

"I love you," he said.

"Shhh," she said. "You just be careful."

"It isn't anything like that," he said.

"Do it anyhow," she said.

They hung up.

Guyer made his last call quickly, before he could think about it too much. There were a lot of reasons not to make the call, all of them to do with self-preservation, but it had to be run out and he was the only one who could do that. He was elected. The bravery in it was incidental, principally it was debt-paying—Elden, List, Edna Foley, somehow Benauti, too—and the one thing that had to be done before anyone could start fresh was get their debts paid.

His call was answered right away. There was no secretary to put him off. No problem or circumstance arose to prevent the meeting. He would, he knew, have accepted excuse by fate, but the dice wanted him there, so he went.

He drove southwest. Slowly, in the right-hand lane. Maybe Mains had somebody on him and maybe he didn't. It wasn't important, it did not matter. Mains would find out soon enough what he was going to do, if he found out by a radio communication from one of his brown Dacron suits, that was okay too. He drove through Leesburg, which stood—stone houses and magnolias—as it had in 1860, and out into Loudoun County. Old Virginia, horse country, soft hills, white fence, and the Blue Ridge Mountains rising hazy in the distance. Following directions, he went from four-lane to two-lane, from two-lane to gravel, and gravel to dirt: a narrow road that crossed back and forth over a tiny stream and finally ended in front of a large, solid frame house painted white. It wasn't a mansion, not quite, but it came from a time when houses were built by carpenters with handsaws. Guyer was just getting out of the car when Joseph Malkin came down a brick pathway to meet him.

Malkin was something of a surprise, Guyer hadn't exactly had clear expectations, but Malkin looked like a man who years ago had settled in to being chairman of a history department at a small midwest college. He wore an old yellow sweater over a striped shirt, stomach bulging above his pants, which hung comfortably low. On his feet were an ancient pair of tennis sneakers worn over brown socks. He was approximately in his fifties, bald on top, with a halo of wild gray hair sticking out above his ears. He had tortoiseshell glasses and was smoking a cigar.

In reality, Joseph Malkin was a journalist. Some years earlier he'd had a widely syndicated column, but had dropped that in favor of stories for a variety of national magazines—almost always lead stories with Malkin's name prominent on the cover. He was generally acknowledged to be among the five or six most informed American writers on the subject of the international intelligence community.

He led Guyer into his study: Stacks of papers a foot high, piles of newspaper clippings, books everywhere, ashtrays full of dead cigar butts, battered throw rug with a sleeping cocker spaniel who opened one eye to look at Guyer then closed it again and, at the center of it all, an immaculate and very expensive-looking word processor. Malkin's twelve-year-old daughter brought them iced tea, though it was very late in the year for that Guyer felt that it was somehow obligatory, and it was exactly what he wanted.

Malkin wouldn't let him start right away. Instead he asked questions, what Guyer thought about the Middle East, what Guyer thought about Afghanistan, what Guyer thought about the Redskins quarterback situa-

[266]

tion. Guyer felt himself grow more and more comfortable, and he knew that he was being read like a book, but he didn't mind. The light faded, there was more iced tea, the cocker spaniel changed his position and sighed deeply, somehow a perfect mixture of contentment and sorrow. Finally, Malkin settled back in his chair and said, "Well, if you've got a good spook story, I'd like to hear it."

Guyer started by explaining the concept, how people looked like other people and what could be done with that, using intelligence-grade filming techniques. About ten minutes in, he paused to see what Malkin might think about it.

"Yes," Malkin said, "it makes sense." He nodded his head slowly, in comprehension. "Some years ago my wife was spirited away and a KGB agent was substituted for her. I began to suspect that when I kept finding microdots in my pancakes."

Guyer had expected something like that. Unfazed, he took pencil and paper and began to sketch out elementary probability tables. He reproduced one of List's sermons about computer capability, talked a bit about gene pools and common ancestry and ethnic similarities, touched on the nature of black and white film, and wound slowly to a halt. Malkin lit a fresh cigar and stared into the distance.

"It's a *Time* cover," he said, "I'll grant you that."

"How do you mean?"

"Oh, like *One of These Men Is Alexander Haig.* Something like that."

"There's more," Guyer said.

"I'm sure there is," Malkin said, sitting back again.

He wasn't specific. He didn't mention Elden's name, and he avoided Benauti entirely. He concentrated on Mains. He was open about the fact that he himself was culpable, but the terms of his culpability he left in the shadows. He caught Malkin, at one point, smiling at him in an evil sort of way. A smile that said he'd spent a great deal of time in this study listening to intelligence officers try to say and not say things at the same time. He was most specific in the area of the car-bombing, how it was done for Delatte's benefit, that Delatte was alive someplace, and that *another person* had died in his behalf. Mains, he said, was behind all of it.

Malkin sighed through his nose. "What we probably have here is the empaneling of a federal grand jury. That's second best, because all we get are artists' reproductions and sealed records and leaks from assistant DA's. Best case, of course, is a congressional investigation. Senate subcommittee on intelligence oversight. Now there's television, and I make money. So do you, by the way. Because we both write books. By the way, who's your agent?"

"I'm not going to do that."

"No? Then tell me, Mr. Guyer, what do you want?"

"Francis Mains."

"Tarred, feathered, and hung on a pole. Eh?"

"That's right."

"Maybe you're lucky. You have in me a sympathetic and biased listener. I've known Francis for a long time and he has always given me a bad case of the squirms. What worries me, though, is that you really don't have anything concrete. What I see is a tiny island of hearsay floating in the mists of deniability."

"When isn't it like that?"

"Sometimes. Once in a blue moon. Most of the time it's *highly placed sources* and *reliable informants*. We're reduced to decisions as to what constitutes a good smear or a bad one."

"Then?"

"Tell you what I'll do for you. Two things. First, I'll give you the best dinner you ever had." He glanced at his watch. "In about a half hour. Second, I'll agree to poke around a little. But if I'm to poke, you have to do something for me."

"What's that?"

"Call him."

"Okay."

"It's after seven, he's home. I'll dial if it's all the same to you." He thumbed through a Rolodex, dialed a number, gave Guyer the handset, lifted a third-party receiver off the side of the phone and held it to his ear. Then he pursed his lips and tapped them with an extended index finger. Guyer understood he wasn't to tell Mains that Malkin was listening.

"Mains residence."

"Francis Mains, please. My name is Guyer."

"Hold the phone, please."

Mains came on quickly. "Yes?"

"This is Guyer."

"I know. What do you want?"

"Do you know what I'm going to do?"

"Don't play games with me, please. If you have something to say, say it."

"I'm going to the newspapers. The whole thing."

"You're a fool." The voice was steady.

"Probably. But that's what I'm going to do."

"You'll go to jail, Guyer."

"You too."

"I doubt it."

"Worth a try, though."

"Think of it Guyer. Ten years in Lewisburg. Sitting in a cell with a sleazy magazine and a box of Kleenex. I can't believe you'd really take the chance."

"Just want you to know about it. No, just wanted you to *think* about it. Because it's going to happen."

Mains suddenly sounded tired. "Is that it, then? A threat?"

"Yes."

[269]

"Then good evening." He hung up.

Malkin put the receiver back, stood up and stretched. The cocker spaniel rose and stretched also. "Now, Mr. Guyer, I want to hear your opinion on the subject of *gnocchi verdi*."

"Will I go to jail?" he said.

"Mmmm, no. I don't think so. You'll be the state's witness, after all. You'll be ruined, of course. Financially. Professionally. But, if you won't do the book, there are always lectures. I can recommend the Brookman Agency. Very good. They'll never let you cross two time-zones on successive days. Let's see. Try this on: *Can We Control the Private Intelligence Industry?* No, rather too severe, I think. Something a little more frisky. *Private Cloak and Corporate Dagger.* How about that?"

"Mr. Malkin, are you going to pursue this?"

Malkin headed out of the study, waving Guyer to come with him. "Maybe a little. Just to see who jumps." He smiled at Guyer, a very pleasant and welcoming smile. "C'mon," he said, "let's eat."

Anderson

IT WAS WARM on the island in February. Eighty-five degrees every day, ocean temperature the same, and the trade winds blew steadily from the southeast, rustling the palm-leaf shelters where the steel bands played at night. The island hotels filled up with tourists, mostly from Montreal. Many of them visited the Tabac on rue 22 Mai and bought the *Gazette* and *La Presse* and *Sélections du Reader's Digest*. The Tabac, which had never had any other name, also sold chewing gum and candy bars, cigarettes and pipe tobacco, sunglasses and Le Cube de Rubik. For the rare soul who insisted on tormenting himself in Paradise, it carried *Le Monde* and a variety of serious journals. An occasional American bought the international *Herald Tribune,* and there were always a few papers from Venezuela, Jamaica, Trinidad, and Panama. The store was tiny, only ten by ten, but Maggie and Guyer were rarely in it at the same time, and most of the sales were made through the window that looked out on the street and the ocean. After buying the Tabac, Guyer had asked about the origin of the street name, expecting something grand and patriotic: 22 Mai, however, turned out to be the date the street was officially completed and dedicated, nothing more. It was that kind of island.

At first Guyer had been carried away by retailer's frenzy, nightly studying huge lists of available merchandise supplied by the distributors. The small apartment above the store had one large window, covered by a screen, which faced the foot of the bed. They sat there after dark, listening to the crash of waves on the beach, Maggie reading historical novels, Guyer surrounded by a mound of catalogues. From time to time he would say, "What about stationery?" or, "Did you know we could get Coppertone?" Maggie would mumble something noncommittal and go back to reading. She had tanned beautifully, and the sun had turned her copper hair fiery and brilliant. She was happy, except that Guyer's plans to turn the Tabac into a department store drove her a little crazy. At last, as he was hanging around one afternoon trying to time-date the inventory—"We have to know what's selling"—she left the store for a half hour and returned with a large portable radio.

"You sit on that beach," she said. "Here's a radio. It plays music, news, all kindsa things. You're a smart man, ran a business and God knows what, see if you're smart enough to listen to a radio and sit on a beach and not screw around with a goddamn store."

He found baseball. Spanish baseball. It was, perhaps, the refraction through another language that pleased him. It came from the Dominican Republic and it was constant. That island apparently did little else but play and watch baseball. During Maggie's shift he would sit on the beach, turn the radio up above the roar of the surf, and follow the fortunes of the *Águilas, Cachorros,* and *Gigantes.* The announcers maintained a steady pitch of hysteria—*Hay doble por Luis Vega!*—and were shamelessly partial to the home club. At six he would go to a small restaurant on rue 22 Mai and pick up pie plates of dinner covered with tin foil. Maggie had briefly attempted the cooking, but following a tantrum that ended late at night with Guyer standing on the stove to remove pancake batter from the ceiling, she gave that up as useless. Sometimes they walked on the beach in the evenings.

Guyer had his bad moments. From time to time he would wake up at night soaking wet. Privately, he blamed himself for everything. He should have seen it coming. The people who had worked for him had trusted him to sense danger, and he had failed them. He had worked out for himself that the Richard List he had seen was not the real one. It had been daring for Mains, Langer, whoever else, to show substitutes in real life, but he understood that the situations had been very controlled: his taxi from Kennedy followed, the false List produced only fleetingly. Something similar had gone on outside Maggie's door. And, if they had fooled him in that way, had they not also fooled Richard? What had *his,* Guyer's, phantom done? He could only guess, but what he did know was that the wedge had been successfully driven. List, if he was alive somewhere, probably hated him. Basic destabilization, old technique, tried and true.

Thus Guyer knew, when he allowed himself to think about it, that his paradise was undeserved. It was in some ways the subtlest of punishments. And when the man finally showed up, there was part of him that welcomed it. He had expected it, known it was coming sooner or later, and he thought Maggie knew also, though they never said anything. Theorem: You can't get away forever. He came first to the Tabac and bought a copy of the local paper, *Le Voix-Tribune*. "How's this?" he said. "Okay," Guyer said. The man looked at him just that instant longer than necessary, and the telegraphy was accomplished. He was a very ugly man, in a short-sleeved drip-dry shirt, the transparent kind. Guyer figured him for somewhere over forty. He was tall, about six feet five, Guyer judged, with a big pot belly, narrow shoulders, and a sunken chest. His face was chinless, he wore clear-frame eyeglasses with clip-on sunshields, and his thinning hair, a vague brown color, was blown about in the wind. Guyer watched him walk away, knowing he would see him again.

His Maggie-ordained period of daily relaxation began at 2:00. The sun was much too hot that time of day, but there was a grove of sea grape trees midway down the sand toward the ocean, and Guyer liked the rattle of their leaves. He'd bought an ancient beach chair, frayed canvas hung on teak, that might have once sailed on a cruise liner. That, and his radio, he set up in the shade.

He watched the ugly man coming toward him down the beach. He wore only a bathing suit and carried no towel. Guyer just sat quietly and waited. Where he was, he thought idly, was one of the nicer places in the world to die, if dying was what the world had in store for him that day. The man strolled up, sat on the sand just outside the shade line, and acknowledged Guyer with a brief, formal nod.

"Good afternoon," he said, the intonation Eastern seaboard, Ivy League, "mind if I join you for a few minutes?"

"No," Guyer said, "I don't mind."

"My name is Owen Anderson," he said, but did not offer to shake hands. His bathing suit, Guyer noted, was a pattern of green lions on a tan background.

[276]

"Do we know each other?"

"You're Guyer. That's right, isn't it?"

"Yes."

"I'm an associate of Charles Holland."

Guyer nodded. Holland had, for a time, been his direct superior at CIA. He reached over and turned down the shrieking baseball announcer.

"I hope the visit isn't a shock. You needn't worry about ill will of any sort," Anderson said.

"Okay," Guyer said.

"I was headed this way, actually my wife and I are on vacation, and somebody suggested I stop by and say hello. That's really about all there is to it. I was briefed about some of your former acquaintances. People thought you might like to know."

Guyer looked at him a little sideways, but Anderson seemed not to notice. He went on. "Richard List, for instance."

"Yes?"

"He's in Paris. Working for a computer services company."

"You saw him?"

Anderson shook his head. "No. But it's good information."

"I wonder if you could do me a favor?"

"If I can."

"There's some money I would like him to have. A split of what we had banked, and proceeds of a business sale."

"I don't see why not. If you'll produce a, well, whatever the local version is of a cashier's check, I'm sure I can see that he gets it."

"Thanks," Guyer said.

Anderson lifted his face to the sun for a moment, as though he'd promised somebody he would get a tan. Guyer looked back up at the Tabac. Maggie was framed in the window, making change for a woman in a dreadful tube bathing suit. Casually, Anderson said "You hear about Francis Mains?"

"No."

"Suicide," he said. "Poor man. He shot himself with a little gun. Servant found him. No note or anything, of course." He paused for a moment, face still turned upward. "The press was after him. Or so I'm told."

"Which press?"

"Some of the TV news journals."

"Langer?"

"That terrible man. Sometimes, Guyer, I really do wonder." A young girl, in hardly any bathing suit at all, ran shouting into the waves. Anderson watched her. "That's why I fight communism," he said. "Nobody really knows what became of Jack, but the current wisdom is that he's no longer with us. We know about a meeting with a shipping broker in a hotel in Athens, in the dining room there. They drove away from the hotel in a Peugeot. Nobody's seen him since. It's been, oh, about three months."

"I'm not surprised."

"Nobody was. A man like that, enemies build up, over the years, and it gets to a point . . ." He paused, dismissed the unpleasant thought. "How do you like it here?"

"I like it."

"Can't see how you wouldn't. I haven't known what day it is since I arrived. I don't *care* what day it is. That's a rare beneficence, where I come from."

"Yes. I know."

"I do have a piece of mail I think you might like to have." He unbuttoned the change pocket of his bathing suit and took out a piece of paper and unfolded it. "Silly me," he said, "I almost forgot." The irony in his voice was gentle. He handed the paper to Guyer.

It was a letter, block-printed in ballpoint pen on

cheap-fancy stationery with a blue border. Guyer had to hold it in both hands to keep the wind from playing with it. "Came to your accommodation address in L.A.," Anderson said. "Consider it forwarded." Guyer read it twice.

Mr. Collier:
    I was real disappointed in you, cheating me like that. I thought you were a man of your word, but I can see you fooled me pretty good. Just in case it slipped your memory, I'm writing this letter to remind you that you owe me money. I kept my part of the bargain, you should keep yours.
Sincerely yours,
Bill Elden

"You can keep that," Anderson said.
"What the hell . . ."
Anderson giggled. "Oh it was *ripe*," he said. "Forgive me. It's all the sun and the swimming. Puts me off my stolid demeanor. I really mustn't tell you everything, tempting as that is. Suffice to say that Mr. Elden did not enjoy his visit to New York. He was whisked off his plane at Kennedy, and he spent his glamorous weekend in New York in an apartment on the West Side, playing Scrabble with Company baby-sitters."
"Who was in the car?"
"Delatte. The papers had it right. *Somebody* told him the way back to health lay in a meeting at the Argentine Embassy. Unfortunately, that turned out to be a fib. We permitted Mains's people to do the rest. Their client, who shall be nameless, was not pleased."
Guyer squinted. Anderson let several seconds go by. "We had somebody at Mains, Gulbenyan. We have people throughout the industry. Lately it's all become a dreadful pain in the fanny. Last July, for instance, we discovered that an East German state security group

had purchased, through intermediary layers, a very good little firm in Los Angeles, and had them up to all kinds of tricks. And Frank Mains had done some real mischief, not only in this instance. We simply had to point a moral and tell a tale."

Guyer looked back at the letter.

"Really, I suppose you ought to pay him."

Guyer nodded yes. "Does he *know*?"

"Not at all."

Guyer held the letter up, started to speak, then cleared his throat. Something wound very tight inside him for a long time was unraveling and he didn't trust his voice. "This, what you told me," he said, looking for words, "it's appreciated." He wanted to say more, but there was too much.

Anderson waved off the gratitude. "It was no trouble at all. Glad to do it. As I said, I was stopping by here anyhow. And we consider you a friend."

"Well, I thank you," Guyer said.

"Don't mention it," Anderson said, turning his face a little more toward the sun. "Maybe sometime you can return the favor."